**'Are you m‌‌‌   ‌‌‌‌
is he your**

Margaret di‌‌‌   nd
Roland cam‌‌‌   al,
Grandmama.

'Do you know what you are letting yourself in for?' Lady Pargeter demanded of Margaret, ignoring her grandson.

'I think so, my lady.'

'Good, because I wouldn't want you to be under any illusions. Being married to a Pargeter heir is a dangerous undertaking, especially for a Capitain.' She looked venomously at Margaret. 'Did your mother never tell you that?'

Born in Singapore, **Mary Nichols** came to England when she was three, and has spent most of her life in different parts of East Anglia. She has been a radiographer, school secretary, information officer and industrial editor, as well as a writer. She has three grown-up children, and four grandchildren.

Recent titles by the same author:

DEVIL-MAY-DARE
THE PRICE OF HONOUR
THE DANBURY SCANDALS

A DANGEROUS UNDERTAKING

Mary Nichols

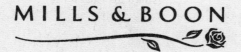

MILLS & BOON

MILLS & BOON, the Rose Device and LEGACY OF LOVE are trademarks of the publisher.
Harlequin Mills & Boon Limited,
Eton House, 18–24 Paradise Road, Richmond, Surrey TW9 1SR
This edition published by arrangement with
Harlequin Enterprises B.V.

© Mary Nichols 1995

ISBN 0 263 79032 0

Set in 10 on 12 pt Linotron Times
04-9505-83067

Typeset in Great Britain by Centracet, Cambridge
Printed in Great Britain by
BPC Paperbacks Ltd

CHAPTER ONE

THERE were two men in The White Hart inn, sitting in a corner with a bottle of wine between them. They did not appear to be enjoying it. One was tall, judging by the length of the buckskin breeches and leather top-boots which stuck out from under the table as he leaned back in his seat. His full-skirted coat with its large button-back cuffs was well cut and, though not exactly the height of fashion, certainly did not proclaim him as anything but a man of substance. He was surveying his companion under well-shaped brows, which at this moment were drawn down in a frown, spoiling what was otherwise a handsome face. He wore no make-up and had a clean-shaven, well-shaped jaw-line and thick dark hair which was unpowdered and tied back into the nape of his neck with a black ribbon. The light of the lantern hanging from the ceiling showed up glints of red-gold in it. His right hand, curling round the stem of his glass, was long-fingered and neatly manicured. He wore a large signet-ring but no other jewellery.

His companion was of an age with him—twenty-six or thereabouts—but somewhat broader. His eyes were grey and he wore a lightly powdered brown wig with long side-curls. His mauve satin coat with its high stand collar was flamboyantly decorated with rows of pleated ribbon. He wore more jewellery than his friend—a cravat pin, a fob across his braided waistcoat and a quizzing-glass, as well as several rings. In London he would not have been considered over-dressed, but in this sleepy town he shone like a beacon. He grinned at his morose friend.

'Cheer up, Roly, old fellow; you'll turn the wine sour.'

Roland, Lord Pargeter, smiled, and his rather taciturn countenance lightened, so that it was easy to see the charming man he could be if he chose. 'It's all very well for you, Charles; you haven't got an insoluble obstacle in the path of your happiness.'

'No, thank heaven, but then I don't believe in witches and curses and nonsense like that.'

'I wish it were nonsense. It's been true for the last four generations, so my grandmother tells me, and that can surely not be coincidence.'

'You know,' Charles said slowly, 'what you ought to do is marry.'

Roland looked at his friend in exasperation. 'Haven't you listened to a word I've said? I have just finished telling you why I cannot do so.'

'You have told me why you cannot wed Mistress Chalfont. What's to stop you marrying someone else?'

'I don't want to.'

'Yes, you do. Think about it, Roly. You cannot marry Susan because you care for her——'

'I love her too much to——'

'Don't interrupt. So why not marry someone you do *not* care for? A complete stranger, in fact. It won't be forever, will it? A year. What's a year?'

Roland looked thoughtful; it was just what his grandmother had said when she had warned him to choose his bride carefully. He had not told her of his intention

towards Susan because the time had not seemed propitious, what with his father so recently dead and
heaven knew what arrangements to be made about the
inheritance. And he had been obliged to return to
London to clear up certain financial matters and consolidate his position at court. He could not assume that
because he had inherited the title and the estates he
had also inherited his father's position and privileges.
Having secured those, at least for the time being, he
was on his way back home. 'No, I cannot. And who
would have me in the circumstances?'

'Oh, anyone,' Charles said airily, waving his empty
glass round the oak-panelled room. 'You would be a
very good catch. You ain't bad-looking—at least not
when you smile—and you're not short of a penny or
two. I reckon you would have no difficulty.'

'It's a mad idea.'

'But growing on you, eh?' Charles paused to look
closely into his friend's face. 'If it meant happiness with
Susan in the end. . .'

'It would have to be someone desperate enough not
to care why I married her. I don't think I could
pretend. . .'

Charles grinned. 'Not even a little?'

'No.' Roland paused, realising it was desperation
which had led him to humour his friend, but the idea
really was out of the question. 'How could I live with
someone for a year, face her over the dinner-table, talk
to her, smile at her, knowing what I had done to her?'

'You don't have to, don't you see? As soon as the
wedding is over, you leave for London, say you have
been called back to your regiment—after all, there is
still trouble with the Jacobites—stay away the whole

year. She will be happy enough playing lady of the manor here without you.'

'I could not do it.'

'Not even for Susan? If it were me, and it was the only way I could have Kate, I'd do it. I wouldn't have any scruples at all.'

'I am not you,' Roland said, thinking of Susan as he had last seen her in September, waving goodbye to him from the steps of her father's mansion in Derbyshire and calling out that she would see him in London in April, if not before. April, five months from now and a whole year after he had received that wound at Culloden, a year in which he had gone from being so badly wounded that he was not expected to live, back to full health, and it was all because of the devoted nursing he had received at her hands. Well, perhaps not all at her hands because there had been nurses and servants too, but she had been the one to sit with him hour after hour, reading to him and amusing him as he slowly recovered. It had been almost inevitable that they would fall in love. He had left her to return to his regiment in London, full of confidence that, when the time came to propose, she would accept and they could look forward to a happy future together. In London he had learned that his father had died and he had hurried home, and that had led to the interview with his grandmother, and now here it was December and he was miserable. Charles was trying to cheer him up but with little success. Roland smiled at him, humouring him. 'Where would I look for such a one?'

Charles shrugged. 'Anywhere. There's a little waif just come in on the stage. If you turn round slowly,

you will see her sitting in the chimney-corner with all
her worldly possessions in a bag at her feet.'

The room, which had been empty except for the two
men, had filled in the previous two minutes from a
coach which had clattered into the yard and disgorged
its passengers, most of whom had come into the inn to
stay the night before continuing their journey north in
the morning.

Roland turned in leisurely fashion, searching out the
girl Charles had mentioned. The hood of her black
cape hid most of her face, though he could see the line
of her chin and a firm mouth. Beneath the cape, her
mourning gown was neat rather than fashionable, but
it did not disguise a figure which was slim, bordering
on thin.

'Half starved,' Charles commented.

'Do you know who she is?'

'No, but that's the beauty of it. A complete stranger
to these parts.'

'How do you know that?'

'It would be easy enough to find out.'

'No, Charles, I forbid it.'

The girl looked up suddenly and met Roland's gaze.
She had clear violet eyes and very dark hair which
curled over her forehead beneath the black lace which
lined the cape's hood. Her face was pale and she
looked apprehensive, though not exactly frightened.

'She seems a little lost,' Roland said pensively. 'Like
a kitten that's strayed from its mother.'

'Perhaps she has. She is in mourning.'

Margaret Donnington could not hear what they were
saying but she sensed they were talking about her and
she felt herself blushing. She turned away in confusion.

She should not have come into the building at all. It had made her the object of curiosity.

She had never in her life before been into an inn alone; it was not something a well-nurtured young lady should ever have to do and, though she was not really afraid, she was certainly nervous. She had been uncertain whether to come in at all, debating whether to enquire the way to Winterford and see if she could find someone to take her there at once, or to use some of her precious savings on a meal and a room for the night, and continue in the morning. She had written to Great-Uncle Henry advising him of her arrival, and had expected that he would send a conveyance for her, but there was no conveyance, no Uncle Henry, nothing, and if she turned up on his doorstep at this time of night there was no telling what sort of welcome she would be accorded, especially if he had not received her letter.

Until a week ago, she had not even known of his existence and she was not sure he had known of hers. She was beginning to wish she had never left London, but it was too late now; she had burned her boats. She had given up the tiny apartment she and her mother had occupied, and spent all but a guinea or two of her savings on the journey, so there was no going back. Besides, what was there to go back for? Her darling mama had died and she had no relatives in the whole world except Great-Uncle Henry Capitain, her mother's uncle. Mother had made her promise to go to him. 'He is family,' she had said, that last day when not even Margaret could convince herself that her mother would get better. 'He will not turn you away.' She had gone on to explain that Henry Capitain lived at

Winterford, a small village in the Fens, not far from Ely.

Margaret had been too concerned with making her mother's last hours comfortable to ask questions about the unknown relative, and only after the funeral had she found herself wondering what was to become of her. There was no money, hardly enough to pay the rent they owed. Mama had been ill for some months and unable to work herself, and though Margaret had had a position with one of London's leading milliners, which was just enough to keep them both, she had been forced to give it up to nurse her mother. Walking away from the simple grave, Margaret had been overwhelmed by grief, and not until she had returned to the tiny apartment that had been her home did she realise that she no longer had a home. The landlord had been adamant, telling her that he had not pressed for payment because of Mrs Donnington's illness, but now the time of reckoning had arrived. He wanted the back rent and he wanted Margaret out; he had others waiting to move in who would pay more, and regularly too.

She had sold everything except her clothes and one or two pieces of inexpensive jewellery which had been her mother's, and paid him, then taken a stage-coach to Cambridge. In Cambridge she had changed to another coach, a very heavy old-fashioned vehicle which had jolted its passengers unmercifully over the rutted tracks which went by the name of roads, making her wish she had never set out. The feeling had been heightened as the coach had taken them through the bleakest countryside she could ever have imagined. True, it was winter, not the best time to see it, and there had been a cold mist which hung over the fields and obscured everything except one or two houses which stood very close to the road. And even these signs of habitation had disappeared as night fell. In common with the other passengers, she had been glad when they'd finally turned into the yard of The White Hart, but she was still short of her destination.

She called the waiter over to her and smiled, determined not to be cowed. 'Would you please tell me how to get to Winterford?' she asked.

'Winterford?' he repeated. 'It's a fair step. Eight miles, I reckon. You weren't aimin' to go tonight, were you, mistress?'

'Eight miles.' Her smile faded. 'Then is it possible to hire a vehicle to take me there?'

'I doubt anyone would want to turn out at this time o' night,' he said. 'Whereabouts do you want to go? There's nobbut there but a fen, a church and a handful of houses. And Winterford Manor, o' course. . .' He paused, looking her up and down, wondering if anyone going to the Manor would arrive without being met, but then, his lordship was sitting on the other side of the room; he would surely have come forward if the young lady were his guest. 'You weren't going to the Manor, were you?'

'No. Sedge House.'

'There!' His manner suddenly changed. 'That ain't even in Winterford. Right out on the edge of the fen, it is, miles from anywhere, and there's many that's thankful for that, everything considered.' He looked at her again. She seemed on the verge of tears, not the sort of girl who normally visited that old reprobate, Henry Capitain. Sedge House guests were usually colourfully dressed, painted and be-wigged, and licentious, to say the least. 'Are you sure you mean Sedge House, miss?'

'Yes. Is something wrong there?'

'No,' he said hurriedly.

'You haven't answered my question. How can I get there?'

'I should send a boy with a message in the morning and Master Capitain will send his carriage for you.'

It seemed a reasonable suggestion and Margaret resigned herself to waiting until the following day, and asked for a room for the night, something she had wanted to avoid doing. But tomorrow, perhaps, the sun might be shining and everything would look better; even her prospects might seem rosier, though she doubted it. She stood up and picked up her valise to follow the man up the stairs.

'There!' said Charles as she disappeared from sight. 'Did you hear that? She is going to old Henry Capitain's and no one with an ounce of good breeding would be going there. She is some waif he has picked up and invited to visit him. You could save her from a fate worse than death.' He gave a cracked laugh when he realised what he had said. 'Well, a short life but a merry one, eh?'

'It is not a matter for jest.'

'I am not jesting.'

'We don't know anything about her.'

'We don't need to know anything, apart from the fact that she is not already married, because that would certainly be an insurmountable obstacle.'

Roland laughed harshly. 'And what about Susan?'

'What about her? She is miles away in Derbyshire

and she won't come here in the middle of winter, considering the state of the roads and the fact that you have not yet issued the invitation.' He paused, looking at Roland with his head on one side. 'Have you?'

'No, but are you suggesting I should keep news of my marriage a secret from the woman I love?'

'That's up to you, old fellow. You aren't exactly betrothed, are you? You have not yet offered for her?'

'No, but I believe there is an understanding. . .'

'What good is an understanding to a young lady who has her heart set on a wedding-ring, not to mention babies? If my estimate of the fair sex is correct, she will not wait forever, so why not do something to hasten the day?'

Roland had polished off the best part of two bottles of claret or he would never have embarked on such a conversation, let alone taken it seriously. But he was in a fix and it seemed like a way out. If he married a complete stranger, someone he found not in the least attractive, as different from Susan as chalk from cheese, perhaps it would work. 'And where did I meet this new bride of mine?' he asked. 'I can hardly tell Grandmama I picked her up in an inn.'

'You've just come back from London, haven't you? You've been away for weeks on business. You were introduced by Lady Gordon at one of her soirées, or something of that sort. You brought her home with you.'

'*Now*?' Roland was astounded. 'You mean me to take her home now?'

'No, tell the Dowager you left the young lady at the inn while you went on ahead to break the news to her.

By the time you come back I shall have made the acquaintance of the woman in question.'

'You assume she will agree.'

'Well, yes, there is that,' Charles conceded. 'But it's worth a try. In any case, it does not have to be this young lady; we can find others. You could advertise.'

Roland laughed, but it was a cracked sound and not in the least mirthful. '"Wanted, a wife for a year. Must be of mean appearance and desperate, not to say a little mad." They will flock to answer it.'

'Have you got a better idea?' Charles demanded, miffed. 'Apart from remaining a single man for the rest of your days?'

'Forget it,' Roland said, rising unsteadily and picking up his tricorne hat. 'I wish I had never told you. I'm going home. Are you coming?'

'No, I'll stay here for the night and come on in the morning.'

Roland looked at him suspiciously. 'What are you going to do?'

'Nothing, my dear fellow. Simply ask a few questions, see how the land lies.'

'I wish you would not.'

'It can't do any harm, can it? I will not commit you to anything.'

'I should hope not,' Roland said fervently. 'What shall I tell Kate?'

Charles looked up in surprise. 'She is not expecting me tonight, is she?'

'How do I know?' Roland was beginning to feel irritable. He supposed it was his friend's unfailing good humour which irked him, his ability to find something to smile at even in the worst situations, but it was unfeeling of him to make a joke of Roland's predicament. 'You are the one who writes to my sister, not I. What did you tell her?'

'That I would see her before the week was out. This is only Thursday. Tell her you saw me in London and that I was just going to Tattersalls to buy a horse. That's true, because you did. Tell her I will be with her tomorrow. Send your curricle in for me.'

'Very well, but I want your promise that you will not propose to the little kitten on my behalf.'

'As if I would.' Charles laughed. 'You can do your own proposing.'

'Never. I bid you goodnight.' With that, he clapped his hat on his head and left the room to go to the stables, where he confidently expected that an ostler would have changed the horses on his travelling carriage.

Charles sat on while the room he asked for was prepared. A faint smile played around his lips. Roland would never have his heart's desire if someone didn't take him in hand.

Margaret opened her eyes to bright sunshine, and hurried to the window. It looked out on to the market, which was dominated by the great cathedral. The street was muddy and unpaved and was busy with carts loaded with produce, carriages, farmers on horseback, and men herding cattle and sheep to the pens from which they would be sold. Men and women hurried past and a coach rolled down the street and under the archway below her window. Perhaps when it had changed its horses it would be going on, and pass somewhere near Winterford. She washed and dressed and went downstairs.

The coffee-room was full, as it had been the previous night, and the waiters were hurrying to and fro serving breakfast. She hurried over to the one she had spoken to the previous night. 'The coach that just came in. Does it go anywhere near Winterford?'

He turned from serving a gentleman with ham and eggs, and smiled thinly. 'No, nothing goes out there; there's nothing to go for. You'll have to hire privately or walk——'

'Excuse me, did you say Winterford?' the man he was serving interrupted.

Margaret turned to him, a smile on her lips which faded when she realised it was one of the men who had been surveying her so openly the evening before. 'Yes,' she said coolly, to let him know she deplored his insolence.

'I am going there myself. I could take you.'

'We do not know each other, sir.'

'I beg your pardon. Let me introduce myself. I am Charles Mellison, of Mellison Hall in Huntingdonshire. You may have heard of the family.'

'I have not.'

He smiled. 'Ours is an old family with the very best of antecedents, I assure you. I am going to Winterford Manor, the country home of Lord Pargeter. You and your maid will be quite safe in my company, I promise.'

'I have no maid,' she said, and then wished she had not admitted it when she saw a little gleam of triumph in his eye. 'But that does not mean I will allow myself to be taken up by a perfect stranger.'

'No, of course not,' he said. 'I only thought I could

help you out of a difficulty. Lady Pargeter would not like to think a guest of hers had been left to make her own way.'

'I am not a guest of hers.'

'No? Then I do beg your pardon.'

'I am going to Sedge House. Mr Henry Capitain is my great-uncle.'

'But the Capitains and the Pargeters have known each other for centuries!' he exclaimed, as if that made everything right. 'You must allow me to escort you. . .'

'Well. . .' She hesitated. Was she in a position to look a gift-horse in the mouth?

'Have you broken your fast?' he asked suddenly. 'Do join me. Waiter, set another cover at once.'

He would not accept no for an answer. As they breakfasted, he drew her out, little by little, and by the time the meal was finished he knew almost all there was to know about her, and she had relaxed. It seemed perfectly proper to allow him to escort her to Winterford in the curricle which appeared as if by magic when they went outside.

There had been a sharp frost overnight, and the hedges and trees as they left the town were covered in sparkling rime. In no time, they seemed to have left these and all other signs of civilisation behind them and were on an uneven lane, going straight as a die, towards a flat expanse of nothingness which stretched for miles, with hardly a hillock to be seen. There were no trees either, except a few frosted willows and alders growing along the banks of the ditches. There were a great many of these dykes, where geese and ducks swam on gaps in the ice. Strange windmills with buckets, instead of paddles, were dotted about the landscape, their sails hardly turning in the windless air. But the sky was magnificent, layer upon layer of dark cloud rising from a horizon that was so wide, it seemed to take on the curve of the earth itself. Each cloud was streaked by fire, red and mauve and awesome. Margaret found herself admiring it at the same time as it frightened her. She felt tiny and insignificant.

'Most of this land was drained in the last century,' Charles told her. 'All but a few acres are owned by the Pargeters. Lord Pargeter is a good man, a fine fellow all round.'

'What of Sedge House?'

'That is not exactly in Winterford, but two or three miles further on. Have you not been there before?'

'Never.'

'It's a bleak place, right on the edge of the unreclaimed fen, and Henry Capitain has done nothing to improve it. I doubt you will like living there.'

'I have no choice.'

'Everyone has a choice,' he said softly, wondering whether to broach the subject of Roland and his dilemma. 'You could marry.'

'One day perhaps,' she said with a sigh. 'At the moment I cannot bring myself to think of it.' She smiled. 'Are you married, Master Mellison?'

'I am betrothed to Lord Pargeter's sister. We hope to marry soon. His lordship is unmarried, though his grandmother has been pressing him to find a wife for some time. He has to secure the lineage, you understand.'

'Does he not wish to marry?'

'Oh, yes, but he cannot find anyone prepared to live in this out-of-the-way place. But whoever becomes

Lady Pargeter would have to, you see, at least three-quarters of the year. Roland is almost resigned to never marrying.' He hoped his friend would forgive him the half-truth.

'I am sorry,' she murmured politely.

'I shall introduce you to him.' He turned to her as if suddenly thinking of it. 'I'll wager you would deal well together.'

'I thought the days of matchmakers were gone,' she said, smiling and revealing a twinkle in her eye and a dimple at the side of her mouth he had not noticed before; it gave him a twinge of conscience.

'Sometimes it is necessary. Shall we stop at Winterford Manor, so that you may make his acquaintance?'

'No, thank you,' she said firmly. 'I am flattered that you should think me worthy, but we are strangers and I am in mourning. Making calls will have to wait until I have settled down.'

He sighed and turned the curricle away from the village they had been approaching and down a narrow rutted track which ran alongside a high bank, on the other side of which was a wide ribbon of water which was too straight to be a river. Halfway along it was one of the strange windmills she had noticed before.

'What are those for?' she asked, pointing.

'The land round here is often flooded in winter. The windmills take the water off the fields in the buckets and tip it into the dykes.'

'How clever.'

They rode on in silence, Charles wondering how he could further Roland's cause without frightening her away, and Margaret apprehensive of what she would find at the end of her journey.

She realised he was making for a speck on the horizon which, as they drew nearer, was revealed as a house. It was a big square brick building which stood almost abutting the lane. On its other side, an overgrown lawn went down to a boat-house and a tiny jetty where a rowing-boat was moored in the water of the fen. The road went no further.

'Do you want me to wait?' he asked as he pulled the horses up at the door.

'No, thank you. I am grateful for your trouble, but I shall manage now.' She did not want a witness to her first encounter with her great-uncle and was glad he took her at her word.

'Very well. But if you change your mind about meeting his lordship, do not hesitate to let me know.'

As soon as she had alighted he turned the vehicle round and was soon bowling away along the flat road, back to Winterford. She sighed and turned to knock on the thick oak door.

She was taken completely aback when it was opened by a girl with a white-painted face, full red lips and several patches. She wore a pink satin open gown whose laces strained across her bosom, and a petticoat of red silk, beneath which Margaret could see white stockings and red high-heeled shoes. She stared at Margaret. 'Well, you're a little out of the ordinary, I must say.'

'I beg your pardon?'

'Different, I mean. You look as if you couldn't say boo to a goose.'

'Then my looks belie me,' Margaret retorted, putting

her chin in the air. Who did the hussy think she was? 'Is Master Capitain at home? I wish to speak to him.'

'Henry!' the girl yelled over her shoulder. 'Come on out here and see what's turned up.'

There was a shuffling noise behind her and a man pushed past her to stare at Margaret with myopic eyes. He wore white small-clothes which were stained with wine or tea, or something of the sort, and a shirt which was opened almost to the waist, revealing an expanse of flabby white flesh. His legs were clad in dirty white stockings but he wore no shoes. He had discarded his wig and his thin white hair stood up at all angles round his head. He had about six chins which wobbled down into a thick neck. 'Who are you?' he demanded. 'Did I ask you to come?'

'No, but I wrote to you. Did you not receive my letter? I am Margaret Donnington.'

'Margaret who?'

She countered with a question of her own. 'Are you Master Capitain?'

'Yes, of course I am. Who else would I be? And I don't remember any letter.'

'I am your great-niece. I am Felicity's daughter.'

'Great Jehosophat! I thought she was dead.'

Margaret gulped hard to take control of herself, though she felt like fleeing back down the road. 'She is dead. She died two weeks ago.' She paused, but he seemed unable to take in what she was saying. 'Before she died, she told me to come to you.'

'Why, for God's sake? We ain't seen each other in. . .' He racked his brain to remember. 'It must be nigh on thirty years. I did hear she had married. What did you say your name was?'

'Margaret Donnington.'

'How did you arrive here?'

'I came by stage to Ely and then a gentleman going to Winterford Manor brought me on.'

'Pargeter!' There was no attempt to disguise the contempt in his voice.

'No, it was one of his guests.' She paused, waiting, then added. 'Are you not going to invite me in?'

'The house is all in a muddle,' he said. 'Not fit to be seen. This slut——' he indicated the girl at his side, who had continued to stare at Margaret with unveiled amusement '—Nellie, here, don't go much on keeping house.'

"Tain't what I came for,' the girl retorted. 'I'm not a servant. If you don't like it you know what you can do.'

Margaret was wondering if she was ever going to be allowed over the threshold, and he was looking at her with bright little eyes, almost buried in the flesh of his cheeks, as if he wished her anywhere but on his doorstep. It was a wish she shared. At last he said, 'Better come in, though this ain't the place for a well-brought-up young lady.'

The girl he had referred to as Nellie laughed as she led the way through a dusty hall to an even dustier drawing-room with heavy old-fashioned furniture and faded velvet curtains. 'That's a fact and no argument,' she said, with a chuckle that hinted at something Margaret was not sure she wanted to know.

'Get us all a drink,' Henry ordered the girl, then, turning to Margaret, indicated the settle. 'Sit down. Tell me what happened.'

The telling did not take long, and he was silent at

the end of it, his many chins resting on his chest and his eyes glazed. The glass in his hand was empty and so was the girl's, but Margaret had not touched her wine.

'My, that's a turn up for the books,' Nellie said. 'What are you going to do now?'

Margaret looked from her to her uncle, who did not deign to answer for several seconds.

'I don't know,' he said at last. 'I don't know. Ain't you got anyone else you can go to?'

'No, or I would, believe me.'

'Where's your father?'

'He died in India. I was born out there in 1727, but the climate did not suit my mother and, when my father died, she brought me back to England. I was only a baby then; I do not remember him.'

'Nineteen years old,' he murmured. 'Felicity took her time about producing, considering she left here in '15.'

'My parents were married two years before I was born, no more.'

'Hmm,' he mused. 'Fancy that little chit managing on her own all that time. What did she do? For a living, I mean.'

'She was a mantua-maker, and a very good one.'

'Is that so? Hardly the occupation of a lady of breeding.'

'Perhaps she had little choice,' Margaret snapped in defence of her beloved mother, though she had no idea what had happened in the past. If Great-Uncle Henry was a sample of her family, then she did not blame her mother for never mentioning them.

'And you expect me to welcome you with open arms?' her uncle asked.

Nellie giggled. 'Why not? You do everyone else. . .'

'Shut up, you witless cow,' he said to her, then to Margaret, 'You'd do better turning right round and going back where you came from.'

'I can't. I've no money.'

'Neither have I and that's a fact.' He sighed. 'You'd better stay, I suppose. Just until we can think of something else. Nellie, my dear, show her where she can sleep and tell Mistress Clark there'll be one more for dinner.'

The house, neglected as it was now, had once been very fine, Margaret decided as she followed Nellie up the carved oak staircase and along a wide landing. The people who had built it must have been quite wealthy and had some standing in the community; the building materials would have had to be transported some distance because, apart from willows and a few aspen, there were no trees locally. The proportions of the house were on a grand scale too; lofty ceilings and long windows with leaded panes. Some of the doors along the landing were standing open and revealed large rooms full of worn furniture which had once been good.

One room was obviously in use. It was even more untidy than the rest of the house—the bed was unmade and garments were scattered all over the bed and the floor. Margaret could not help noticing that there was a man's night shirt and hose as well as women's clothes. She averted her gaze hurriedly; so Nellie was her great-uncle's wife! She was younger than Margaret herself and she was certainly not a lady of breeding. But who was she to criticise? Margaret asked herself as she followed her hostess into a bedroom at the far end of the corridor.

'You won't be disturbed here,' Nellie said. 'I hope you're not used to being waited on, because there aren't any servants except Mistress Clark, and she don't sleep in.' She laughed suddenly. 'She don't approve of Henry's goings-on, as she calls them, but she stays on account of she knew the old master.'

'My mother's father?'

'Yes; I suppose it would have been Henry's brother. He was a few years older than Henry. Before that, of course, there was your great-grandfather. Henry don't talk about them.'

'Is there no one else in the family?'

'Not that I know of, but then I ain't known Henry that long.' She paused, looking round the room. 'It's a bit dusty. It ain't one of the rooms we use often.'

'Do you entertain much, Mistress Capitain?' Margaret asked, going over to the wash-stand and noticing the scum on the top of the water in the jug.

Nellie threw back her head and laughed. 'Bless you, I ain't Henry's wife.'

Margaret was shocked to the core. She was not blind to some of the things that went on in the less salubrious parts of London; she knew men took mistresses and some wives took lovers, but she had never expected to find it happening in her own family, nor in the family home away from the capital. She sat down heavily on the bed, sending up a cloud of dust.

'Don't look so stricken,' Nellie said. 'Henry and me, well, we're just good friends. I came down here 'cos I needed to get away for a bit, understand?'

Margaret didn't and she said so.

'Never mind,' the girl said, and laughed again. 'You're like a fish out of water, here, ain't you?'

'Yes.'

'I'd find somewhere else to go, if I were you.' It was said almost kindly. 'Later on, or mayhap tomorrow, there's a whole lot more coming.'

'More like you?' It was out before Margaret could stop it.

'Yes, only worse. Men and women—they're coming to gamble and. . . Well, you know.'

Margaret shuddered. Her mother could not possibly have known it would be like this when she'd told her to come here. Now where was she to go? For a fleeting moment she thought of Charles Mellison and his friend, Lord Pargeter, looking for a wife who would be prepared to live in this outlandish place. She had heard that fen people were all slightly mad, and she was beginning to believe it. What could she do? She lifted her chin. 'Perhaps you should be the one to leave,' she said. 'After all, you have no ties here.. . .'

It was a silly thing to say and she realised it as soon as Nellie began to laugh. She was still laughing as she went back downstairs, leaving Margaret alone in the grubby bedroom.

It was a corner room, having windows on two sides which would have made it a pleasant bedchamber if it had been clean. It had a bed, a dressing-table and a cupboard, standing on a carpet so faded as to be colourless. She did not unpack, but went to the window and looked out on a landscape so bleak that she didn't know how anyone could like it. She saw nothing but acres and acres of flat land, some of it meadow, some of it ploughed, intersected by dykes, whose banks were higher than the surrounding land. From the other window the view was of water, with clumps of frost-blackened sedge and reeds. A rowing-boat rocked on its moorings beside the landing-stage. Overhead, in the great bowl of the sky, a heron flew. But her mother had loved her childhood here and had spoken of the special magic of the fen country—its glorious sunsets and red dawns, its plentiful wildlife, fish and fowl, its close-knit communities and hardy, superstitious people. What she had never told Margaret was why she had left and why she had never been back. As she stood at the window, a little of the atmosphere communicated itself to her and for the first time she began to understand.

But that did not mean she wanted to stay. Her uncle evidently did not want her and she was certainly not impressed with him, but what else was there for her to do? She had no money to return to London. Suddenly she found herself thinking again of Charles Mellison, who had suggested she should marry, and his long-legged, handsome companion, who was looking for a wife. She did not want either of them to be given the opportunity of crowing over her. She smiled and turned from the window; she would just have to make the best of the situation. Straightening her shoulders, she returned downstairs and made her way to the kitchen, intending to ask for mops and buckets to clean her room.

CHAPTER TWO

MISTRESS CLARK was thin and dark, reminding Margaret of a scavenging crow as she darted about the kitchen picking up utensils and bowls. She was muttering to herself, but stopped suddenly when she saw Margaret. 'Miss Felicity!' The bowl she had in her hand dropped to the floor and shattered. Margaret bent to pick up the pieces.

'It's a judgement, that's what it is,' the woman went on, crossing herself. 'I knew it would all end in tears; I told you so.'

'I'm not Felicity, Mistress Clark. I'm her daughter, Margaret.'

The cook let out her breath in a long sigh. 'My, you gave me a fright, mistress. The image of your poor mother, you are.'

'My mother is dead.'

'And you thought you would come back home, did you?'

'It was Mama's last wish. I'm sure she didn't know it would be like. . .' She paused, lifting her arm to indicate the house. 'Like this.'

'No, she wouldn't. She was only a young girl when she left home. I told her; I told her it would end in misery. . .'

'Mama wasn't unhappy, Mistress Clark. She and my father were very happy until he died and then we managed very well, she and I.'

'Well, I'm glad to hear it. But you aren't thinking of staying here, are you? This is an evil place and that one. . .' She pointed with a wooden spoon at the wall dividing the kitchen from the rest of the house. 'That one is the devil. Get out. Get out before he drags you under his wicked spell. He'll——'

She was interrupted by a bellow from the corridor outside, and the door was thrown open to reveal Henry Capitain, more tousled than ever. 'Are you going to stand there gossiping all day? I want my dinner.'

'It's coming,' the cook said, but there was no servility in her tone. 'Do you think I've got ten pairs of hands?'

'And you mind your manners, or you'll be out on your ear.'

Her answer was a laugh of derision.

He ignored it and turned to Margaret. 'Get back where you belong. Seeing's you're here, you can be my hostess. You can't be any worse at it than Nellie. Come on, now, we've company.'

Margaret followed him back to the drawing-room, where she found three men and three women who had arrived while she had been talking to the cook. They were all so grotesquely painted that it was impossible to tell what their features were like, and they wore huge wigs which disguised the colour of their hair. The men's clothes were as vivid as the women's, in pinks and purples, greens and mauves. They reminded Margaret of a flock of parrots.

'Margaret, I want you to meet our guests,' he said, waving a hand at them. 'Entertain them while I go and dress.'

He disappeared, leaving Margaret unable to utter a word. They stared at her; one of them even lifted a quizzing-glass and moved it up and down inches from her face. 'Ain't seen you before,' he said. 'Where'd old Henry find you?'

'He didn't,' she said coldly. 'I am his great-niece.'

This was followed by another long silence, until Nellie came in and diverted them with cries of welcome. 'It's been dull,' she said. 'There's nothing to do. . .'

'Nothing to do, Nellie?' one of the women laughed. 'Don't Henry satisfy you any more? Well, now we're all here, things will liven up, don't you think? Is the niece part of the entertainment?'

'My, I could be entertained by that one,' drawled one of the men, looking lecherously at Margaret. 'It might be amusing, don't you think? The quiet ones often turn out to have hidden fire. I had a mistress once, young she was, hardly out of the schoolroom and carefully brought up, but my, was she a demon in bed!'

He laughed heartily as Margaret turned and fled.

She ran up to her room, grabbed her bag and hurried down the back stairs to the kitchen. Mistress Clark was just taking a roast fowl from the oven. Margaret dashed past her and out of the door. They would surely catch her if she tried to go back along the only road. She turned and ran over the grass to the landing-stage. They could not follow her if she took the only boat. She threw her bag in the bottom, climbed in and cast off.

She had never rowed a boat before, but she had seen it done on the Thames and she bent to the oars with a will. At first she went round and round and kept bumping into the bank, but at last she found a kind of rhythm and discovered how to steer. Her direction was clear enough because Ely Cathedral stood out clear against the skyline. She had no idea how far away it was, because distances were deceptive where there were no landmarks except a few windmills, and the light was so strange. She rowed out of the wide water of the fen into the cut. She kept going until her back felt like breaking and her hands were covered in blisters, but still the great tower of the cathedral seemed no nearer. She knew that if she stopped the current would take her back the way she had come. She forced herself to continue, and inch by inch drove the boat forward towards a group of buildings surrounding a church, which she guessed was Winterford. There was a small landing-stage and sloping lawns to a large house. Thankfully, she pulled in and, throwing her bag before her, climbed on to dry land. And then, to her great consternation, she found her legs had become so numb with cold that she could not stand.

The house was two hundred yards away and much bigger than she had at first supposed. Built of grey stone, it seemed to have been put together haphazardly, with a tall main building and two wings, one with a lower roof-level which jutted out along the frontage and the other set at right angles. The central frontage had half a dozen evenly spaced mullioned windows and a massive wooden door, heavily studded. She began crawling over the grass towards it, dragging her bag with her, but, before she could reach it, she found herself looking at a kid-booted foot and a dark blue woollen skirt and heard the voice of a young woman. 'Goodness, you poor thing, whatever happened to you? Charles, come here and help me.'

'Mistress Donnington!' Margaret recognised the

voice of Charles Mellison, though she was all but fainting and could not see him clearly. 'How did you get here?'

'Never mind how she got here,' the young lady said, before Margaret could find her tongue. 'Help me get her indoors.'

He lifted her easily and carried her into the house and into a small sitting-room. Margaret saw nothing but the glowing embers of the fire, felt nothing but the warmth enveloping her, and then she fainted.

When she came to herself, she was lying in a beautifully furnished bedroom, covered with clean sheets and warm blankets, and the young lady was sitting in a chair beside the bed watching her. She smiled when she saw Margaret was awake.

'I'm Kate Pargeter,' she said, picking at the lace edging of the tiny apron she wore over a flower-patterned silk day-gown. It was almost a nervous gesture, as if she was unsure of herself, but then she laughed and revealed the mischievous look of a young girl. 'Charles told me you were coming to visit us, but I never dreamed you would arrive in so spectacular a fashion. My brother is out on the land but he'll be back soon. Wait till I tell him you could not wait for him to send for you and made your own way here.'

'I wasn't. . .' Margaret stopped, wondering what Charles Mellison had said about her. Why should Lord Pargeter send for her? 'I'm sorry, I'm confused,' she said.

Kate's tinkling laugh came to her as if through a fog. 'You are nothing like as mystified as I am. I thought you came from London, from Society, but you can evidently row a boat with the best of fen women.'

'I didn't know I could.' Margaret smiled. 'I don't think I am very good at it.' She turned her hands over, but the blistered palms had been covered with salve and bandaged.

'No, you poor dear. But how brave you were to try.' She picked up a glass from the small table by the bed and leaned forward to help Margaret drink from it. 'Charles said you had to go and visit your uncle before you honoured us with a visit, but he was quite sure you would not want to stay there. . .'

'He was right about that.'

'Is it as bad as they say?' The question was asked with a conspiratorial giggle.

'What do you mean?'

'Oh, there are all sorts of rumours. Visitors, you know, riotous behaviour——'

'Kate, you should not be bothering our guest with questions like that.' The speaker stood in the doorway, tall, angular almost, in country breeches and muddied top-boots. He was not smiling.

'Roly, you're back. Look who's here. Aren't you pleased to see her?'

'Very,' he said laconically, without stepping over the threshold. 'But I believe Mistress Donnington should be allowed to rest. You can question her all you like after I have spoken to her.'

Margaret looked up at him, recognising Master Mellison's companion of the evening before and guessing he was Lord Pargeter. They must have been talking about her or how did he come to know her name? If they had, what had they been saying? And why did Kate say she was expected? The strange conversation

she had had with Charles Mellison came to her mind
and made her mouth lift in a little quirk.

'I am glad to see you are able to smile,' his lordship
said. 'Now, please sleep. We will talk as soon as you
feel stronger.'

She wanted to say that they should talk now, that
whatever mysteries there were to be solved should be
uncovered at once. She felt like a pawn being pushed
around on a great chess-board, not in control of the
situation at all, and she did not like it. She turned to
Kate, who stood up with the empty glass in her hand.
Margaret just had time to register that it must have
contained a sleeping-draught before her eyes closed.

The next time she awoke, it was snowing. She could
see huge flakes of it sliding down the glass of the
window, but the room was warm from a fire which
blazed in the grate. Her bag had been unpacked;
underclothes, white stockings, a cambric petticoat and
a round gown of blue merino wool were laid over a
chair near the blaze to warm. She turned her head. A
maid was pouring hot water into a bowl which stood
on the wash-stand in the corner. It was the sound of
that which had disturbed her.

'Oh, did I wake you, mistress?' the maid said. 'I'm
sorry.'

'What time is it?'

'Ten, mistress.'

'Ten?' Margaret sat up. 'You mean ten in the
morning? Have I slept all night?'

'Yes, mistress. I'm Penny; I'm to look after you. His
lordship said I was not to rouse you, but as soon as you
waked to say he would like you to take breakfast with
him in the morning-room.'

'Yes, of course.' Margaret looked at the window. 'Has it been snowing long?'

'All night, mistress. I reckon the roads are about impassable. If it freezes harder, we'll have to get the skates out to go anywhere, but the ice isn't thick enough yet.' She turned towards Margaret and smiled. 'Still, we're snug enough here. Shall I help you wash and dress?'

'What? Oh, no, I can manage.'

'But your poor hands. Let me help you, mistress. His lordship will be put out if he hears I left you to struggle with them little buttons on your own. And you shouldn't put those hands in water, not till they've healed.'

Margaret acquiesced, and half an hour later Penny conducted her downstairs and showed her into the morning-room where Lord Pargeter sat alone, eating a late breakfast. He uncurled his great length from his seat and held a chair for her. 'I trust you slept well, Mistress Donnington?'.

'Very well, thank you.'

'Please help yourself to whatever you want.' He indicated the many chafing-dishes on the table. 'Or would you prefer me to do it? Your hands must still be painful.'

'Hardly at all, my lord.' She took a little ham, concentrating on her plate because she knew he was looking at her pensively, as if wondering how to make conversation with her. 'I am afraid I do not make a very good oarsman.'

'You did very well. Am I to assume you found Sedge House not to your liking?'

'It was not the house,' she said, 'though it was in a

parlous state.' She looked round the room as she spoke. It was elegantly furnished in mahogany and walnut, some of it exquisitely inlaid with satinwood. The seat of the chair she sat on, like all the others, was covered in damask. The fireplace was of marble and the plastered ceiling was decorated with gilded scrolls. It exuded wealth and status; there could not have been a greater contrast with Sedge House. 'My uncle was not expecting me and he had other guests,' she went on, in a effort to excuse the behaviour of her unsympathetic relative.

'Just so.' He lifted a pot. 'Chocolate?'

'Thank you.'

He poured a cup of the thick dark liquid for her. 'Your great uncle is a Capitain, just as you are,' he said, as if that explained everything.

'How do you know so much about me, my lord?' she asked, though she could guess his information came from Charles Mellison, and that made her feel uncomfortable. She began to wish she had not been so open with the young man.

'Master Mellison told me of his conversation with you,' he said. 'He told me you were going to live with your uncle.'

'That does not mean I could condone. . .' She paused, not wanting to put a name to what she had seen in her uncle's house. 'I never knew I had any relations until my mother was dying. Now I wish I had never come.'

'What would you have done if you had not?'

'I could have found work and lodgings, looked after myself.'

She could not read his expression. One minute it was

solicitous, another almost malevolent. His dark eyes never moved from her face; it was as if he was studying every line of it, committing it to memory. What did he see there? she wondered. Was he trying to read signs of debauchery which would tell him she was like her great-uncle? Was he wondering if he dared keep some-one like that under his roof? He broke the silence at last. 'What kind of work have you done?'

'I am a milliner, my lord.'

'I doubt there is much call for hat-makers in Winterford, Mistress Donnington. We are a very rural community. The village used to be on the edge of the winter inundation; it was the only place where the fen could be safely crossed, which is how it got its name, but a hundred years ago, while Cromwell and the king battled it out for supremacy, the Adventurers fought against nature and won. Now Winterford is simply a slight rise in the surrounding land, all of it very fertile, but a long way from the beau monde of London.'

'I was not thinking of setting up as a milliner here, my lord.'

'What, then?'

'I do not know. I am adaptable, my lord.'

He smiled and his sombre expression changed; his mouth softened and his eyes twinkled. 'Just so long as it does not entail keeping house for your uncle, eh?'

'He already has a housekeeper.'

Her smile dimpled her cheeks very attractively, he decided, though she still looked tense, half afraid. 'Where would you live?'

'I would have to find lodgings.'

'Live alone? I hardly think that would serve.' He

paused, then asked slowly, 'Have you thought of marriage?'

She smiled. 'Doesn't every young lady dream of it?'

'Is there no one?'

'No, my lord. I have been too busy. . .' She stopped suddenly, remembering her conversation with Charles Mellison.

Encouraged, he went on, 'I believe Master Mellison told you a little of my situation.'

'My lord, he would not be so indiscreet.'

He chuckled suddenly. 'You obviously know how to be discreet yourself, but you need not worry, I am not asking you to betray him; I know my friend very well and I can guess he told you I was looking for a wife.'

'He did mention it in passing, my lord.'

'Only in passing? I am persuaded he went out of his way to speak to you about it.'

'I cannot think why he should do that,' she murmured.

'Did he not say we would do very well together, you and I?'

'My lord!' she protested.

'Oh, please do not be alarmed.' He stopped speaking to offer her warm bread in a cloth-lined basket. She shook her head, and he went on, 'But he is right about my wanting to marry.'

'I am sure you could have no trouble finding a suitable wife, my lord,' she said demurely.

'As to that, I am not so certain,' he said. 'You see, I am very particular and very difficult to live with. In truth, I am impossible.'

'Surely not,' she said, because she thought it was expected of her.

Her answer produced a short bark of a laugh. 'Indeed I am. I am short-tempered, ill-mannered and I am wont to go off by myself for hours at a stretch. And as for making polite conversation. . .' He shrugged. 'Most of the time I find it tedious.'

'You do not paint a very agreeable picture of yourself, my lord.'

'I want you to know the truth.'

'Why?'

'Because. . .' he went on, leaning slightly towards her and making her heart beat in her throat and flooding her face with colour. Surely he was not. . .? No, she was being absurd. 'I believe you are in something of a fix yourself. . .'

'Not so desperate that I have to resort to trying to live with a man who, on his own admission, is impossible to live with,' she said with some spirit. 'I pray you, do not assume that because I am in a little difficulty I have to throw myself at the first man who crosses my path. I listened to Master Mellison because politeness demanded it, but that does not mean I understood or wished to comply with whatever it was he was suggesting. I may be a Capitain, as you put it, but we are not all like my great-uncle, I assure you. My mother was a lady right to the end, in spite of being forcibly separated from all she held dear and having to earn a living.' She pushed her chair back and stood up. 'I am grateful for your hospitality, Lord Pargeter, but I should like to leave now.'

'Leave?' he queried, raising one dark brow. 'I am afraid you can't do that.'

'I insist.'

He smiled. She was very angry indeed. Her cheeks

were flushed and her eyes sparkled; she was not a lost kitten but a spitting one, and he found the transformation somewhat disturbing. 'I am sorry,' he said. 'As soon as the roads are cleared of snow, of course you may leave. I would not dream of detaining you against your will. Please sit down and eat some breakfast; I can't have you fainting again.'

She subsided into her chair, though she did nothing to obey his command to eat. She was sure that food would choke her.

'That's better. Now, let us begin again. You are very welcome to stay as long as you like, but there are certain things you should know.' He looked closely at her, wondering how to go on. 'Firstly, my friend Mellison.'

'What about him?'

'He is betrothed to my sister Kate.'

'I know; he told me.'

'He is also impetuous. Once he has an idea in his head, there's no shifting it.'

'About you needing a wife, you mean?'

'Yes. He is quite convinced you are the very one.'

'I am flattered,' she murmured, but she didn't sound very convincing. 'But haven't you got a mind of your own?'

His smile disappeared and his frown took over. 'My mind is my own, Mistress Donnington, make no mistake about that. Unfortunately Charles was so sure of himself that he told my grandmother to expect you. . .' He paused. 'He said I had met you in London, at Lady Gordon's. . .'

Margaret attempted to laugh, but it came out more like a strangled cry. 'I have never met Lady Gordon.'

'Please do not interrupt. Grandmama was overjoyed to know I am going to settle down at last.' He grinned suddenly. 'I am twenty-six years old and she was beginning to think it would never happen.'

'It hasn't,' Margaret said sharply.

He ignored her interruption. 'Lady Pargeter is very old and not always in good health. The doctors say she must not, on any account, be upset.'

'I am sorry for that and, of course, I would not wish to upset her, but——'

'Her ladyship has been led to believe I have brought you here to meet her. She wants to see you.'

'Master Mellison had no right. . .'

'Exactly what I told him, Mistress Donnington, but I am afraid he is unashamed. He is quite convinced he is in the right of it and you will agree to marry me.'

'You have not asked me, have you?'

'I am asking you now.'

'In order to please your friend or your grandmother?'

'I please myself.' Again there was that angry set to his mouth which spoiled his looks.

Margaret found herself laughing hysterically. The events of the last two days had been so strange, the people she'd met even stranger. It was like being in a madhouse.

'I am glad it amuses you,' he said coldly, though he could not help noticing the dimple deepening near her mouth; he found it strangely alluring.

'I am sorry,' she said, taking a handkerchief from her reticule and dabbing at her streaming eyes. 'But I never dreamed my first proposal would be so. . .so romantical.'

He stood up suddenly, crashing his chair back. 'And

I never expected the lady in receipt of my offer would laugh in my face.' He strode to the window to look out on the white landscape and calm himself. Charles was right about one thing. There was no question of Susan's coming down in this weather and neither could he go to her. The thought of never seeing her again filled him with impatience which could not be relieved unless he followed his friend's advice and found someone else to marry. And Margaret's laughter had served to harden his heart; and the fact that she was a Captain went some way to salving his conscience. He turned back to her, once more in command of himself. 'Please forgive me. I deserved your derision, but let's not beat about the bush any longer. I need a wife and you need somewhere to live, so shall we begin again?'

The look on his face stopped her laughter. He was regarding her with an expression almost of loathing, and yet there was pain behind the dark eyes, as if the hate was more for himself than her. 'I do believe you are serious!'

'Certainly I am. After all, arranged marriages are nothing out of the ordinary and, if you have no one to make such arrangements for you, is there any reason why you should not make them for yourself? I am wealthy and I am not an ogre. I will make no great demands on you. You will have your own suite of rooms, a wardrobe befitting my wife, jewellery, carriage and horses, an allowance. To all intents and purposes, I will be the loving husband. . .'

'And what do I have to do in return?'

'Be a dutiful wife in the eyes of the world, at least while my grandmother is alive. After that——' he shrugged—'you may annul the marriage if you wish, so long as it has lasted at least a year. You will be amply recompensed in that event.' He did not know how difficult an annulment would be, but, as he did not anticipate having to put it to the test, it was an easy thing to suggest.

She understood that the marriage was not to be consummated. It seemed extraordinary that he should not want an heir. And what significance was there in stipulating a year? 'My lord, this conversation is becoming nonsensical,' she said.

'It will make more sense if you think about it,' he said. 'Do not dismiss my proposal out of hand and, as it looks as though you might be snowed up here for a little while, perhaps you would do me the courtesy of allowing yourself time to consider it.'

Agreeing to that could do no harm, she decided. 'Very well, my lord. I will think about it.'

He smiled and returned to the table. 'Thank you, but I must ask you to maintain the masquerade for my grandmother's sake when you meet her.'

She was his guest, and an impoverished one at that; she agreed reluctantly. She didn't see how deceiving Lady Pargeter would be any help at all if the marriage never took place. He was so willing to lie that she supposed he would soon invent a story of a lovers' tiff and the engagement being all over.

She met her ladyship at dinner, which was taken at three in the afternoon, but, even as early as that, it was almost dark and the long dining-room was bathed in the glow of several chandeliers.

Physically Lady Pargeter was a tiny, very frail woman who had to be helped to her chair, but mentally, Margaret was sure, she was strong as iron and just as unbending. She wore a white powdered wig with a cap trailing ribbons sitting on top of it. Her undress gown of patterned silk flowed in pleats from an embroidered yoke, which did little to disguise the fact that she was little more than skin over bone. Her face did not look painted, although it was chalk-white and the cheeks sunken. But her brown eyes were alive, darting about the room, taking everything in, missing nothing. She lifted the lorgnette which dangled from a ribbon on her wrist and peered through it at Margaret.

'So,' she said, when everyone was seated and the silent footmen began to serve the meal, 'are you my grandson's choice or is he yours?'

Margaret did not know what to say, but before she could think of a suitable reply Roland came to her rescue. 'It was mutual, Grandmama.'

He had changed into a lilac satin coat over a long embroidered waistcoat. His white breeches were tied with a bow below the knee. Pristine white ruffles adorned his throat and wrists and white stockings graced his elegant calves. He wore a powdered wig with side-curls and ringlets tied at the back with a black ribbon. He looked very stylish, but Margaret found herself thinking that she liked him best in plain country clothes which seemed to suit his muscular physique better. She blushed suddenly when she realised he was looking at her. Could he possibly have read her thoughts?

'Do you know what you are letting yourself in for?' Lady Pargeter demanded of Margaret, ignoring her grandson.

'I think so, my lady.'

'Good, because I wouldn't want you to be under any

illusions. Being married to a Pargeter heir is a dangerous undertaking, especially for a Capitain.' She looked venomously at Margaret. 'Did your mother never tell you that?'

'No, she never mentioned Winterford at all, not until. . .until the day she died.'

'Hardly to be wondered at.'

'Grandmama, you are making something of nothing,' Roland put in before Margaret could ask what she meant. 'We will hear no more of it. Tell me, what have you been doing today?'

'What is there to do in this God-forsaken place? Hannah read to me a little while and I worked on my needlepoint, but my eyes are not good enough for that now. I don't know why I continue with it. Obstinacy, I suppose. I do not like being beaten. Oh, and I sat for a time looking out of my window.' She gave a cackle of a laugh. 'A wonderful view I have from my window—nothing to behold but the horizon and the sky.'

'The sky is very beautiful,' Margaret said. 'I never realised it until yesterday.'

'I did see something today, though,' the old lady went on, ignoring Margaret's comment. 'I saw a woman in a rowing-boat, coming upriver from that. . .that *place*. She stopped at our jetty.'

Kate giggled and Charles said, 'I didn't see anyone, did you, Roland?'

'At our jetty?' he queried. 'No, I did not.'

'It's funny she should turn up again,' the old lady said, peering at Margaret. 'You have a look of her. . .'

'No, she hasn't,' said Roland quickly. 'Mistress

Donnington is nothing like her. And it was years ago, Grandmama. . .'

'Is it? Oh, time means nothing to me now. Sometimes it drags, and weeks seem like years, and sometimes it is the other way round.' She sighed. 'What it is to be old. Everybody standing about waiting for you to die.'

'Rubbish!' said Roland.

'Oh, Grandmama!' said Kate. 'You must not talk like that.'

'Why not? I am long past the age when I should be in my coffin. My daughter-in-law has been dead these many years and now my son is gone. Why have I been left behind?'

'Because we love you and do not want to part with you,' Kate said.

'There's more to it than that,' she said. 'It has something to do with this young man here.' And she poked Roland's arm with her lorgnette. 'I have been preserved, pickled in wine and brandy, simply in order to see the Pargeters with a new heir. I shall go to my grave in peace when that happens.'

Roland looked at Margaret as if defying her to deny the possibility. She concentrated on her plate, picking without appetite at fish in oyster sauce. What was going on? They were all talking in riddles.

'So, when is the wedding to be?' her ladyship continued. 'I think it should be soon.'

'But I am in mourning, my lady,' Margaret put in, reluctant to talk of a marriage she never intended should take place, but she remembered just in time Roland's warning to humour the old lady. Arguing with her might bring on a seizure. 'My mother died less than two weeks ago.'

'Where?'

'In London.'

'Your father? Was he one of the Donningtons of Devon?'

'I don't think so, my lady. He died when I was very small. In India.'

'Oh, a merchant!' There was contempt in her ladyship's voice, and Margaret was tempted to defend the father she had never known, but changed her mind.

'I believe so.'

'Was he successful?'

Margaret forced herself to smile. 'If he had been, I would not be here now.'

It was not an answer which pleased her ladyship. She drew her lips down into a thin line and tapped Margaret impatiently on the back of her hand with her fan. 'My grandson honours you, and you would do well to remember it.'

'Indeed, I do, my lady.'

'Good. Have you any other kin, besides that reprobate Henry Capitain?'

'I know of no one, my lady.'

'Then who is there to complain if you marry while you are in mourning?' She turned to her grandson. 'I want it done and I want it done quickly. I have no time to waste, even if you think you have. And you haven't, you know. Twenty-six and still single. You are not even a widower, which might excuse you.'

'Oh, I say,' Charles broke in.

'I call spade a spade,' she said. 'And we all know it sometimes takes two marriages to produce an heir.'

Margaret was perplexed. 'What does she mean?' she whispered to Roland, who sat next to her.

'My father's first wife died in a fall from a horse soon after they married, and they had no children,' he answered in an undertone. 'My sister and I are the result of his second marriage. Grandmama is a little confused; she sometimes relives these little dramas. Pay no heed.'

The meal ended silently. It was as if the old lady's talk of death had put a constraint on them all, and Margaret was glad when it was over and her ladyship rose to leave the table. Hannah, the old lady's companion, who had shared the meal but not the conversation, was immediately at her side to help her to her room, leaving Kate and Margaret to go to the withdrawing-room together.

'Oh, I am so glad you came,' Kate told Margaret. 'It gets dreadfully dull here sometimes.'

'What do you do for amusement?' Margaret asked her.

'Sometimes we go to Cambridge or to the races at Newmarket. And there is always the fen.'

'The fen?'

'Boating and fishing and wildfowling. I don't shoot, of course, but Roland is a crack shot, and Charles nearly as good. It isn't surprising when you consider they both served with distinction in the army. They were in the same regiment—did you know that?'

'No,' Margaret said, choosing her words carefully. 'His lordship and I had very little time to get to know each other. I had to nurse Mama.'

'Of course, I understand. But you must think of the future now.'

Margaret didn't want to think about it. 'Tell me about yourself,' she said.

'Roland is eight years older than I am, you know. I believe my mother had several miscarriages between the two of us. I don't remember her, but Roland says Papa was so delighted to have a daughter after so long, he spoiled me dreadfully.' Her voice became sad as she added, 'He died five months ago. Roland was missing at the time—it was just after the battle at Culloden— and we did not know what had happened to him. It was only when Charles got leave in the summer and came to tell us Roland had been wounded, and was being cared for by the Chalfonts in Derbyshire, that we knew he was alive. As soon as he was well enough to travel he returned to his regiment, and then of course he learned of Papa's death and came straight home to take up his inheritance.' She laughed lightly. 'You know, sometimes he treats me like a daughter instead of a sister. He can be very pompous when he chooses.'

'Yes, I can imagine that,' Margaret said with a wry smile.

'But you are not at all haughty and you will not treat me like a child, will you, even when you marry Roland? After all, you cannot be much older than I am.'

'I am nineteen.' She knew that she would soon be past marriageable age, especially as she had no dowry, but that didn't mean she was desperate. 'But I have not agreed to marry him.'

'Oh, but you will, won't you? You will be so good for him, I know you will. I knew it as soon as I saw you. Charles was right; all Roly needed was a little push in the right direction.'

Margaret felt herself being drawn further and further

into the web and yet she seemed unable to do anything to free herself, and the longer the charade went on, the more difficult it became to speak out, to say she had no intention of marrying Lord Pargeter. She was about to pluck up her courage to do so, when Roland and Charles joined them.

They had some desultory conversation, and then Roland suggested showing Margaret over the house.

'Capital notion!' Charles said, grinning. 'Kate and I will amuse ourselves with a little piquet. Hannah will be down again directly to chaperon us.'

Margaret followed Roland from the room, determined to tell him she would not fall in with his outrageous scheme. Although it was little past four o'clock it was already quite dark, and he picked up a lamp from the table in the hall and held it aloft. It revealed a vaulted gallery that towered the whole height of the building, panelled and hung with portraits.

'My ancestors,' he said, indicating the pictures. 'The baronetcy was granted by Elizabeth when we lived in Ely and owned land on the higher ground above Winterford. As the fens were drained, so we acquired more. We have been in residence in the Manor since the Commonwealth.' He led the way up the wide staircase. 'The house is built in the shape of a crooked E. The staircase forms the central bar and most of the rooms we use are in the west wing, which is more protected from the prevailing wind than the east side.' They reached the gallery, where they stood side by side, looking over the banister to the vestibule below. It was lit by two lamps near the door, and a huge fire whose warmth did not reach them.

'Your great-uncle was here,' he said.

'Uncle Henry? When?'

'Last evening. He came looking for you.'

'How did he know where I was?'

'One must suppose he guessed.'

'I did tell him that Master Mellison had been kind enough to escort me to Sedge House,' she said slowly. 'What did he say?'

'Oh, he was full of bluster and talk of abduction and a great deal more.'

'He thought you had abducted me?' she queried in surprise. 'Why, that's nonsense.'

'So I told him. He said if I had not abducted you I would have no objection to your returning with him.'

'What did you say to that?'

'I said, of course, I had none, but that you were sleeping off the effects of your ordeal, an ordeal brought about by his immoral behaviour, but, if you wished, I would take you to him when you had recovered.' He paused, turning to face her. 'Do you wish to go back?'

She thought about it for a moment. Was that what she ought to do? It might get her out of the extraordinary situation she found herself in here at the Manor, but the memory of her uncle's lecherous guests decided her. 'No, certainly not. I cannot think why he should think I would. He did not exactly make me welcome.'

'He said something about the child of his beloved niece and blood being thicker than water. I am afraid that he angered me so much that I became a little indiscreet.'

'Oh, what did you say?'

'I cannot repeat the words I used, Mistress

Donnington.' The fury he had felt when he'd seen
Capitain shaking the snow off his hat and stamping his
booted feet on the hall rug of Winterford Manor had
evaporated, leaving him icily calm. Pargeters and
Capitains had not spoken to each other for years and,
for the most part, ignored one another's existence;
Roland could hardly believe that charlatan could have
had the effrontery to call at Winterford Manor and
demand to see him. Demand! He had been about to
throw him out, when he had realised there was a way
to crush him completely. He had told the insolent
fellow of his intentions towards Margaret. It had
silenced him just long enough for him to comprehend
the implications. There had been a great deal more
ranting about being Margaret's legal guardian and his
permission being needed for such a step, but that was
all it was, nothing but bravado. They had come to an
arrangement which guaranteed silence and involved a
certain sum of money changing hands. The man would
gamble it away in less than a month, but by then the
marriage would have taken place. If Roland had had
any doubts about the rights and wrongs of what he was
doing, they had been dispersed by that visit.

CHAPTER THREE

'THANK you,' Margaret said quietly. 'It was kind of you.'

'No, it was not!' Roland sounded almost angry. 'I am not kind, I am just the reverse. My motives were purely selfish.'

'Oh,' she said, understanding. 'You told him. . .'

'That we were to be married, yes.' His tone had moderated; it would not do to take his anger out on her.

'Why?'

'He insisted he was your legal guardian and could force you to return to him. I could not let you go back to him, could I?' That was true; he could no more have handed her back to that debauched old man than he could have drowned a kitten, and she was homeless and penniless, but did that mean he had the right to coerce her into marrying him?

'Thank you, but did you need to go to such lengths?' She looked at him with her wide violet eyes and made him feel a hundred times worse. 'Now it is not only your grandmother who is being deceived, but my uncle too.'

'There need be no deception. You said you would think about my proposal. . .'

'I have considered it very carefully, my lord, and I am very conscious of the honour you do me, but the answer must be no.'

'Why? Are you nursing dreams of falling in love, Mistress Donnington? I assure you it is a fantasy that only marriages based on love are successful.' He paused, hardening his heart. 'Do you want me to hand you over to your great-uncle? I believe he has plans for you. . .'

'What kind of plans?'

'Need I go into detail? You saw his paramour and his guests. . .' He shrugged, leaving her to imagine the worst. 'The choice is yours.'

'I can go back where I came from.'

'Do you have enough money to pay the coach fare, find lodgings and keep yourself until you find work suitable for a gentlewoman?'

'No,' she said slowly. 'I wonder, would you be kind enough to lend me——?'

'No, it will not serve.'

'You are despicable!'

He laughed. She was angry again, but anger became her, made her eyes sparkle and colour flood her cheeks. He had to grit his teeth to go on. 'No, simply practical. Don't you see, it would be the answer to both our dilemmas? I promise you I will do everything to make your life here as agreeable as possible.' He meant that, every word of it. 'Is such a prospect so dreadful?'

She did not answer immediately because a little imp inside her was telling her that she could grow to like the idea. He was handsome and courteous, if you ignored his bouts of ill-humour, and they soon passed. And maybe it was simply that he could not understand her reluctance. Why was she so reluctant? Could it be that he was right and she had been fantasising about falling in love? She ought to know better than that; she had not been so carefully nurtured that she did not know anything about the real world. You could not live and work in London and remain ignorant of it. She should be glad she did not have to return to that world, where she might end up like Nellie, desperate enough to consent to anything.

Seeing her hesitation, he gave a twisted smile. 'I promised to free you at the end of a year and, God willing we both survive, I shall keep that promise. And I will make sure you have a dowry, enough to seek out the man you believe you are destined to fall in love with. I will not stand in your way.'

'Why a year?' she asked, curious in spite of herself.

'It will soon pass,' he said, evading her question. 'And I will not trouble you with my presence. I have to go back to London almost immediately and shall not return except very occasionally, when I come home to see that all is well and pay my respects to Grandmama.'

'Why?' she asked again.

'I have my reasons.' His tone was clipped.

She turned to look into his face, dimly lit by the lamp he held, trying to search out answers he did not seem to be able to voice. What sort of man was he, that he could so cold-bloodedly talk of ending a marriage before it had even begun? Unfeeling in the extreme, she decided, a man with no warmth. And yet there were times when there was a light in his eyes which revealed humour and vitality, and there was about him a suppressed energy which excited her. She could so easily fall under his spell.

He returned her gaze, hating himself. She was helpless, forced to ponder on the imponderable because of her circumstances. And she was beautiful, something which had not been evident when he had first seen her in the White Hart; she had a clear skin which had never been spoilt by paint, huge, expressive eyes which seemed to bore into his very soul, a mouth made for kissing, and a determined chin. Life with her would not be dull. If she had been anyone but a Capitain, he would have retracted, given her money to go wherever she wished and put her from his mind. It was all Charles's fault. No, he chided himself, he should not blame Charles. *He* had done nothing but put the idea into his head. Charles had not been the one to lead Lady Pargeter to believe he would marry Margaret; he had done it himself. Lies! Could she see that in his eyes?

'Very well,' she said quietly. 'I accept your terms.'

'Good.' He smiled briefly as he took her arm to guide her along the gallery.

She was not sure if it was the touch of his hand or a feeling of foreboding which made her shudder. She did not know why she should be apprehensive—perhaps it was because marriage was something she had not even been considering forty-eight hours before, perhaps it was the cavernous entrance hall with its upper gallery and dark corners where no lamp could reach, or perhaps it was just the weather, which imprisoned everyone, whether they willed it or not.

'You are shivering,' he said. 'Are you cold?'

'A little.'

He put the lamp on a chair and took off his coat to drape it round her shoulders. His touch was gentle and his breath was warm on her cheek as he bent to draw the coat close under her chin. She looked up and their eyes met and held, his dark and brooding, hers bright with tears which she did not know why she was shedding. It was as if both were searching for knowledge, for reassurance, for hope. He lowered his head, drawing closer, his mouth only inches from hers. She waited, trembling like a frightened bird beneath his hands.

'No,' he murmured, and drew away.

'No?' She could hardly speak for the tumult in her breast.

'You are cold. I think we should postpone the rest of our tour for another time.'

'Yes,' she said, bewildered by his strange behaviour. He had proposed, in the coldest fashion possible, a marriage of convenience and then had warmed sufficiently to behave like a prospective husband and kiss her, and then decided against it. Ice; he was made of ice. And fire.

He picked up the lamp again and escorted her to her chamber door. 'Goodnight, Mistress Donnington.' He took her hand and bowed over it but he did not lift it to his lips. It was almost as if he was afraid to do so.

She went to bed, her insides churned up by the knowledge that she had wanted him to kiss her, which was foolish in the extreme. She had agreed to his terms and they took no account of feelings, either his or hers. It was not a love-match. Then why was she crying?

He returned downstairs to join Charles and Kate in a childish game of cards which caused them great hilarity but failed to lighten his mood. Kate soon lost patience with him and declared her intention of going to bed. 'One would think Mistress Donnington had rejected you,' she said.

'On the contrary, Mistress Donnington—Margaret—has done me the honour of accepting.'

'Then smile, for heaven's sake,' she said. 'It should make you happy.'

'Yes, cheer up, man,' Charles said. 'Think of the future.'

Yes, he decided, forcing a smile for their benefit, it was only thinking of Susan and their future that kept him sane.

Kate retired and the men went into the library, where a decanter of good French brandy and glasses had been put out on a small table by the window.

'There is something you forgot when you thought of this diabolical plan,' Roland said, pouring drinks. "Marry a complete stranger", you said, but you forgot that when two people are together for any length of time they cannot remain strangers. Even after one day, I have come to know Margaret a little. She is brave and independent and she has a sense of humour that is refreshing. I am sure she can read my guilt in my eyes.'

'Then stay away from her until the wedding. You are leaving immediately after it, aren't you?'

'I had planned to.'

'What do you mean, planned to? Have you changed your mind?'

'The weather may prevent it.' How could he explain to his friend what he did not understand himself, his remorse, so strong that he had been almost tempted to tell Margaret the truth? The only reason he had not done so was because he would lose any respect she might have had for him, and he was surprised to discover how much that mattered to him. He told

himself he wanted to see her comfortable and happy in
her new home before he left it.

'It was only an idea, to help you out.' Charles's voice
broke in on his brooding. 'You didn't have to do it.'

'No, and do you know what decided me? It wasn't
my own predicament; it wasn't thinking of Susan; it
was the sight of that depraved villain, Capitain, standing in my vestibule demanding to have her back. I was
furious.'

'Whatever the reason, it's done now. If you have any
twinges of conscience, just remind yourself of the
benefits.'

'To me, but not to Margaret.'

'She will have a year of being Lady Pargeter, a year
of plenty that most young ladies would give their teeth
for, and what she doesn't know cannot hurt her, can
it?' He paused to take a mouthful of brandy, smiling
over his glass at his friend. 'Besides, she may survive
the year. After all, you do not love her and she does
not love you, so it won't count, will it? Nothing will
happen. It will all come right in the end and no harm
done to anyone. But you really must look happier at
the prospect, my friend, or questions will be asked.'

'I must go to Derbyshire and explain to Susan.'

'No.' Charles spoke sharply. 'It will look decidedly
odd.'

'It will look even odder if I don't, particularly to her
parents. I am sure they were expecting me to offer for
her before I left.'

'Why didn't you?'

'I don't know. The time didn't seem propitious.'

Charles laughed. 'You mean you were not sure of
your feelings?'

'Of course I am sure.'

'Then wait,' Charles said implacably. 'The roads are impassable and, you never know, by the spring. . .' He stopped and surveyed his friend. 'Harden your heart, Roland, harden your heart. Think of your true love, think of the Capitains. Don't all Capitains deserve your hatred?'

'Yes, by God. If it weren't for a Capitain, I wouldn't be in this fix. Here's a pox to all Capitains.' He tipped the contents of his glass down his throat and poured himself another and then another, followed by several more until the bottle was empty.

He did not remember staggering up to bed, but he woke in his own room next morning with a blacksmith's shop in his head. He groaned and sat up. Johnson had laid out a double-breasted velvet coat and buff breeches and there was hot water in the washing bowl. He ignored the clothes, washed, and went to the wardrobe where he found warm wool breeches and thick stockings. He scrambled into them, put on a huge black overcoat which came almost to his ankles, and went downstairs. He passed the open door of the morning-room, where the table bore witness to the fact that everyone else had already breakfasted, and went out into the snow. Perhaps the biting cold would knock some sense into him.

The village, with a few large trees surrounding its green, stood on ground a little higher than the surrounding fen, which meant the inhabitants were rarely troubled by flooding except in very severe weather. There had been fresh falls of snow during the night, which might cause problems when a thaw set in. He dug into the snow with his cane to assess its depth and the amount of water they might expect, then looked back at the house, which was two hundred yards from the cut and about ten feet above its present level. Was ten feet enough if the cut became swollen with melting snow from the hills away to the west? And what about the village itself? The men ought to begin building a barrier now, not waiting until disaster struck.

Putting aside his headache and his impending nuptials, he tramped off over the snow towards the group of clay-lump cottages which stood close to the church.

Unlike Roland, Margaret could not put the forthcoming wedding from her mind. Kate would not cease chattering about it, laughing and making plans, oblivious to the fact that Margaret was not joining in.

'When is it to be?' Kate asked as they sat together in one of the smaller sitting-rooms, which was easier to keep warm than the huge drawing-room and had some comfortable upholstered chairs. She had some embroidery in her lap, but she had done no work on it since Margaret had joined her.

'The twenty-first, four days before Christmas. Her ladyship wants no delay and his lor—Roland agrees with her.'

'But that's less than a week away! How can you possibly be ready by then?'

'It is not difficult. I have no family except Great-Uncle Henry, and there will be no invitations issued, although Roland has said he will invite the villagers to attend the service. They will help to fill the church.'

'Don't you mind? A wedding should be a grand affair, a cause for celebration. It is almost as if you are ashamed to have it known.'

'No, not at all. You forget, I am in mourning.'

'Oh, yes, I am sorry, Margaret, how thoughtless of me. Does that mean there will be no wedding-trip either?'

Margaret gave a light laugh and was surprised that it sounded so natural. 'We'll go nowhere while this weather holds, but later, perhaps, we may go to London. Roland tells me he has business there.'

'Business!' Kate gave a grimace of disgust. 'You know, he really is the dullest man.'

'Not at all,' Margaret said, and meant it. Whatever she thought of Roland, she did not find him dull. If only he were not so tense, as if he was deliberately holding himself aloof, he would be an entertaining and charming man. She began to wonder if the fault was with her, but if he found her not to his liking, why had he asked her to marry him? 'We can combine business with pleasure, surely?'

'Yes. There will be routs and balls, and no doubt Roland will present you at court. Have you decided what you are going to wear?'

'To court?'

'No.' Kate laughed. 'At your wedding.'

'Roland has insisted on buying me a gown. Is there anyone in Ely who could make me one? Nothing extravagant, of course.'

'There is a dressmaker, but I have rarely been to her.' Kate sounded doubtful. 'I usually buy all I need when we are in London.'

'There is no time for that. I am a good needlewoman, so if it isn't to my liking I can alter it.'

No wheeled vehicle could use the roads so they went into Ely by sled, drawn by a sturdy little pony, with one of the grooms at its head wearing huge flat snow-shoes and Roland and Charles riding alongside. Wrapped up in fur cloaks and muffs and with several sheepskins around their knees, the two girls enjoyed the ride. The sun sparkled on the snow and icicles hung from the hedges, and for a time Margaret forgot to be sad. It was good to be outside, to breathe the icy air; it made her tingle with new life. She looked up at Roland, riding so easily alongside, his hands loosely on the reins; there was no doubt he was a very handsome man and she had made quite a catch. If only they had met in different circumstances; if only. . . He glanced towards her, almost as if he had read her thoughts, and their eyes met briefly, reminding her of the kiss that never was, before he turned back to negotiate an ice-covered pot-hole.

'We should be able to skate tomorrow,' Kate was saying. 'Not on the river, of course—that's too danger-ous—but on the fen. There is a shallow stretch of water which is flooded every winter and is perfectly safe. Would you like that?'

Margaret pulled herself together. 'I would certainly like to try, though whether I can stay upright remains to be seen.'

Kate laughed. 'If the ice holds we'll go tomorrow, and then we shall see.'

The Isle of Ely was a surprisingly small place, considering the size of the cathedral, and its roads were no more than muddy lanes, made slippery by frozen snow. Set on a small hill which had been an island in the days before the fens were drained, it had the usual quota of basket-makers, candle-makers, butchers, dair-ies, fish-sellers, blacksmiths, carriage-makers, coopers and the like, besides more than its fair share of inns and taverns. There was, as Kate had said, a dressmaker and, because it was a place of learning, a bookshop, tucked in the ancient walls close to the cathedral.

Once Margaret and Kate had been delivered at the door of the dressmaker's tiny establishment, the two men went off on business of their own, promising to return in an hour. The dressmaker, a tiny little woman in a plain grey wool dress which did not fill Kate with confidence, dashed around laying out patterns and materials, talking the whole time to cover the fact that she was flustered to receive such illustrious customers. 'If only I had known you were coming,' she said. 'I could have ordered more samples. Would you like me to send for some?'

'No, I am afraid there is no time,' Margaret said, deciding not to tell the woman that the gown was intended for her wedding; she was not sure if the dressmaker was capable of anything elaborate. If her mother, who was a first-class seamstress, had been alive, she would have had a wedding-dress the envy of the world. She sighed. If her mother had been alive, she would not have been in Ely choosing a wedding-gown in the first place. 'I need something simple.' She picked up a swatch of pale lilac taffeta. 'This, I think.'

'Margaret, it's too plain!' Kate exclaimed.

'It can be trimmed with satin ribbon bows and lace in the neck and sleeves. I am in mourning, after all, and I don't want anything too bright.'

Roland returned at that point to fetch them and Kate turned to appeal to him. 'Look at this,' she said, holding the swatch out to him. 'Margaret wants to wear this.'

'She may have whatever she chooses,' he said, barely glancing at the material. 'I am sure whatever she wears will look very well.'

There was no more argument and, having been promised that the gown would be ready in time, they joined Charles for nuncheon at the White Hart.

Kate chatted happily to the men and no one seemed to notice that Margaret was very quiet. She was thinking of the last time she had been there. Was it only two days before? So much had happened since then and her life had been turned round in a way she could never have foreseen. Was it for the good? Or had she put her head in a snare of her own making? If she had been able to see into the future, would she have ever left London? It was a question she could not answer.

Kate was laughing and talking about her own wedding, fixed for early spring. 'I can hardly wait,' she said, looking at Charles. 'Can you?'

He reached across and put his hand on hers. 'No, and I see no reason why we should. Shall we bring it forward? Shall we have a double wedding?'

'Could we?' Kate's eyes were bright. 'What do you think, Roland? After all, I am in mourning for Papa.'

'Your father approved the match,' Charles said. 'He would not have objected.' He turned to Roland with a boyish grin. 'What do you say?'

'I don't see why not.' Roland lifted an enquiring eyebrow in Margaret's direction. 'Would you like that?'

'I think I should like it very much,' she said, then to Kate, 'But are you sure? Were you not thinking of a grand occasion with a great many friends and a big banquet?'

'If you can go without that, then so can we. My gown

is ready and has been hanging in my closet for weeks. It is red taffeta, embroidered with pearls and scarlet ribbons.' She jumped up excitedly. 'Oh, let's go back and break the news to Grandmama.'

Five minutes later, they were once again tucked up under the sheepskins on the sled and on their way back. Kate's obvious happiness and the fact that she was known and liked locally would ensure that the dual wedding was a joyful occasion and might divert attention from Margaret herself who, try as she might, could not bring herself to rejoice. She was being thoroughly nonsensical, she told herself; she should not be sad. Many a young girl had gone to her wedding without being in love and it had turned out well in the end. Love was not a prerequisite for a successful marriage, never had been, never would be; what was important was to respect and admire the man you were to marry and know that you would be treated with courtesy and kindness. And it was not difficult to admire him, though she certainly did not understand him. He was riding alongside now, deep in thought, as if he were struggling with some weighty mathematical problem.

When they arrived back at the Manor, they were told that a package had arrived for Mistress Donnington, which had been put in her room.

'A package?' Margaret queried. 'But no one knows I'm here.'

'Someone evidently does,' Kate said, hurrying upstairs, leaving Margaret to follow more sedately. She was puzzled. No one knew where she was except the people at the Manor and Great-Uncle Henry, and she could not imagine him taking the trouble to wrap anything and send it to her. She entered her chamber to find that Kate had flung off her heavy cloak and draped it across a chair and was standing by the bed gazing down at a rather large box, tied with ribbon.

'Oh, do hurry and open it,' she said. 'Is there a message?'

Margaret suppressed her own curiosity in order to take off her coat and boots and put them tidily away as she always did; servants or no, it was a habit she would find hard to break. Then she carefully untied the ribbon, lifted the lid of the box and pulled aside its cotton lining. 'Oh!' Carefully she drew out a magnificent open-skirted gown in a heavy ivory satin. The bodice was square-necked with three-quarter sleeves which ended in a froth of pleated lace. The hem and neckline and the stiffened stomacher were heavily beaded in a rose pattern. 'Oh, it is exquisite!'

'A wedding-gown,' Kate whispered in awe, while Margaret delved into the box and drew out a piece of paper, half expecting a note from Roland saying he had decided against the gown she had chosen in Ely. It would explain his cursory glance at the material. But why had he not said anything at the time? And where could he have come by such a lavish creation? She found herself wondering if it had been meant for someone else, but she pushed the thought from her; she did not want to think about that.

'What does it say?' Kate asked eagerly.

'It is from Great-Uncle Henry,' Margaret said, stifling her disappointment that it had not come from her groom. 'He says my mother was to have worn it at her wedding, but there was no wedding, not in Winterford at any rate. I didn't know that; she never told me. Oh, poor Mama! He says it has been in a trunk in a box-room at Sedge House all these years. He sends it with his felicitations.'

'Oh, how romantical! Try it on, do! Does it have a petticoat?'

Margaret looked in the box. There was a white silk petticoat and a bonnet of matching slipper-satin, trimmed with ribbon. She slipped out of her clothes and put them all on. They fitted perfectly, as she had known they would. She and her mother had been very alike, both in looks and figure. She stood before the long pier-glass, swaying this way and that, admiring the richness of the fabric and noticing the brightness of her eyes and the colour the cold air had put into her cheeks. Suddenly she felt happy. How could anyone clothed in such a wedding-dress not be happy?

'Oh, let's go and find Roland and tell him,' Kate said.

'No!' Margaret said suddenly. 'I want it to be a surprise.'

'Oh, what a lovely idea! I won't say a word, I promise.'

Margaret took the finery off and hung it carefully in the mahogany wardrobe and dressed again in her simple blue merino; then they went downstairs to find that Roland had put the idea of a double wedding to Lady Pargeter and obtained her agreement. What he would not countenance was that Henry Capitain should be invited to the ceremony.

'But he is my only relative,' Margaret said, feeling that the least she could do was to allow her great-uncle to see her in the gown. 'Surely it cannot do any harm?'

'I am surprised you can suggest it,' he said. 'You know what he is like.'

'I know he is a little ill-groomed, but I am sure he would dress suitably for such an occasion.'

'And bring his doxy with him, I don't doubt.'

'You could ask him not to.'

'No,' Roland said, so firmly that Margaret knew further argument was useless. She said no more, but made up her mind to write a little thank-you note and have it sent to Sedge House.

She saw little of Roland in the next few days because he was busy directing the digging of a new drain and the building of a flood barrier, but he did return to accompany Charles and the girls skating.

The huge field was two or three miles away and the girls went in the sled, while the two men rode. The narrow roads were crowded as everyone from miles around converged on the area which had been set aside for the skating. Men with brooms had been out sweeping it free of debris and already there were people on the ice, young and old, competent and novice. There were friends of Roland's there, who came over to speak to him, asking him if he intended to enter for the championship.

'I'm a little rusty,' he said, laughing. 'But why not?' Then, turning to take Margaret's hand, he asked, 'May I present you to Mistress Donnington, who is staying at the Manor with us and is shortly to become my wife?'

'Roland, you old dog!' they cried as they bowed to Margaret. 'Where have you been hiding her?'

'Where the likes of you could not claim her first,' he said. 'Now, if you don't mind, I have a skating lesson to give.'

He sat on the edge of the sled to strap his long fen

pattens on over his boots, and then turned to help Margaret on with hers. 'Now stand up,' he said, holding out his hands. 'Hold on to me. Tight as you like; I won't fall over.'

Tentatively she took a step forward and fell into his arms. He laughed and righted her, then stood facing her, holding both her forearms in his broad, strong hands. 'I'll go backwards and pull you along,' he said. 'Just concentrate on keeping upright. I know you can do it.'

Skating backwards, he towed her out on to the ice and soon her natural sense of balance took over and she found she could push one foot forward and then the next, but when he let go of her she floundered and then found herself sitting on the ice with her feet straight out in front of her. He hurried to help her up. 'Are you hurt?'

She laughed. 'Not at all, my lord.'

'Come, we will skate side by side. So.' He took her right hand in his and put his left around her waist and pushed his left foot forward. 'Come, follow my steps. You are quite safe; I will not let you fall again.'

She felt secure in his arms, secure enough and brave enough to glide along beside him, two people moving as one in perfect harmony, oblivious to the crowds who laughed and jostled about them, aware only of each other, their minds and bodies perfectly in tune. The cold air brought a colour to her cheeks and a sparkle to her eyes. She turned to look up at him. His brooding look had gone and he was smiling. 'You are doing very well. Shall we attempt to turn before we run out of ice?'

She laughed and gripped him the harder as he leaned

over to make the turn to take them back the way they
had come. Behind them the sharp edges of their skates
left two parallel sets of lines, followed by two perfect
curves. In no time at all, they were back where they
started, to find Kate and Charles waiting for them.
'Well done!' Kate cried as Margaret slowly skated back
to the sled and sat down.

'I think I'll just watch for a while,' she said.

Roland followed her and carefully tucked the sheepskin rug round her. 'You mustn't catch a chill now.
Are you sure. . .?'

'Yes,' She smiled. 'Go on, let me see what you are
made of.'

He laughed boyishly and set off after Kate and
Charles, who were already out in the middle of the
arena. Kate skated gracefully, turning pirouettes with
ease, while the two men raced each other across the ice
at such a frightening speed that Margaret was sure they
would be unable to stop and would end up in the river
which ran alongside the field.

In the afternoon the ice was cleared for serious
racing and people came from miles around to watch
the champions test each other's mettle. Roland, urged
on by Kate, entered one of the heats and Margaret, on
the sidelines, found herself cheering him on as he
flashed past where she stood, and clapping excitedly
when he won. He returned to her, sliding easily over
the ice and stopping in front of her to hold out the
rosette he had been given as a trophy. 'For my lady.'

She laughed and tucked it into her hair. 'In medieval
times the lady would have given her knight a favour
before the joust.'

'What favour have you to give me, my lady?' he

asked, half in fun, half serious. 'I have yet to compete in the final.'

She took a lace handkerchief from her pocket, one she had made herself in the days when her mother was alive and she was happy. 'Here, my lord. Do well.'

He took it and tucked it into the top of his shirt, then, with a long, lingering look at her, skated off to join the line-up for the final. The moment the signal was given, he went into the lead and he never lost it, though his fellow competitors went after him and closed on him at one stage. He felt rather than saw them behind him and surged forward again, his hands nearly touching the ice as he turned the bend at the end for the return run.

'He's done it!' cried Kate as the cheers went up for a popular win, and Margaret found herself clapping and smiling as if she had had no little hand in the success.

It was growing dark when they returned to the house for dinner with cheeks glowing and eyes sparkling. If anyone had asked her, Margaret would have told them she was very happy, but, deep inside, there was still that apprehension, the feeling that all was not as it should be. And it was all to do with Roland's attitude towards her.

On the ice he had been merry and boyish, with no inhibitions, holding her up as she'd taken her first tentative steps and always on hand to help her to her feet whenever she'd fallen, but as soon as they returned to the house he changed, and was once again scrupulously polite but distant. It was as if the familiarity they had shared on the ice had been expunged from his memory. She kept telling herself that he had never promised her anything more than courtesy and she had asked for nothing more. It was a business arrangement to give her a little independence in a year's time, and the excursion on the ice had been no more than a pleasant interlude. But oh, how easy it would be to fall in love with him. And how disastrous!

Her uneasiness was not lessened when Kate told her that the road to Huntingdon had become passable and she and Charles were going to leave immediately after the ceremony. 'It will give you and Roland the house to yourselves,' she said, smiling. 'Except for Grandmama, of course, but she will no doubt keep to her rooms. It will be like a honeymoon.'

Margaret suddenly realised why Roland had been so compliant about the double wedding; with Charles and Kate out of the way, she and her husband could have separate sleeping arrangments without arousing comment. Roland obviously intended to stick to his side of their bargain. That was good, she told herself firmly, trying to ignore the fact that his attitude was less than flattering. But flattery did not come into it; she did not want empty compliments.

She would miss Kate, and began to wonder what life would be like in Winterford when the young couple had gone. Would she and Roland get to know each other better? Would they be good companions and pleasant company for each other? It was all she had a right to ask.

There were no more falls of snow and the wedding-day dawned bright and sunny. Margaret rose and went to the window. It was almost impossible to tell where the land ended and the water began; everything was covered in snow, like a great white carpet. Overhead, in the blue bowl of the sky, one or two pink-edged clouds drifted, and below them a whole flock of swans came flying gracefully in, their wings sounding like distant drums. Nearer they came, hundreds of them, like sky-born ships in battle line, necks outstretched, webbed feet tucked under them. They landed, wave upon wave, four hundred yards away on the only piece of open water for miles, almost covering its surface.

'That's a lucky omen, miss,' Penny said. She was standing just behind Margaret, holding a pile of soft towels and a block of scented soap which she had fetched from a cupboard. 'The swans have come to your wedding.'

Margaret laughed and turned from the window to have her breakfast, which had been brought in on a tray. 'Do you believe in omens, Penny?'

'Of course, mistress, don't everyone?'

'I do not think I do.'

'You will if you stay here, mistress,' Penny said. 'You'd have a hard job not to.'

Margaret smiled. She had heard that the fen people were more than usually superstitious but she did not argue with her maid; she had other things to think about.

She was too tense to eat, but managed a slice of bread and butter and a cup of hot chocolate before Penny set about helping her to prepare herself for the most important day of her life. At least, that was what everyone said it was and she had to believe them. But oh, how she wished Roland had done more than give her a curt goodnight when she had left him the evening before. If only he would smile!

Her *toilette* took hours. First she had to be bathed

and anointed with sweet-smelling oils, then clothed in
the finest silk underwear and stockings before sitting at
the mirror to have her hair dressed. 'It would be easier
if you wore a wig,' Penny said, brushing vigorously.

'No, they always give me a headache and I always
want to scratch. Do what you can with my hair.'

It was done at last, a wonderful creation, full of
padding and rolls, and after a final powdering Penny
took off the cape and Margaret was ready to don the
petticoat and put on the magnificent gown. The effect
was magical. She felt inches taller although she had not
yet put on her slippers; her eyes, with their naturally
dark lashes, shone lustrously. Margaret had always
thought of herself as plain, but even she had to admit
that she looked very handsome. She was watching in
the mirror as Penny fastened her mother's garnets
round her throat and set the bonnet on her curls when
Kate came in, radiant in the red taffeta and sweeping
peacock feathers.

'Are you ready? Charles and Roland have already
gone, and the carriage is outside. Roland has had the
servants busy for hours clearing the snow from the road
to the church.'

'Yes.' Margaret took a deep breath, picked up her
handkerchief and fan, and turned towards the door.

The tiny church was crowded with villagers and
estate workers come to wish both brides well, and
Margaret was glad to see them. They made the
ceremony more impressive than it would have been if
there had only been she and Roland and a couple of
witnesses. She really felt like a bride as she walked
slowly down the aisle in that magnificent gown towards
the man she was to marry. He turned to face her and

she noticed, with a little quirk of amusement how his eyes widened in surprise at the sight of her.

He looked elegant himself in a double-breasted brocade waistcoat with silver buttons, matching breeches and a mauve velvet topcoat frogged in silver braid which fitted his muscular figure exactly. His huge turn-back cuffs were also braided and ornamented with silver buttons. The froth of lace at his neck and wrists was pristine. His shoes had silver buckles and he wore a white wig, curled at the sides and tied at the back with black ribbon. She was so much in awe of him that she almost tripped, and certainly was not aware of the congregation, and only half conscious of the presence of Kate and Charles.

Step by step, she moved towards the man who, in a few moments, would become her husband. Forgotten was their bargain, forgotten the temporary nature of the transaction; she was like any bride going to be joined to the man she loved, ready and wanting to make her vows to love, honour and obey. For life.

Not until she reached his side and heard a strange cry did she become fully aware of her surroundings. She turned to see Lady Pargeter standing in the family pew, supported by Hannah on one side and leaning heavily on her cane at the other. She was staring at Margaret, and her eyes were so venomous with hate that Margaret almost recoiled. 'Witch!' Her voice was so weak that no one but those standing near her heard it. 'You will pay!' She lifted a bony finger to point. 'A year, that's all!' Then she fell back on to her seat. Margaret was afraid that she had had a seizure and looked from her to Roland in alarm. He nodded to Hannah who, unseen by the congregation, gave her ladyship a few drops of laudanum, for she was crying hysterically, her voice rising almost to a shriek. She soon fell quiet under the drug and leaned heavily against her companion, her eyes closed. Roland turned to the congregation, who could not see into the enclosed pew and were whispering among themselves, imagining all sorts of calamities—the excitement was too much for the old lady; she was going to announce an impediment to one or both marriages; she was drunk, for everyone knew she liked a drop of brandy, preferably from a keg which had not seen an exciseman. There were any number of conjectures. Roland raised his hand and they fell silent. 'There is nothing to cause alarm,' he said, then, turning to the parson, added, 'Proceed.'

The parson cleared his throat and the service began. Margaret heard the words, made her responses, but none of it sank into her bemused brain. She was sure Lady Pargeter had been looking at her when she had cried out. How could the sight of her have caused such a response? What could the old lady have against her? If she had disapproved of the marriage she would surely have said so before; she was unfailingly outspoken on every other subject and most of the time everyone deferred to her. Was she genuinely ill or was it an act? Roland certainly did not think her condition was serious enough to suspend the ceremony.

She found herself looking down at the ring which had just been placed on her finger and realised with a start that the deed was done. She had become Roland's wife. She was the new Lady Pargeter, mistress of Winterford Manor, but somehow the joy had gone out of the day. She went back down the aisle on Roland's arm, bowing and smiling to right and left, thinking, This isn't happening to me; I am dreaming. She was almost at the porch when she noticed her great-uncle among the crowd of villagers at the back of the church. He was dressed in a dark coat and wore a tricorne hat over a dark brown wig, but she recognised his fleshy face immediately. His little dark eyes were looking at her with something akin to triumph. She shuddered and looked away, and a few moments later was borne away in the family coach back to Winterford Manor and the wedding-feast.

CHAPTER FOUR

KATE was concerned for her grandmother and would have delayed her departure, but Roland would not hear of it. 'She is perfectly well,' he said. 'It was simply too much excitement. Hannah has put her to bed with a sleeping-draught. Go and see her, if you wish.'

Reassured, Kate and Charles left in the early afternoon after a sumptuous banquet, most of which was wasted on Margaret. The house seemed empty without them and Margaret found herself wishing that something would bring them back. Roland was morose, sitting by the fire in the withdrawing-room, a glass of brandy in his hand, staring into the flames, as if the solution to his problems might be found in their depths. And her own thoughts were in a tumult too as she wondered what would happen when the time came for them to go to bed. He had said he would not trouble her. Did that mean not ever? Not even on their wedding-night? Should she stay sitting by the fire as long as she could, delaying whatever it was she was afraid of, or should she precipitate whatever was to happen and suggest retiring? She looked across at him, a smile on her lips, wanting to lighten the heavy atmosphere, to let him know that if only he would confide in her she would try to understand. 'Is anything wrong?' she asked.

He looked up as if her voice had startled him. 'Where did you get that gown?'

She had changed into a simple grey taffeta and looked down at it in surprise. 'Why, in London. Do you not care for it?'

'I meant the one you wore to church. Your wedding-gown.'

'It was beautiful, wasn't it? My great-uncle sent it. He said it was my mother's but she never wore it.'

'Burn it.'

She gasped. 'You cannot mean that. It is too lovely to destroy.'

'I said burn it.'

'Why?' She was perplexed. 'Are you angry because I did not wear the gown you bought for me? I did not think you would mind. I am very sorry if I hurt you.'

'Hurt me?' he asked in surprise. 'I am not hurt.' He could not bring himself to tell her that the lilac taffeta would have done nothing for her complexion or figure, that the cream brocade had lifted her from the ordinary to the magnificent. For a moment, as she had walked towards him down the aisle, he had been half stunned by her beauty. He did not want her to be beautiful; he wanted to be able to dislike her, and he was angry with himself that he could not. He had to remind himself constantly that she was the last of the Capitains and she was making it possible for him to marry Susan. 'It came from Henry Capitain; that is enough.'

'I thought it was very kind of him to send it.'

'Kind of him! He only sent it so that he could gloat over us; kindness did not come into it.'

'Gloat? Why should he do that?'

'A Pargeter taking a gift from a Capitain!'

'You forget, my mother was a Capitain.'

'I do not forget.' His voice rose angrily. 'God,

woman, how could I forget? It's the only reason I
could——' He stopped suddenly, realising he could not
go on.

'Only reason what? Tell me what you were going to
say.'

'No, I was distraught. I meant nothing.'

'You married me because I was a Captain? Is that
it? To punish me, to punish all Captains? But what
have I done to you?'

'You? Nothing, except to be far too beautiful and
generous for your own good.' He stood up and took
two or three paces across the room, then turned and
came to sit beside her, taking her hand. 'No, my dear,
nothing like that,' he said gently, changing his tone
completely and puzzling her more than ever. 'It was
simply that the sight of that gown and those pretty
beads about your neck brought about my grandmother's seizure.' He reached out and lifted them from
her throat, making her tingle from head to foot. It was
like fear and yet it was not fear; she did not understand
the extraordinary effect his touch had on her. 'I am
excessively fond of the old lady.' He dropped the
necklet and leaned back to look at her. 'I do not want
her upset.'

'But why should the sight of me upset her, Roland?
We met for the first time less than two weeks ago and
yet I seem to stir up such a hatred in her.'

'It is not hatred, Margaret.'

'What, then?'

'Unhappy memories.' He stopped speaking, wondering whether to tell her. 'I did not know about it myself
until today, when we came back from church and I
went to see that she was comfortable.' He paused and

then went on. 'You remember I told you she becomes confused sometimes? For a moment she thought you were your mother, just as she did when you arrived in that boat.'

'I know I am very like Mama. . .'

'Then she must have been very beautiful,' he said softly, unable to forget the sight of her walking towards him in the church, angelic in the ivory satin, so slim and so vulnerable. It had come to him then, with terrible clarity, the dreadful harm he had done her. And Susan, too. What would she say when she learned of his hasty marriage? How could he tell her? Oh, why had he listened to Charles and his ill-conceived ideas? No, he should not blame his friend; it was his own fault. 'My father certainly thought she was.'

'Your father?'

'Grandmama told me that your mother and my father fell in love. Against all opposition they were determined to marry.' He smiled wryly at her expression of disbelief. 'You did not know?'

'No. She never told me. But why was there opposition?'

'The Pargeters and the Capitains have been mortal enemies ever since the Civil War.'

'But that was a hundred years ago!'

'Old grudges die hard in these parts, Margaret. Before the war the Capitains owned Winterford Manor; it was their ancestral home. The Pargeters lived in Ely and farmed land near by. They were friends until the war, when we were staunch Parliamentarians and the Capitains were for King Charles. Their home and much of their land was sequestered and given to the Pargeters by a grateful

Parliament. When the monarchy was restored, the new king saw no reason to restore their lands to them and there has been enmity ever since.'

'Surely if there are grudges they are on the Capitain side? They lost most for their loyalty.'

'I am only recounting the story, not judging the rights and wrongs of it. The Pargeters prospered, and they have been instrumental in improving the lot of the villagers who had been parlously neglected by the earlier lords of the manor. Perhaps that is why the Manor was not returned after the war.' He paused and added, 'We have been good squires, Margaret.'

'I do not doubt that, but surely you could have done something towards a reconciliation?'

He smiled wryly. 'It seems our respective parents tried. And failed. Family feuds go on for generations in the Fens.'

'Perhaps, but is there any need to perpetuate them? They will never die if we do.'

'You are right, of course, but to Grandmama it happened only yesterday.'

'What happened?'

'My father and your mother were very young and headstrong. They arranged to marry in secret. It was not the present cleric but his predecessor who agreed to perform the ceremony. They reached the church. Your mother was wearing that gown and those garnets, a wedding-gift from my father. My grandparents had found out about it and were waiting. They persuaded— nay, ordered—the parson not to proceed on the grounds that Felicity Capitain was a suspected Jacobite.'

'That's nonsense. Mama was a good Protestant, just as I am.'

'Father was persuaded that she had deceived him. He left the church and shortly afterwards your mother went away.'

'Poor, poor Mama, I think she never truly recovered. She was over thirty when she married my father. They went to India, where I was born, but he died. I do not know the cause. Perhaps he could not compete with the memories.'

'My father married soon afterwards. It was an arranged marriage and lasted less than a year. Then he met my mother and they were happy together until Mama died ten years ago.'

'What has all this to do with you and me?'

'Nothing,' he said brusquely, 'I was simply explaining about my grandmother and why that gown is unlucky.'

'Unlucky!' she cried. 'I can understand people like Penny believing in lucky and unlucky omens, but you, my lord, surely not?'

He grinned, almost shamefacedly. 'I simply meant that I do not want it turning up again in another thirty years.'

'It won't,' she said, remembering the transient nature of their marriage. In a year's time she would be gone, put from his mind, forgotten. 'When I leave it will go with me,' she said, her voice thick with the effort not to cry, 'as a reminder of my mother and what love did for her.'

'Love,' he said, and gave a crooked smile. 'It leads to all manner of problems. Perhaps it is as well to put one's trust in arranged marriages.'

'But why me?' she asked, conscious as she spoke

that it was a question she should have asked long before. 'Why another Captain?'

'I did not know you were a Captain when I first saw you sitting in the White Hart looking like a lost little kitten. I thought you needed a home.'

'I find that difficult to believe.'

'As you please. It's all the explanation I can offer.' He rose and offered her his arm. 'Now, it is late. Let me escort you to your room.'

She stood up and laid her fingers lightly on his sleeve and together they ascended the stairs. Outside her room he stopped and turned to her. 'You will not be disturbed, my dear. Sleep well.' Then he was gone, slipping into his own room and closing the door with a soft click. The gesture had a finality about it that left her in no doubt that he meant what he said. She turned and went into her own room, wondering why his rejection hurt so much. She had no right to feel hurt; he had not promised to love her, had not even said he would stay with her. She would have to find an occupation which would fill her days and mitigate the aching loneliness in her heart, something which would keep her busy for a whole year.

The next morning she woke determined to make the best of things—a favourite dictum of her mother's—and, dressing carefully, went down to breakfast. Roland was already there, sitting at the head of the table with a cup of coffee in front of him. She smiled, pretending everything was as it should be. 'Good morning, Roland.'

He looked up and she was struck by how tired he looked. His eyes were heavy as if he had not slept, but he smiled pleasantly. 'Good morning, my lady. Did you sleep well?'

'Yes, very well,' she lied, helping herself to a coddled egg from the sideboard and sitting down opposite him. 'Are you leaving for London today?'

'No. I must oversee the completion of the flood defences before I go, and there are one or two other matters to be dealt with. Can you bear my company for another day or two?'

'Of course, my lord. It will be a pleasure.'

'What will you do today?'

'There must have been a great deal of food left over from the wedding-feast,' she said. 'I thought I would pack a basket and take it to the villagers; there is no reason why it should be wasted.'

'I have already given orders for it to be distributed,' he said, pleased that she had thought of it too. 'Two of the menservants have been told to take it round to the cottages.'

'Then I should like to go with them, if you do not object? I should like to thank the villagers for coming to church.'

'They take a long time to accept newcomers, Margaret. Perhaps you should wait until I can go with you.'

'There is no need, my lord. I will deal gently with them.'

'Of course,' he said, knowing she would. 'But do not stray from the centre of the village. The snow is very deep.' He stood up to go. 'I shall see you at dinner.'

'And my wedding-gown?'

'Keep it, of course. I am sorry I mentioned it. I was not quite myself last night.'

Not quite himself! What could he mean by that? That he was ill, or out of sorts, or worried? 'Thank you,' she said, dazzling him with a grateful smile. Like a sacrificial lamb, smiling at its executioner, he thought, hating himself.

Margaret went upstairs for boots, cloak and muff, and then down to the kitchen where James and John, the two footmen, were preparing to take the heavy basket of food to the village. She pulled up the hood of her cloak and followed them along the snow-covered road towards the village.

The cottages, which had looked so picturesque from a distance, were nothing but mean little hovels with no floors or proper chimneys, and they reeked of stale odours and wood-smoke. Margaret was greeted with suspicion at first, but her sunny smile and obvious interest in the villagers melted their reserve, and they were soon chatting to her about their homes and their families. They did not seem unhappy, but their lives were undoubtedly hard. They worked on his lordship's land most of the year, or for one of the yeomen farmers in the district, but in winter they spent a great deal of their time on the fen, fishing and catching wildfowl which they took to market to supplement their incomes. Even the children worked, except at this time of year when there was nothing for them to do. There was a charity school in Ely, but few of them attended.

'I think we should have a school in the village, don't you?' Margaret suggested at one home. 'Then the children could attend classes when they are not working and would not be absent from home so long.' The mother looked doubtful and Margaret smiled reassuringly. 'I shall speak to his lordship about it. And about these cottages. They really are in need of repair.' She looked up at the thatch as she spoke; it was possible to see right through it. And the keen wind found its way between the walls and the window-frames.

'My lady, I would not want his lordship to think I had been complaining. . .'

'Of course he will not. Now I must go.' Margaret ducked her head under the low doorway and went out into the snowbound street, glad to breathe fresh air again. The two footmen were waiting stoically. She smiled at them. 'Have we anything left in the basket?'

'Very little, my lady,' one said, trying not to let her see him shivering. 'One small package.'

She reached in and took it out. 'Then I shall take it. You may go back home.'

'But, my lady. . .' he protested.

'I shall be perfectly safe. Now go.'

They scuttled away, and Margaret stood for a moment before turning slowly to continue to the next house, which obviously belonged to the blacksmith. His smithy stood next to the house; its doors were open and she could feel the heat from its fire as she approached. The parson was leading his newly shod horse from the interior. He doffed his tricorne hat. 'Good-day, my lady.'

'Good-day, sir. I have been taking your parishioners a little of the bounty we enjoyed at the Manor yesterday.'

'But surely, my lady, you have not been inside their dwellings? Heaven knows what noisome diseases are to be found there. And they are so dirty.'

'No, they are not, they are simply poor.' She smiled to mitigate the reproof. 'Have you seen my lord?'

'Aye, my lady,' the blacksmith interposed. 'He rode off down the fen road. I reckon he's gone to inspect the new earthworks.'

'Thank you.' She turned to go and he called after her.

'The snow's pretty deep along there, my lady.'

The new barrier had been occupying most of Roland's waking hours for the best part of a week now, and she was interested in seeing it for herself. It was being constructed on the western outskirts of the village to divert flood water into the cut and thence, a few miles further on, into a tributary of the Great Ouse. She smiled wryly as she walked. He was trying to save those miserable hovels when in her opinion they were in no danger. He would do better to try and repair them and make them fit to live in. And she intended to tell him so.

She found about twenty men, digging with a will, but no sign of Roland. After standing watching them for a few minutes, she turned away, intending to go home, but then realised she still had a packet of food in her hand. She undid the wrapping and discovered it was a large piece of bride-cake. She smiled and wrapped it again, before setting off along the fen road towards Sedge House. She would thank her uncle for the gown in person and offer him the cake as a small consolation for not being invited to the wedding-feast. Kate had been right; he could not be all bad, if he could think of sending her that gown and coming to the church to stand among the parishioners to see her married. She was momentarily put off by the thought of his dreadful guests, but decided they would surely have left as soon as the roads had been opened.

She tried to keep to the tracks left by carts and horses and people's snow-shoes, but in some places the wind had drifted the snow and she found herself floundering. The snow got into her boots and froze her toes, and before long she was wishing she had not come. She turned to retrace her steps. It was snowing again now; huge flakes filled the leaden sky and obliterated everything except the blurred shape of the church steeple. She plunged towards it, believing the road was straight. She had not gone far when she realised how wrong she was; the snow was very deep.

She struggled on, almost crying with frustration and anger at herself. A heron flew low over her head and then a flight of swans, making for the open water. Penny had said they were lucky. Penny had been aghast at her insistence on going out alone, but she had never been protected by servants before and she had no patience with women who never stepped outside their homes unless accompanied by a maid and a couple of footmen. She had sent the footmen home; would that alert anyone that she was in danger? She doubted it.

Head down, she struggled on, her one aim to reach the village. For a little while the going seemed to get easier and she thought she had found the road again. She stopped when she realised that she was only a few hundred yards from where the swans had come down. They were gracefully bobbing up and down on the water. She smiled and took a few steps towards them, unwrapping the cake as she went, ready to scatter it. Then there was an ominous cracking sound at her feet and, before she could do anything to prevent it, she had fallen through the ice and was up to her armpits in freezing water.

The cold was so intense that it snatched her breath away and she could not even cry out. There was a current too, so she knew she must be in the cut, and it was pulling at the voluminous clothes she wore, dragging her legs from under her. She found herself being toppled and drawn under the ice, unable to do anything but snatch hopelessly at the edge of the ice to save herself. It broke away in her hand. She was numb with cold, but her head was still just above the water. She managed to scream at last, but it took the last of her srength and she found her grip on the ice weakening. Her hands slipped and the current swept her off her feet and continued to pull her skirts, forcing her down and under the ice. With one last desperate effort she lifted her arms and grabbed a tussock of reed.

'Hold on!' The voice seemed miraculously close at hand, but she dared not turn for fear of losing her tenuous grip. She decided she had imagined it, that she was dying and on her way to heaven. Her eyes closed and slowly the reed slipped from her grasp.

'She's gone,' Henry said. 'You can't save her.'

'Of course I can save her,' Roland grunted, tying a rope about his waist and handing the other end to Henry. 'Tie this to my horse's saddle and, when I shout, move him off.' He moved forward gingerly on to the ice and then lay down, spread-eagling himself to distribute his weight as widely as possible. Slowly he inched his way forward. The ice creaked and groaned, protesting. Margaret had disappeared, but her clothes must have been caught on something because the current had not carried her beyond the hole she had made in the ice; if it had it would have been impossible to find her. He reached out and grabbed a handful of her cloak, enough to bring her face above the water again. The ice cracked ominously, threatening to topple him in with her. She was far too heavy to lift out from that position and he cursed his wound, which had made him less than the powerful man he had been before it. Carefully he undid the rope about his waist and put it around hers. Then he raised his arm to signal to Henry Capitain. Slowly the horse took the strain and, inch by inch, Margaret was dragged clear. The ice broke all about her as she came out and he quickly wriggled back to safety before he fell in himself.

'I don't know why you bothered,' Henry said, when Roland was once more on dry land and wrapping Margaret closely in his own cloak, thankful that she was still breathing. 'You had a God-given opportunity to be rid of her and you go and do the chivalrous thing. I'm damned if I understand you.'

'No, and I don't suppose you ever will,' Roland was breathing heavily, ignoring the pain in his side as he lifted Margaret carefully on to his horse and climbed into the saddle behind her. 'Now stand aside; I must take my wife home before she freezes to death. I thank you for your assistance.'

Henry laughed. 'It was a pleasure. After all, it is not I who wants her dead.'

Margaret, brought briefly to her senses by the jolting of the horse, could never be sure afterwards if she had really heard those words.

She was so cold that even her brain was numbed, and she could do nothing to help herself or protest when Roland lifted her off his horse and carried her indoors and up to her room, shouting for Penny to come at once with mutton-fat and hot mulled wine. In her room he stripped her of every vestige of clothing and began gently rubbing her limbs with smooth, powerful strokes which set her whole body on fire. The sensation was excruciatingly painful and, though she tried not to, she could not help crying out.

'Good,' Roland said. 'You are coming back to life.'

'Oh, my lord, what has happened?' Penny came running into the room in answer to his summons.

'You may well ask,' he said grimly. 'Why were you not with your mistress? I've a mind to have you whipped.'

'No,' Margaret whispered. 'I would not let her go with me.'

'We will talk about it later,' he said, then to Penny, 'You know what to do?'

'Yes, my lord.'

He stood aside so that the maid could approach the bed, where she set about covering Margaret in mutton-fat, working it all over her, before wrapping her in several sheepskin rugs and withdrawing.

'It smells dreadful,' Margaret murmured as Roland sat down on the edge of the bed, the cup of mulled wine in his hand. 'I wonder you can bear to be near me.'

'Oh, I can bear it,' he said with a grin, putting his hand beneath her head to raise it and help her to drink. 'It is a time-honoured method and I've been saved by it more than once myself. . .'

She sipped obediently. 'You've been through the ice?'

'You would be hard put to it to find a healthy, adventurous fen boy who has not, some time or other, nearly drowned.' He laughed suddenly. 'We have a great deal of water.'

She smiled crookedly. 'Yes, so I have discovered.'

'Do you know how near you came to drowning?'

'Yes.' She shuddered involuntarily. 'I am sorry to have put you to so much trouble.'

'It was a very narrow escape, my dear,' he said gently, putting down the empty cup.

'I know. I owe you my life——' She stopped suddenly because he had turned away to look out of the window as if he could not bear to face her.

The snow was still falling steadily; it would delay his departure again. So much for Charles's theory that he could turn his back on her and the consequences of what he had done. He could not. 'Where did you think you were going?' he asked, turning back to face her.

'I had a piece of bride-cake left and decided to take it to my uncle, but the snow was too deep and when I turned to come back I lost the road. Then I thought I had found it again. . .'

'You were on the cut.'

'I know that now.' She shivered. 'I don't know what would have happened if you had not come along.'

'I will tell you what would have happened; you would have drowned and your frozen body would have been washed out into the sea on the tide below Highmere Sluice. It was providential that I was riding along the drove looking for signs of a thaw, when I caught a glimpse of you through the blizzard.'

'My uncle was there too, wasn't he? I didn't dream it?'

'Yes.' He was frowning again. 'He said he was watching the swans through his spy-glass and saw you go through the ice.' He didn't believe Capitain's story but, as he could think of no other reason why the man should be standing at his window using a spy-glass on such a day, he put it from his mind.

''Then I have him to thank too.'

'I have done it on your behalf. You will not go down that drove again, whatever the weather, do you hear?'

'Why not?'

'Because it is not seemly. Your great-uncle's companions are not people I would wish my wife to associate with.'

'I thought they might have left.'

'Mayhap they have, but doubtless others will arrive. You must not go there again.' His dark brows were drawn down in a straight line, but she could not tell if he was worried or angry. She supposed she deserved a scold, and put a hand out of the sheepskin to touch his arm.

'I am sorry, Roland; it will not happen again.'

He picked up her hand and stroked it gently with his thumb before putting it back under the covers and tucking them round her. 'You do not understand the fen, Margaret. It is our master. . . Oh, you may smile, but I assure you it is. It will punish anyone who tries to defy it, particularly someone who knows nothing of its ways. You must learn to respect it.'

'You make it sound almost human.'

He chuckled, dispelling his frown. 'Perhaps it is; perhaps it is a deity, perhaps the devil, who knows?'

'I had heard that fen people are superstitious, but I did not realise it applied to——' She stopped, unwilling to make him angry again.

'Someone like me?' He managed to look sheepish.

'Oh, I tell myself I am immune, but I have not lived in this part of the country all my life without seeing and hearing things which make it impossible for me to remain aloof. I am part of it, part of the fen, of the village——'

'If that is so, why are the villagers' cottages in such bad repair, with leaking roofs and broken windows?' She paused, then hurried on before he could answer. 'Roland, you cannot be ignorant of their condition.'

'Of course I am not,' he said curtly. 'But you forget I have only lately returned home. There has been no time——'

'No, I do not, but you have been home long enough to set the men digging ditches when it would be far more to the point to rebuild those hovels they live in. I feel guilty that I am warm and comfortable and have more than sufficient to eat when they are in such straits.'

'The "ditches", as you call them, are very necessary. As soon as the snow melts, there will be floods, and we must be prepared. It is more important than a little thatch falling off a roof.'

'To save your fields.'

'To save their livelihoods. Without their work in the fields, they would be in worse straits. The houses will be repaired as soon as the dyke is finished. The men understand that and so do their wives. Now, you will not interfere in what does not concern you, is that understood?'

'Very well, but what does concern me? There seems little point in learning to keep house when I am not expected to stay beyond a year.'

'Then you may do as you please.' He stood up

abruptly and moved away from her, unaccountably annoyed that she had reminded him of the transient nature of their relationship. 'Within the rules laid down.'

'That means I do nothing,' she said flatly.

'Have you no needlepoint or reading matter?'

'Of course, but I want to do something useful. I thought I could set up a schoolroom for the village children. Let me do it, Roland, please.'

He smiled crookedly. She looked more than ever like a kitten—a drowned kitten—with her little pointed chin and big violet eyes and hair stuck to her scalp. He could never bring himself to drown a kitten, however unwanted; he would always try to save it. It had been his natural instinct to rescue her from the ice and he knew he would always do all he could to keep her safe, but it made nonsense of his reason for marrying her. It was all very well to talk of the death of a stranger, but this woman was no longer a stranger; she was a warm and generous human being who had already shown how much she cared for those around her, even that reprobate uncle of hers. The guilt which had been tormenting him ever since she'd arrived on his doorstep, exhausted and with bleeding hands, had become unbearable. Whatever happened, he must protect her, but how long could he go on defying destiny? He reached out and smoothed her hair back from her forehead. 'Of course, my dear, when you are fully recovered. Now I can hear Penny coming with warm water to wash that grease off you. After that, you are to rest.' He stood up and made way for her maid, who had arrived with a steaming jug of scented water.

Margaret submitted to being washed, and dressed in

a lavender-scented robe, and took the dose of physic Penny put into her hands before leaving her to sleep off the effects of her ordeal. Margaret didn't want to sleep; she wanted to lie there and think of Roland. His hands had been gentle as they had coaxed the life back into her limbs, and his eyes had had a worried look as if he really cared what happened to her, and yet his words had been brusque, almost harsh. He was a strange mixture of domineering male and tender lover. . . She checked her thoughts hastily. How could she think of him as a lover? He had given her no cause for that, not even when he had been gently rubbing her bare flesh. His hands had set her limbs on fire and not all of it because of the icy water, but he had not been in the least roused. He was as cold a fish as had ever been pulled from the fens.

Not even the combined efforts of Roland and Penny could keep Margaret in bed longer than a day, and she was up and about by Christmas Eve. The snow had stopped but there had been no thaw; everywhere was blanketed in white and no one could get into the village from outside. Nor could anyone leave. Roland was still at home and would be until after the festivities. There was a great flurry of preparation in the kitchen but there was little she could do there but get in the way. She turned to leave, and from a window saw two of the menservants carrying home the yule log and greenery from the little copse of trees on the far side of the village, accompanied by a crowd of ill-clad children, dancing along on the hard-packed snow, apparently oblivious of the cold. They reminded her of her inten-

tion to start a school, and she went to the kitchen door
to meet them.

'Come into the warm, children,' she called out to
them. 'I want to speak to you.'

They looked doubtfully at each other and came
forward reluctantly, but when they realised she only
wanted to give them marchpane and cordial they held
out their grubby hands and started to smile.

'What are your names?'

'I'm Christopher, this here's Ben and that's Jenny.'
The boy, who must have been about ten years old,
pointed to the girl in the group, who held a toddler by
the hand. 'And the baby's Tilda.'

'Do you go to school?'

'Nah. Ain't one. 'Sides, what's the sense? Pa says
he'll learn me all I need to know.'

'I am sure he will.' She paused, not wishing to be-
little his father. 'But reading and writing and reckoning? I doubt he has much time to spare for that, does
he? Would you like me to teach you?'

'I don't know, miss.'

'My lady to you,' Cook snapped, poking the boy in
the ribs with the wooden spoon she held in her hand.
'Mind your manners.'

'After Christmas I shall talk to your parents about
it,' Margaret said, giving the servant a reproving look.
'How many children are there in the village?'

He didn't know but he wasn't going to admit his
ignorance. 'Hundreds and hundreds,' he said airily.
'Can we go now?'

She pressed more sweetmeats into their hands and
let them go. They fled across the courtyard and out of
the gate, calling gleefully to each other.

'You'll have half the village here in no time, my lady,' Cook said. 'All wanting sweetmeats.'

'Then give them to them.'

Cook sighed. 'Yes, my lady.'

Margaret smiled. 'It is Christmas. Now, where shall we put all this greenery?'

For the next two or three hours she occupied herself decorating the house with holly and mistletoe, though the servants discarded any ivy which clung to it. ''Tis unlucky,' they said. She was almost tempted to insist on putting it up, to prove how silly their superstitions were, but thought better of it; she did not want to alienate them.

Roland came home in a cheerful mood and, seeing her up and about again, bowed politely over her hand and said he was glad to see her recovered. She smiled and put her fingers on his arm to go in to dinner.

'Is there any sign of a thaw?' she asked.

'Not at the moment, for which we should be thankful. The dyke will take another day or two yet.'

'And then the village will be safe?'

'Let us hope so.'

She wanted to ask if he intended to leave as soon as it thawed, but decided she would not risk spoiling his good humour. If he felt happy and relaxed in her company, that was good. When he was in a good mood and trying to be agreeable, as he was now, she knew he would make an admirable husband and she could be happy with him, might even love him, but when he was broody and quick-tempered, as he sometimes was for no reason at all that she could see, she found it difficult even to like him. And then she reminded herself that the arrangement had a time-limit and it would be best not to delve too deeply. She must try and hold herself aloof and live each day as it came, accepting the good and enduring the bad.

Fish and roast lamb were brought in to them, with salsify and boiled potatoes, and they talked of the village and its people, the church, even a little of politics and Roland's time in the army, everything except what she most wanted to know. Why had he married her?

On Christmas Day they went to church, leading the whole household, except Cook and the kitchen-maids, who were needed to prepare the dinner. Even the Dowager Lady Pargeter emerged from her room to accompany them, a rare occurrence since the wedding. They returned to a dinner of goose and pork and plum pudding and tarts filled with minced meat and spices, after which the old lady returned to her room and Roland suggested to Margaret that they resume their postponed inspection of the house. 'I haven't been in the east wing for years,' he said, 'Shall we explore it together?'

She agreed readily and he took up a lantern, while she wrapped a shawl about her shoulders, for the unused parts of the house were unheated. Some of the rooms were still furnished with heavy oak chests and sideboards, tables covered in dust and long blackened settles which must have been there a hundred years or more. There were cobweb-covered pictures on the walls and cracked mirrors, but no carpets. One of the rooms had a long window which looked out on to an overgrown garden.

'This would be just the thing for a schoolroom,' she said, smiling up at him in a way which wrenched at his heart. 'It can be reached from the garden; the children do not need to go through the house. It already has a sturdy table and we can have chairs and stools brought in from the other rooms and the fire could be lit. Do say yes. I've already asked the parents and they agreed, so long as the lessons do not intrude on the children's working hours.'

'And the Parson, have you asked him?'

'Asked him, my lord? Do I need his permission?'

'It would be wise to obtain it. He will want to satisfy himself that you are not teaching sedition.'

'Sedition? Does he take me for a papist?'

'No, but it would do no harm to consult him, especially if you mean to teach the Scriptures.'

'I shall leave religion to him. I want the children to be able to read and write, to know a little of science and the world outside the Fens, then perhaps they will grow up to rely less on superstition and more on their own abilities. . .'

'Beware of playing with fire, my lady.'

She looked at him sharply. 'You may be sure I shall tread carefully.'

'I am sure you will.' She was so enthusiastic that he found himself smiling with her.

'I will need horn-books, slates and chalk, a bible and one or two prayer-books.'

'I've no doubt they can be purchased or ordered in Ely. I have some business there myself. We will go tomorrow.'

They went in the sled, well-wrapped up against the chill air, but, though her body was warm and Roland sat close enough to touch, he seemed, once again, distant and cold. She sensed he was distracted by thoughts he could not share, and would not welcome conversation, so she sat silently beside him as they covered the eight miles to the city. When they arrived, he pulled up at a tiny shop set in the wall of the cathedral buildings, where he left her to browse and talk to the cleric who came out from the back to greet them. By the time he returned, she had bought most of what she needed and arranged for one or two books to be sent from Cambridge.

'They'll be here in a week,' she told Roland as they left the shop. 'I am afraid I asked for everything to be charged to you. I have no money. . .'

'Naturally, I expect to pay,' he said, helping her back into the sled for the return journey. 'And you ought to have a little pin-money of your own. I will see to it.'

His generosity did not stretch to giving of himself, she thought as she thanked him. He was as cold as the snow which seemed so slow to thaw. She stole a glance at him as he carefully negotiated the horses around a great ice-covered pot-hole. His jaw was set and his dark eyes looked troubled, and she longed to ask him what was wrong, but his brows were drawn down in the familiar way he had when he did not want to be questioned or crossed. She remained silent, watching his skilful hands on the reins, they way the horses obeyed each little movement as if they could read his orders before he even uttered them. Man and animals were at one and she felt excluded.

As soon as they returned and the pony and sled had been handed over to a groom, he ordered a riding horse to be saddled and set off in the direction of the village. She stood at the door and watched him go, knowing she would not see him again for the rest of the day.

Roland set off along the bank of the cut, going he knew not where, though he pretended he was going to inspect the dyke. He was in despair. The earthworks were finished and the roads would be open any day now, and he ought to leave as he had said all along he would, turn his back on Margaret, spend the next fifty-one weeks as far away as he could get. He ought to do it for her sake, not his. What he had never envisaged, when he had agreed to Charles's preposterous plan, was that he would fall in love with his wife. What had his friend said? 'You do not love her and she does not love you, so it won't count, will it? Nothing will happen.' But he was in love with her and could no longer pretend otherwise. Whenever he was with her, he wanted to make love to her, to sink himself into her, to merge with her, to become part of her living, breathing body, as she was his. But to do so would be to kill her, as surely as he was a Pargeter and she was a Capitain. He rode on, leaving the village behind him, his horse picking its way sure-footedly over the hidden paths towards the fen. He did not need to guide it with any more than a light hand on the rein; he did not need to see where he was going. In any case, he could not; his eyes were too full of the tears he would have died rather than let anyone see. Love and guilt were impossible bedfellows.

CHAPTER FIVE

THE school was set to open on the following Monday and, as soon as breakfast was over on that day, Margaret hurried to the schoolroom to make sure everything was in readiness. Nine o'clock came, and then half-past, and there was no sign of her pupils. Surely the children were not making game of her and had no intention of attending? At ten o'clock, she left the house to see what had delayed them, but, before she had gone beyond the Manor gates, her ears were assailed by a cacophony of noise and then a crowd came into view, men, women and children. Many of the men were dressed in their wives' skirts and had painted their faces with powder and rouge. On their heads they wore ladies' wigs. They were pulling an old plough, and it was bumping and scraping over the hard-packed snow and the ruts in the lane. Women marched beside them banging tin trays, and they were followed by what seemed every child in the village. Margaret was obliged to stand aside as they marched past her towards the Manor. She hurried after them, wondering what it all meant. In the courtyard they stopped.

'Out with you, good master,' they shouted. ''Tis time to pay the ploughman. Come out and pay up or take the consequences.'

The door opened and Roland appeared. Margaret was afraid there would be an angry confrontation, but a great cheer went up as he threw several guineas into the quart pot which was thrust under his nose. 'There's a fat porker and a barrel of beer at the kitchen door,' he said. 'Enjoy it, but make sure you are at work tomorrow.'

They roared their appreciation, collected the largesse and went on their way singing. Margaret tried to speak to one of them, but he could not hear her above the din. She grabbed Christopher's arm to pull him round to face her. 'Why did you not come to school?'

'Tomorrow,' he said, wrenching himself away. 'Tomorrow we'll come. Today we feast.'

She gave up and went down to join Roland at the door. 'What are they doing?' she asked him. 'Why are the men dressed like that?'

'It's Plough Monday,' he said, watching the departing villagers. 'It is a very important day in the country calender. The men are dressed as plough witches. The big fellow at the front is the Molly. They are taking the plough round the parish boundary in order to ensure there are good crops in the coming year.'

'Witches, fertility rites,' she said, too annoyed to mind her tongue. 'I never heard such heathen rubbish. They would do better to come to school and learn more sense.'

'You will not get them to school on a feast day,' he said mildly. 'Why did you not inform me you had decided to open the school today? I could have told you it would be useless.'

'You were busy and I did not want to bother you.'

He looked down at her with a slightly quizzical expression. 'Am I so unapproachable?'

'No, but surely one of the servants could have told me about the festival?'

'I expect they all assumed you would know.'

'And what else am I expected to know?' she asked tartly. 'What other important dates will find my class-room empty?'

He smiled suddenly, realising this kitten could spit when she chose, and it brought a fire to her cheeks and a sparkle to her eyes which he found very disturbing. 'Haymaking and harvest, of course, when they are required to work, and Easter Day. You would not deprive them of their egg-hunt?'

'No,' she said slowly, realising her anger was unjustified. 'I am sorry for my bad temper; I was disappointed, that's all, and no one told me. . .'

He smiled. 'They have nothing against school; they do wish to learn, you know. It is simply that the old traditions are important to them.'

'Will they come tomorrow?'

'They will come tomorrow.'

He was right; nearly all the children below the age of eight arrived promptly next morning and she set them to work. Half an hour later the Reverend Mr Archibald arrived to see how they were going on, and stopped to help. He was a young man, new to the parish and anxious to please, and he and Margaret were soon in the throes of planning future lessons. For the first time since her arrival, she felt she had a purpose in life. During the day, she ceased to wonder why Roland had married her and concentrated on the work in hand, but at night, alone in her bed, when the house was quiet, she could not keep her doubts from surfacing. A month of her year had passed; could she live through eleven more and then walk away from it, from Roland himself, who filled her head and heart to the exclusion of almost everything else?

One day he was a gentle friend, the next distantly courteous, but always he was solicitous of her health. She was obliged to tell him almost daily that she had never felt better. Even the tiniest sneeze would have him giving orders for her to be put to bed and dosed with laudanum. She hated the stuff and was convinced it did more harm than good, though old Lady Pargeter swore by it as a cure for all ills.

Margaret contrived to throw any dose she was given into the bedroom fire or out of the window. She could not understand why Roland was so worried about illness; it was not as if he was over-anxious about his own health or even that of his grandmother; his concern was for Margaret. She would have felt flattered if she did not think there was something more to it than a simple solicitude for her welfare.

It might have been easier for her peace of mind if he had gone back to London as he had said he would; he could have reached Cambridge on horseback, and the roads were open the rest of the way. There was nothing that she could see to detain him. While one half of her mind reasoned coolly, the other acknowledged with something akin to panic that she did not want him to go, any more than she wanted to leave herself, and that she could not envisage a life without the enigmatic man she had come to love. And she wished, more than anything, that she were his wife in every sense, and not just in name. The realisation came as a shock and she found herself shaking from head to foot, not made easier by the fact that she was, at the time, helping

Cook to chop onions and the tears were streaming down her face. And then he made matters worse by coming into the kitchen from the yard, where he had been talking to one of the grooms, and hurrying to her side to put his arm about her.

'Margaret, what is wrong? Why are you crying? Are you hurt?'

She sniffed and smiled. 'It's only the onions.'

'Thank God. But, my dear, there is no need for you to do menial tasks. Leave that to Cook.'

'Oh, Roland, it helps to keep me busy.' She did not add that the lively chatter of the kitchen staff also helped to keep her mind off her troubles.

'Leave it. I wish to speak to you.'

'Can it not wait a moment? I have nearly finished.'

'Now!' He grabbed the knife from her hand, and it slid across the backs of her fingers and cut them, clean as a whistle, sending the blood flowing down her hand.

'Oh, my God!' He looked down, paralysed for a moment, then, pulling himself together, grabbed a cloth from Cook and bound it round her hand, talking all the time. 'Oh, my darling, what have I done? Forgive me. I am a clumsy oaf. . .'

'It was an accident,' she said, her heart lifted by the endearment. 'It is a clean cut, nothing serious, no more blood than a surgeon would take at a letting.'

He commanded Penny to fetch salve and bandages and carefully bound the wound himself. 'Up to bed,' he said when he had finished. 'Rest until you recover.'

'I am perfectly well, thank you.'

He scooped her up in his arms and carried her to her room. 'I could have killed you. I don't know what devil got into me. If anything should happen to you. . .' He

laid her on the bed and sat on the edge, with her hand
nestling in his like a trapped bird. His expression of
concern, and something that looked very akin to guilt,
heartened her, even if they were a little out of place.
The cut was deep but it was clean.

She smiled to reassure him. 'Nothing will happen to
me. I am as strong as an ox and I can spare a little
blood.'

'But it is my fault, all of it, not only that cut but
nearly drowning under the ice. I should never have
brought you here.'

She laughed. 'You did not bring me; I came by
myself, if you remember. And I cannot see how you
can blame yourself for my ducking. You will tell me
next that it is all some terrible omen. . . .'

She could not have said anything more calculated to
bring home to him the dreadful thing he had done, and
she did it so guilelessly. He dropped his head into his
hands and groaned aloud.

She sat up and took his hands from his face. 'Look
at me, Roland. I do not believe in luck, except that it
was chance that brought me here. We make our luck
by what we do.'

He looked up into her eyes and recognised the truth
in what she said; he knew also that Susan had fled from
his mind and his heart. Her place had been taken by
the woman who held his hands so fearlessly in her own.
He loved her. He could not deny it, did not even want
to. His body ached with longing for her. All the will-
power he had so steadfastly exerted in the past few
weeks fled and left him defenceless. He groped for her
through a mist of tears and she came into his arms, as
easily as if she belonged there. He held her closely

against his chest for some time, not moving, not speaking, feeling her soft breath on his neck, her fluttering heart beneath his hand. Slowly, oh, so slowly and carefully, he unfastened her gown and slid it off her shoulders, revealing small rounded breasts and nipples that stood at his touch. He bent to kiss them one by one. She shivered and clung to him as he moved his head back to look at her.

'Margaret——'

'Don't talk.' She put a finger on his lips to stop him; it did not seem to be a time for words. He took her hand away from his mouth and kissed her fingers one by one, then bent to kiss her lips, gently, almost afraid that she would fly away and he would be left with empty arms. But she was flesh and blood and had no wings to fly with, would not have done if she had; she wanted to heal this big, hurting man with her love. She opened her mouth to his, telling him without words that she was his, always and forever. His response was urgent and powerful and yet careful of her too, and she gave herself to him willingly and lovingly. Everything that had held them apart, his strange proposal and talk of ill-omens, faded to insignificance in the face of this new, unfathomable delight, which came to an end in an explosion of passion which left her satiated and pleasantly exhausted.

He lay beside her, his arm beneath her shoulders, staring up at the ornate ceiling, wondering if he would ever be forgiven for what he had done. He had taken her because he loved her and wanted her, but in doing so he had thrown her life away, selfishly sacrificed her to the curse. She had said they made their own luck. But how? How could he change it? Should he tell her?

He turned his head to look at her. She had fallen asleep, her hair tumbled about on the pillows and a faint smile on her lips, as if she was dreaming of the pleasure she had just enjoyed. Or of more to come? How could he make love to her again? But how could he not, without breaking her heart and his own along with it?

He slowly withdrew his arm and carefully left the bed without waking her. He dressed silently and went downstairs, picked up his gun and called to his dog. The best place for him, until he could pull himself together, was out in the open, among the village men, working on the dyke. Taking a turn with a shovel might help to release the terrible tension within him.

In the middle of February the thaw set in, and Roland's work on the new drain was put to the test.

'It's holding,' he told Margaret one day, coming back to the house at ten o'clock for his breakfast; he could not break a lifetime habit of rising early and going out with his fast unbroken. 'Though the levels of the cut are two feet above normal.'

'What about Great-Uncle Henry? His house is very low-lying.'

'What about him?' He did not like her reminding him of the man. 'I have seen nothing of him these last two weeks. No doubt he has left and taken his fine friends with him.'

'And the villagers?'

'All high and dry. Would you like to come with me and see?'

It was the first time he had asked her if she would like to accompany him, and she gladly accepted, hoping that with the melting snow would come a thawing in their relationship. She had hoped it might improve as a result of their lovemaking, but she had been doomed to disappointment. Nothing had changed, except that perhaps he was even more remote, even more troubled. She had tried to ask him what was wrong, but he had denied that anything was bothering him beyond the usual business of the village and his duties as a Justice of the Peace. She could not reach him and could only pray that whatever it was would pass and he would come to her again.

As soon as they had eaten their fill of boiled ham, coddled eggs and oatmeal porridge, she hurried to put on fur-lined boots, cloak and muff, and rejoined him at the front door. He took her arm and they set off on foot through the village towards the flood-defences on the other side.

Margaret was surprised and delighted to see that several of the village houses had new thatch, and on others the walls were being repaired. 'Oh, how glad I am to see you are a man of your word,' she said.

'Did you think I was not?' he asked mildly.

'No, I knew you were.'

He did not answer. He had broken a far more important promise to her, and the guilt would not go away. It was made worse because she was so obviously trying to please him, to make a success of their marriage, to interest herself in things that concerned him, to give him a loving home to come home to after a day in the village or on the fen. In everything she did, she showed over and over again that she loved him and had forgotten that impossible pledge he had made to release her at the end of a year. He could no more release her now than hold back the dawn of each day, drawing the year inexorably onward. He forced himself to smile at her as she spoke cheerfully to the villagers, who had come to know and like her.

'What are those bricks made of?' she asked, pointing to a pile of greyish-brown blocks.

'Clay lumps,' he said. 'Come. I'll show you how they are made.'

He took her to a yard at the end of the village street where a group of men were busy mixing clay, chopped straw and cow-dung in a trough and puddling it into a dough with bare feet. She grimaced and he laughed. 'It makes capital bricks. When the mix is just right, they cut it into slabs and dry them out.'

'Can they withstand the weather?'

'Very well. The completed walls are washed over with diluted chalk and salt and then given a colour-wash. They last for years.'

She watched while Roland had a word or two with the men, then they continued on out of the village to arrive on its western side where the new drain had been cut and the displaced earth formed into a six-foot barrier along the bank. He took her hand and helped her to scramble up the slope so they could see down into the water. It raced along in a torrent, taking with it lumps of ice and broken branches, bearing them away towards the river and leaving the village dry, though some of the outlying fields had been inundated. Margaret smiled to see the men walking over this flooded land on stilts, herding the cattle to higher ground, as well-balanced as if they had been on their feet. The strange windmills were busy scooping the water into their buckets and tipping it into the dykes

which bordered the field. Beyond them, clumps of
blackened reeds stood twisted and drooping, half in
and half out of the water; willows and alders, tracing
the line of the cut, stood starkly against a strangely
luminous sky. 'Where has all the water come from?'
she asked. 'Surely it is not all melted snow?'

'Yes, but it has come from hills many miles to the
west, brought down the rivers and canals to the fens.
Before they were drained, all this——' his hand swept
the acres of sodden fields, '—would have been under
water. Now it only happens in severe winters, and then
only if we are not prepared.'

'As you were.'

'As we were. There was some flooding, but nothing
dramatic.'

'Where does it all go?'

'To the sea, eventually.' He pointed in the direction
of Highmere Sluice. 'The sluice is opened and away it
goes.' He paused, noticing her shiver. 'Are you cold?'

'No, not at all.' Not for a minute would she have
confessed that her toes were numb; she wanted to
savour this intimacy, the shared interest in the welfare
of the village, their togetherness.

'Would you like to go out to the fen? Then I could
really show you some water.' He smiled and added, 'I
promise you won't have to row.'

'I should like that very much.'

He led her down the bank at the end of the new
dyke and helped her into a small boat which was
moored there. He was cheerful, almost boyish, as he
picked up a quanting-pole and propelled them along
the cut and out on to the permanent water of the fen.

Here all signs of civilisation vanished. They glided

along through the rustling reeds, the only sounds the lapping of the water against the sides of the boat and the croaking of frogs. Roland pulled the craft in to a patch of reeds, shipped the quanting-pole and, leaning over the side, began pulling at a narrow osier basket which was anchored just below the surface. It had no bottom but a huge net, and in the net were hundreds of squirming eels. Involuntarily she shrank from it.

'Don't you like eels?' he queried, dropping the net back into the water.

'Not live ones, though Mama used to cook eel pie when we lived in London. She bought them from the market.'

He smiled. 'They are still alive when they reach London, Margaret. They wouldn't remain fresh otherwise. They are sent to London in barrels of water, which is changed at every stop when the horses are changed. Your mother would have known that.'

'Yes, she would, wouldn't she?' It was pleasant to be talking to him about her mother in such a calm way, but then, it was not Roland but his grandmother who could not bear the mention of her. 'There is so much about her I didn't know. I could not understand her love for her home, which I had always thought of as bleak and unfriendly, but it isn't, is it?'

'You either love it or you hate it,' he said. 'There is no middle road.'

'Then I love it,' she said, warmed by his smile which seemed to be reaching out to her, drawing her to him. 'I want to learn all I can.'

'Then where shall we start?' he asked. 'With the way the men earn a living?'

'Yes, please.'

'Farming, of course, because this is some of the most fertile land in the country, but they supplement their living on the fen as their forefathers did, long before the fens were drained. Fish and fowl and reeds for thatching. Eels are not the only delicacy from the fens to find their way to the tables of London,' he said. 'Ducks are sent too, sometimes thousands at a time. They are enticed into netted enclosures by tame decoys.'

She laughed. 'You are teasing me.'

'No, on my oath. The tame ducks know there is an abundance of food in the enclosures because the duck-hunters scatter it there. They lead the other birds to it. When the net is drawn in, the tame ducks are identified and set free to entice more wild birds back to the nets. They do not know their fellows have ended up on dinner-tables.'

Suddenly, as if to prove his point, the sky was filled with a great cloud of wildfowl, flying in arrowhead formation, low and silent, except for the beating of their wings. As she watched, they dived down towards a distant reed-bed, quarking and squabbling. 'They do not know they will never fly again,' she said wistfully, and could not suppress a shudder of apprehension. Had she been enticed into a trap? Would she ever be free again? Did she even want to be?

'You are cold?'

'A little.'

'It is time we returned,' he said, looking up at the sky. In the past half-hour it had filled up with huge black clouds, tier upon tier, whipped up by the wind which tore across the open space.

'Will it rain?' she asked.

'Perhaps.' He picked up the pole and in no time, it seemed to Margaret, they were back on dry land, but by this time she was very cold indeed and could not stop shivering. 'I am sorry I should not have taken you out,' he said. 'You are not used to this raw weather. If you catch a chill. . .'

She smiled through chattering teeth. 'If I can escape a chill after going through the ice, a little cold air won't hurt me.'

'We will not take the risk.' Suddenly he was the distant Lord Pargeter again, not the laughing boyish Roland in whose company she had just spent two delightful but chilly hours. 'Why did you not tell me? We could have come back long ago.' He took her arm and hurried her towards the blacksmith's shop where he knew it would be warm.

'I was so interested, I hardly noticed how cold I was,' she said, following him into the smithy. 'Please don't worry.'

The blacksmith's name was Silas Gotobed. He was a huge man, with long dark hair which fell loosely about his broad shoulders. His features were craggy from being alternately in great heat and cold winds, but his eyes were intelligent and friendly. He dusted down a stool and set it close to the fire. 'Sit awhile, my lady,' he said. 'The wind is lazy today, but it will blow the clouds away. I doubt it will rain.'

She laughed. 'Lazy?'

'It cannot take the trouble to go round you,' Roland said with a smile. 'So it blows right through you.'

'Oh, I know exactly what you mean.' She sat down and stretched out her cold toes to the warmth, while the blacksmith continued to fashion a piece of red-hot metal. 'What are you making?'

'A weathervane, my lady. The one on the Manor has fallen down.' He held it up to show her. It was a witch riding on a broomstick. 'She always rides with the wind, do you see? Her cloak is flying out behind her.'

Margaret turned to Roland, who was standing at the doorway surveying the sky, as if searching for something in the shapes of the clouds. 'Why a witch, Roland?'

'Why not? There has been a witch on the gable-end of the Manor these last hundred years. It keeps her associates away. They are afraid of iron.' He laughed suddenly. 'And who am I to deny the beliefs of my forebears?'

'So they are perpetuated.' She was annoyed with him, but she was unsure why. Did he really believe such nonsense? 'If you are going to be superstitious about it, you could say that her being blown down was a sign that witches have lost their potency and she should not be replaced.'

'Would to God you were right,' he said morosely, and turned to face her. 'Come, Silas is right; it's too windy to rain.'

She rose and followed him out into the road, where the gale whipped her skirts against her legs and took her breath away. 'What do you mean?' she asked, miserable because the friendly intimacy they had shared on the fen had disappeared with their return to habitation. Perhaps he was really only happy on the water. 'Are you afraid of something?'

'No, of course not,' he snapped.

'But you are. You are afraid of some fairy-tale nonsense. Oh, Roland, how could you?'

He did not answer, but took her arm and propelled her forward, so that it took all her energy to keep up with him and she certainly had no more breath for speech. As soon as he had seen her safely indoors, he turned on his heel and went out again.

He could not bear to stay with her, to see the reproach in her eyes, to know there were questions on her tongue he did not dare to answer. He loved her and had by his selfish actions condemned her to the fate he had been so careful to avoid for Susan. And thinking of Susan and her expectations, even if those had not been put into words, made his wretchedness worse. He picked up his gun, powder and shot, called to his dog and hurried down the lawn, squelching through the melted snow towards the boat-house. Out on the loneliness of the fen was where he wanted to be, somewhere he could contemplate without those kitten eyes watching him, accusing him. He untied the boat, jumped in and pushed off. He would get up a sweat and bag a few ducks, which was what he had intended in the first place before his impulsive invitation to Margaret to join him, and maybe he would feel better after that.

He rowed down the cut towards the river, passing Sedge House on the way. That building was the symbol of his misery; he wished it would fall into the water, as it had been threatening to do for years. He glanced towards it as he rowed. The flood-water had reached the back door, though he doubted it would go higher. Anyone in the upper rooms would be perfectly safe and he need not trouble his conscience about them. He caught a glimpse of someone moving across one of the bedroom windows; so the old fellow had not gone after all. More fool him! He thought he saw a man at another window, a tall, thin man with long golden hair. He paused in his rowing and cupped his hands to his mouth and shouted, 'Master Capitain! Do you need assistance?'

The window was flung open and Henry's head appeared. 'None, an' if I did I'd not seek it of a Pargeter.'

Other heads appeared at other windows, Roland noticed. 'Would you all drown first?'

'We will not drown, have no fear of that. If we are threatened, I shall know what to do.'

'Your skiff is not big enough to take you all. I see three or four of you.'

'Then your eyes deceive you. An' I was not thinking of running away. If you think to save your fields by overfilling the river, then I give you fair warning; if the water-level rises by so much as an inch more, your new bank will come down.'

'And do you expect the people of Winterford to stand by and let you do it? You are a fool, Henry Capitain, if you believe that. I have the right of it.'

Henry was about to retort, when someone tugged at him from behind. 'Desist, Henry, desist.' He said other things that Roland could not hear, but the result was that Henry's head disappeared and the window was banged shut. Roland picked up his oars and rowed on.

The encounter with Henry Capitain did not make him feel any better about Margaret; nothing did, nothing could, not even a few hours spent on the fen with no company but a dog and a fowling-piece. The eerie silence, broken only by the croaking of frogs, the beating wings of ducks as they flew overhead and the light splash of his oars, served only to amplify his thoughts until it seemed he was shouting them aloud. He was cursed and he did not know how to break out of it. If he died. . . If he fled far away. . . If he confessed. . . The dog looked at him in surprise; there were ducks in plenty and not once had his master fired. He wagged his tail to encourage him but all that happened was that a tired hand was laid on his head. 'Good dog, I'm not pleasant company today, am I? Best be getting home before they send a search-party out looking for us.' There was nothing to be done but watch and wait and protect Margaret with every ounce of his will and strength. From now on, he promised himself, he would try to be a loving husband, try to pretend nothing was wrong, for her sake. He picked up his oars and rowed home, without firing a single shot.

Spring arrived at last. Swords of bright green pushed their way up out of the muddy water; blackened sedge was replaced by new green shoots. The alder sent forth fronds of pale lime and golden catkins dangled on the willow. Daffodils bloomed on the lawns of the Manor and snowdrops and yellow aconites carpeted the woods. The winter wheat was inches high, and the men were out on the open strips, sowing barley. They plodded rhythmically up one furrow and down the next, each pace exactly the length of the one before, each handful of seed covering exactly the same area. Behind them a small boy with a harrow covered the seed, and small children danced and shouted and clapped their hands to scare away the birds which flocked about them, daring to swoop on the banquet after the winter shortage. The sky was a light blue and there was more warmth in the sun. Everything seemed to be alight with new life, and Margaret felt it flowing through her, giving her a zest and energy that nothing seemed to suppress. She had put on a little weight and her hair, worn in ringlets and unpowdered, shone with health. Her cheeks glowed and her eyes sparkled. A quarter of her year at Winterford had gone and, but for one thing, she would have said she had never been happier. Roland had said nothing about what would happen at the year's end, had not said he wanted her to stay. And surely, now that they were husband and wife in reality as well as name, he did not still expect her to leave? But she was too afraid of what he might say to mention it herself.

She woke one night from a deep sleep to find Roland gone from her side. Before she could wonder what had woken her, she heard the sound of shrill cries coming from along the passage, followed by footsteps and a door banging. It seemed to be coming from the Dowager's bedroom and Margaret, wishing to help if there was something wrong, left her bed, put a dressing-gown on over her night clothes and crept along the passage towards her ladyship's room. As she reached it a high-pitched shriek convinced her there was something very much amiss, and she pushed open the door to see Roland and Hannah struggling with the old lady.

'Hush, Grandmama, hush,' Roland said, pushing his grandmother back on to the pillows. 'There is no one here but Hannah and me. Go back to sleep.' He nodded to Hannah, who went to a table and fetched a cup of dark liquid which he took and held to his grandmother's lips. She gulped it greedily, then sighed and looked up to see Margaret, in her floating gown, standing in the doorway. She shrieked. 'I told you so. There she is. There's the witch.'

Roland looked round and saw her too. 'Go back to your room, my lady.'

'Can I not be of help?'

'No. Go at once.'

His tone brooked no argument and she went back to bed, lying awake, listening, but there were no more noises and, before she knew it, she had fallen asleep again. She did not hear the soft click of the door-latch or Roland's footsteps as he crossed the room to look down at her tousled head; she did not know, until she woke next morning, that he had gone back to his own room rather than disturb her again.

She rose as soon as she woke, without waiting for her breakfast to be brought to her, and hurried to join her husband in the morning-room. He looked up in surprise, but said nothing except, 'Good morning, my dear. I am sorry you were disturbed last night.'

'Oh, that's of no consequence.' She helped herself from a chafing-dish and sat down opposite him. 'How is her ladyship this morning?'

'Quiet again, though I fear she will not long be with us.'

'Roland, I am concerned for her. She takes far too much laudanum. I am sure it is that which makes her confused.' It was not only Lady Pargeter who took opium; the villagers used white poppies grown in their own gardens to concoct their insidious medicine. 'Could you not find something else to soothe her?'

'No, she has taken it all her life; it is too late to make changes now. It comforts her and that is reason enough to give it to her.'

'But it is killing her.'

'How dare you, madam, how dare you accuse me. . .?' There was a gleam in his eye, and a dull red spot on each cheek, which told her she had gone too far.

'I am not accusing you. Why are you so touchy? I am simply saying——'

'Then I wish you would not. Do you think I wish my grandmother dead or would do anything to hasten the day? My God, Margaret, do you take me for a monster?'

'No, of course not.' She pushed her chair back and rose to her feet. 'I am obviously distressing you. I beg your pardon.' She walked to the door with as much dignity as she could muster, glad that she had her back to him and he could not see her tears.

She went to the schoolroom, but there was only a handful of children there, being examined by the Reverend Mr Archibald on the Scriptures. He was pleased with their progress, although he had a few strong words to say to Christopher Gotobed about his tardiness in arriving at church the previous Sunday.

Margaret smiled; she knew the boy liked to take his dog for a scamper across the meadow and sometimes he forgot the time and was late back.

'Young people are no great minders of time,' she said with a smile, when the children had been sent home for their dinner and they were tidying up the books. 'And, without timepieces, it is extraordinary how seldom they are late.'

'That is why we have a bell, my lady,' he said, though he smiled. 'A bell for school and bells for church.'

'Yes, of course, though I sometimes think the people have in-built clocks that tell them the time. It is a sort of instinct.'

'The sun is a clock, my lady, and there is a sundial on the village green, put there by an ancestor of his lordship, just to remind people that their time on this earth is short and they should make the most of it.'

'They are a very superstitious lot, aren't they?' she said, deciding he was the best person to talk to about it. 'More here than in other parts of the country. In London, they throw spilled salt over their left shoulders, but that is about the extent of it. Here, their whole lives seem to be governed by the need to keep evil spirits at bay and encourage the good ones.'

'You are making a study of such things, my lady?'

'I am interested. Do people still believe in witches?'

'Oh, yes, indeed, and always will.'

'Do you?'

'No, my lady, but I have had an enlightened education, as I am sure you have.'

'Why do the people of the Fens believe in omens so strongly, even the most devout church-goers?'

He put the pile of books he was carrying on a shelf and turned to smile at her. 'Their lives have always been hard, my lady, especially in earlier times, before the fens were drained. They had to be tough to survive. Their livelihoods depended on what they could glean from the water—fish, fowl, osiers for baskets, reeds for thatch—and the water was a hard taskmaster; it was muddy and putrid, freezing cold in winter and full of pestilence in summer. The people were victims of disease and ague and it is small wonder they turned to folklore and superstition to make their lives more bearable. In order to avert the disasters which overtook them all too frequently, they would believe in signs and omens. They would try to set aside portents of evil with good-luck charms and incantations.'

'Surely they could have turned to the Church?'

'The churches were often some way off, and in winter inaccessible and, when they were not, ten to one the incumbent was absent. Because he did not like the pestilential atmosphere, he would visit his flock infrequently.' He sighed. 'The witch-hunters of a century ago thought to eradicate witches with purges and hangings, but that did no good, and in more recent times we have tried to replace the superstition with education, a love of God and a faith in His goodness, but the beliefs are so deeply ingrained that we have only partially succeeded.'

'Do you know anything of the enmity of the Pargeters and the Capitains? It seems to go back as far as the Civil War.'

'I had heard something of it. That sort of thing was particularly prevalent in this area at that time because Oliver Cromwell was a local man and East Anglia was at the centre of hostilities. People who had, until that time, lived happily side by side became mortal enemies; things were said, threats made, evil deeds done, and it was easier to blame those in the pay of the devil than one's own weakness.'

'Do you think that is how it started? It seems very foolish to me.'

'So it is. The feud has been handed down from

generation to generation, so that even the people who perpetuate it cannot remember how it started. Stories grow up around it and are added to with every telling. It is unfortunate, in a way, that old Lady Pargeter has lived to be such a great age. She is only two generations removed from the original trouble and she grew up hearing about it, but now, perhaps, it will die for want of telling.' He smiled suddenly. 'The two families are united now in you and his lordship; that is surely a good sign.'

'An omen, sir?' Margaret teased.

He laughed. '*Touché*, my lady.'

'I do hope you are right, but my husband is less sure.'

'Then you must have faith enough for both of you.'

He bade her good-day with a smile and left, as he had come in, by the garden door, and Margaret turned her attention to preparing the following day's lessons, but she could not give her mind to it and reluctantly gave up.

Something had to be done to ease the dreadful tension in the house, or everyone would turn as mad as old Lady Pargeter. It was like a great stormcloud poised for a crack of thunder to release its power, or a keg of gunpowder waiting for a fuse to blow everything sky-high. Much as she loved him, she did not know how she could go on living with a man who was under so great a mantle of darkness that it obscured his reason. Perhaps she ought to go back on her bargain to stay a year and leave Winterford at once, for Roland's sake. To give him peace. . .

* * *

But before she could speak to Roland the Dowager Lady Pargeter died.

Kate and Charles came down for the funeral, which was attended by the whole village and many dignitaries from Ely and Huntingdon. Although it was a sad occasion, Margaret was very pleased to see Kate; she seemed to bring a breath of sanity to the house, and they spent some time laughing and chatting and bringing each other up to date on what they had been doing. Kate was saddened by her grandmother's death, but she was pregnant and so pleased with herself over it that she could not mourn for long. She and Charles stayed two days, and the old house came to life for a time, but sank into gloom the minute they left. Roland seemed to take their departure as a signal to disappear himself for hours on the fen.

Margaret assumed he had a problem to wrestle with and until he had solved it he had to be alone, but she could not stop herself wondering if it had anything to do with her. Had his grandmother's death reminded him of their bargain? Would he send her away at once? It would break her heart into a thousand fragments if he did; whether he loved her or not, she could not face life without him. She held her breath, waiting. . .

CHAPTER SIX

THE days passed, one upon the other, growing longer and warmer. Roland did not mention leaving himself, nor asked Margaret to leave, and she began to relax, to hope for a reprieve, especially as he seemed to enjoy making love to her. Each time they seemed to find new ways to delight each other, fresh sensations to add to those that had gone before. She was a flower opening to the sun, each perfect petal unfurling to reveal the nectar that would quench the thirst he had for her. The night belonged to them, the lovers, but the day, as far as he was concerned, was for remorse and guilt and shame, not because he loved her but because he knew it was inevitable that she would be hurt by it.

She spent her days with the school—though that was very poorly attended now that there was work for the children to do on the land—and going for long walks, always accompanied by Penny. She explored the old footpaths, once the only routes through the fens but now high above the surrounding fields that sprouted with new corn. She never ceased to wonder at the hard lives the fen people must have led before drainage had brought the land under the plough and prosperity to the farmers, and only wished more of it could be spread downwards to the people who really did the work. Roland did his best; his cottages were now sturdy and weatherproof and his workers had a little land of their own to grow vegetables, fatten a pig or keep a milking cow. But they were first and foremost wildfowlers, fishermen—fen slodgers, they were called, as much at home on the water as they were on the land. They caught tench, pike, eels and otters, and hunted snipe, moorhens, ducks and geese. Their barges, called fen lighters, towed in gangs of five or six, carried cargoes of coal, peat, grain, vegetables, stones for the road and passengers, towed along the haling way by heavy horses. She came to admire these hardy fen people more and more. Roland, for all his wealth and position was one of them. If only she could understand him!

Every day, as she moved among the fen people, she learned more about their ways and their strange beliefs, until she almost began to believe them herself. There were tales of ghosts and fairies and strange flickering lights out on the fens which had no human source, and no one dared go out when they were about, so Mistress Coulter told her. Two of the Coulter children were ill and, because their mother had to stay at home to nurse them, she had lost her wages. Margaret, who had remonstrated with the farmer who employed her to no avail, had taken a basket of food to supplement the barley gruel which was all Mistress Coulter could afford for her large family. She had stayed to talk, encouraging the woman to tell her about the fenman's superstitions.

Witches, she was informed, were afraid of iron and water, so each cottage had an inverted horseshoe nailed to the door, an iron implement under the doormat or a jug of water in the hearth to stop them coming in through the chimney. Fairy-stones—flints picked up from the fields and riverbanks which had a hole through the centre—were worn round the neck or hung over stable doors to bring good luck. But bad luck had its own omens—a clock that suddenly stopped, a bird tapping on the window, a falling picture, a ticking spider, a coffin-shaped piece of soot hanging in the chimney, a blazing fire with a black coal in its centre, called a 'fire-hole'. And the most dreaded of all was a big black dog, the size of a small calf, called Black Shuck. He had bright yellow eyes—sometimes only one—which glowed in the dark and he would spring out on a lonely road and then disappear before the terrified watcher could blink. 'He foretells death, my lady,' Mistress Coulter told her.

Margaret smiled a little nervously as she bade the woman goodbye and left the little reed-thatched cottage, musing on what she had been told. If Roland had been brought up surrounded by such tales, no wonder he held so fast to them, though if you were forever trying to encourage good luck or warding off evil you would have little time for anything else.

Roland's reaction, when she recounted her conversation with Mistress Coulter over the dinner-table, was to smile. 'She is one of the more gullible of the villagers.'

'Then you do not believe in these omens?'

'It depends. Three things you must watch out for—a dead donkey, an out-of-work parson and a contented farmer. The first two are rarely seen and the last one never.'

'I will remember that.' Margaret was relieved that he could make a joke of it. Was that a sign that he was over his own fears? She smiled at herself; now she was the one looking for omens.

Sometimes, when she was out in the village, she saw

Nellie, hurrying with her shopping, and once they even came face to face. The girl carried a heavy basket of provisions, far more than Margaret would have deemed necessary for two people, and she assumed that her great-uncle had more visitors, though they never came to the village. Margaret smiled, prepared to be friendly, but Nellie turned away and hurried off in the opposite direction.

'She can't look you in the face, my lady,' Penny said. 'She's an evil one.'

'No, Penny, not evil, misguided perhaps. Now let us go home; his lordship will be worrying about us.'

For once Roland was not worrying about her, at least not about her whereabouts. He was in his library, pacing the floor, with a letter in his hand. It had come, the imperious command he had been half expecting from Susan. It had been written in London where she and her parents were to be in residence for several months. Why had he not kept his promise to come to her in London? Why had he not written since Christmas? He was breaking her heart with his neglect of her. 'You must come at once,' she had written. 'Papa is giving a ball for me and I expect you to be there. Oh, I cannot wait to see you again. If you do not come, then I shall come and find out for myself what it is that holds you so firmly in the country when you could be with me. I shall not like to do that because there is so much going on here, so many balls and routs and visits and so many fashionable young men, but I can think of nothing but you and so I am determined.' There was more in like vein, but he could hardly bear to read it. That she had even addressed a letter to him was proof enough that she considered she had a claim on him; young unmarried ladies simply did not write to gentlemen. He wondered vaguely if Sir Godfrey and Lady Chalfont knew about it and how long it would be before someone told them of his marriage. His behaviour would be decreed that of a scoundrel by every right-thinking person; he would be a social outcast and, worse, his position at court would be rescinded, his judicial authority in the county undermined. The only way he could avoid that was to make Susan understand why he had done it, to tell her the truth.

He heard Margaret come in, chatting to Penny as she went upstairs to change out of her walking-clothes. He folded the letter, put it in a drawer of the escritoire and left the room to find his wife.

She was sitting before the mirror in her bedchamber in an undress gown, having her hair brushed by Penny. A green silk overdress lay spread on the bed, together with a cream petticoat and white silk stockings, ready to be donned when her *toilette* was complete. He strode over and took the brush from the maid's hand. 'Leave us.'

Penny scuttled away and he stood behind Margaret with the brush in his hand. She looked up at him in the mirror. 'Is anything wrong?'

'No, not at all. May a man not visit his wife in her boudoir?' He began brushing her hair, making long, smooth strokes down the length of her tresses, wondering how to begin.

'That's lovely,' she said, almost purring.

He lifted her hair and kissed her neck and then wished he had not, because she raised her arm and put her hand behind his head, drawing him closer, making him feel more wretched than ever. 'I have to go to London.'

So it had come; the thing she dreaded most. He was going to leave her as he had said he would. The fact that he had made her his wife in deed as well as name meant nothing at all. He had simply been passing the time in dalliance. Her hand dropped to her lap. 'When?'

'Almost immediately.' He could not bear to see the hurt in her eyes; he had to do something to mitigate it. 'Would you like to come too?' It was a rash thing to suggest but he was rewarded with a brilliant smile. 'I have business affairs to attend to, but they will not take all my time. . .'

'Oh, yes, please,' she said, her spirits soaring. 'It will be pleasant to see some life, go to social gatherings, perhaps a ball. Do you think we might be invited to a ball, Roland?'

'I don't know,' he said, thinking of Susan's letter. That was one ball Margaret must not attend.

'We will both be better for a little recreation and it will lift your low spirits.'

'I am not in low spirits, my dear.'

'Indeed you are. Come, admit you would like a little amusement. I know I should.'

'Perhaps.' He turned her stool back to the mirror and began brushing her hair again, long, sensuous strokes that roused him to a passion which could not be denied. The brush fell from his hand and he knelt at her feet to take her in his arms. She slipped from the stool, to sit on his thighs, laughing as he drew her underdress over her head and threw it carelessly across

the room. Her skin was smooth and lustrous, glowing
in the firelight, her figure so perfect, her senses so
finely tuned to his, that it was as if they moved as one.
She was his wife and he could no more leave her
behind than he could have stopped breathing, even
though he knew he was being utterly reckless.

They set off in the travelling-chaise at the beginning of
May, a week after the wagon which had been sent
ahead with several servants and a mountain of luggage.
The roads had recovered from the soaking they had
had earlier in the year, and were now baked hard into
deep ruts. But the pastures were lush and the cattle on
them thriving. Wheat and barley, coleseed and turnips
were growing strongly in the strips of cultivated fields,
where farm labourers hoed between the rows. Pink and
white candles of blossom clothed the chestnut trees and
the scent of may-blossom filled the air. Margaret
breathed deeply of the balmy air, her contentment
marred only by Roland's silence.

The further they went, the more taciturn he became.
She had been so sure that the oppressive atmosphere
of the Fens, coupled with the death of his grandmother,
was contributing to his depression, and that whatever
was troubling him might be seen in clearer perspective
once they were in London. What they both needed was
a little gaiety. Had she been mistaken?

Pargeter House was a three-storeyed residence in
Mayfair, with a short gravel drive at the front and
round the side, gardens at the rear and stabling and
kitchens in separate wings. Its front door was reached
by a flight of steps, heavily studded and lighted on
either side by flambeaus in brackets. Its evenly spaced

windows had green-painted shutters. Inside it was richly decorated and furnished, with a great deal of mahogany and walnut, inlaid in fine detail with satin-wood and rosewood. The chairs were covered in tapestry and damask and there were valuable paintings and mirrors on the walls. The ceilings were plastered and gilded and the floors covered in rich carpets. The servants had been hard at work for the last two weeks and everything sparkled.

As soon as they arrived, Roland went to his room and changed from his dusty travelling-clothes into a blue satin full-skirted coat with a high standing collar, double-breasted striped waistcoat and darker blue breeches, then went in search of his wife. 'Do not wait dinner for me,' he said. 'I may dine at my club.' He knew he had disappointed her by leaving so soon, but she could occupy herself with unpacking and exploring the house, and he would be back again in no time. And then he meant to make amends. He was going to try to expunge his guilt.

He found a chair to take him to Sir Godfrey's town house in Mount Street. It was a modest establishment but well-maintained, and he was admitted by a foot-man, who took his hat and conducted him to the drawing-room where Sir Godfrey and Lady Chalfont were listening to their daughter playing the harpsicord. She was dressed in a brocade gown with wide panniers and a very low neckline. Her naturally fair hair was covered by a white wig. As soon as Roland was announced, she left off playing and ran towards him, both hands outstretched.

'Roland, you bad boy,' she cried as he bent over her hands. 'Why have you taken so long? You said you would be in town in April. Have you been ill again? Does your wound trouble you?' She prattled on, giving him no time, reminding him what a chatterbox she was and how difficult to deny. 'Come and pay your respects to Mama and Papa, and then you shall come to the Duchess of Devonshire's rout with us. I am sure she will invite you an we ask her.'

He allowed her to drag him over to her parents, where he made his bows and enquired how they did.

'Very well,' Sir Godfrey said. 'Now tell us what you have been up to.'

'Up to?' he queried. Did they know of his marriage? He turned to Susan, but she was smiling agreeably. She had smiled like that when he was wounded and lying helpless in her father's house, smiled her siren's smile and captivated him. Why did he find it less than appealing now? 'The winter was a hard one and I had much to do on my estates. . .'

'But you are here now,' Susan put in. 'We will go everywhere and have such a happy season.' She looked at his clothes almost disparagingly. 'You have time to go home and change before the Duchess's rout.'

'I am afraid I am otherwise engaged.' Cursing himself for a coward, he rushed on, addressing Sir Godfrey. 'Since I had the good fortune to be given succour in your house, much has happened.' He paused and took a deep breath. 'I have acquired a wife.'

'A wife!' Susan shrieked, and sank into a chair.

'Yes.' He tried not to look at Susan, who appeared to be swooning. To go to her now would make it impossible for him to do what he had come to do; he kept his eyes resolutely on her father. 'My grand-mother——'

Sir Godfrey stood up, while his wife comforted their weeping daughter. He was quite a short man and his head hardly came above Roland's shoulder, but his anger lent him dignity. 'You have played fast and loose with my darling and that cannot be forgiven. You are a scoundrel, sir, a blackguard, and I shall see that all London knows it.'

Roland turned towards Susan. She was staring at him with red-rimmed eyes, which surprisingly showed more anger than misery. He had a sudden feeling that she could be vindictive if she chose. 'I never intended to hurt you. It was because I thought so much of you that I could not ask you to be my wife.'

'How could you?' she spat. 'You are not making sense.'

'I came to explain——'

'I wish for no explanations,' Sir Godfrey said. 'I bid you good-day, sir.'

There was nothing for it but to leave. If only he had been able to speak to Susan alone, he was sure he could have made her understand. Now there would be the devil to pay and he would find himself ostracised. He didn't mind that for himself, but Margaret would suffer too.

It was easy to understand why he had imagined he loved Susan. He had been ill and in pain, delirious much of the time, and her cool hand on his brow and her soft voice had soothed him. She was beautiful too, like a painted doll, with perfect teeth and hair and a ready smile. He had been more than grateful and, when he had felt better, so anxious to please her that it had been easy to imagine himself in love. He had stayed longer than he should, enjoying her company and growing steadily stronger until he could no longer put off the return to his regiment. Now, seeing her again, he was still grateful, but gratitude was not love.

His love was for his wife. She was beautiful too, but in a quieter way, and she had courage, mountains of it, and a quiet composure which he found restful. She liked his country home and the people on his estate, the fenmen and women, perhaps because she was her mother's daughter and therefore one of them. They liked her too and that must mean she had qualities over and above beauty. Sir Godfrey's condemnation was nothing to the castigation he heaped upon himself. He could not go home, could not go back to the reproach in Margaret's eyes. So he took himself off to White's and proceeded to become very drunk indeed.

It was to become the pattern of his days. He rose late, went out riding alone and then spent hours in his club playing cards and drinking, leaving Margaret to occupy herself as best she might.

Reluctantly she realised that whatever had troubled Roland in Winterford was a hundred times worse in London. No one came to call and she could find nothing to do but shopping, accompanied by Penny, or riding in St James's Park, escorted by one of the grooms who rode a few paces behind her, almost like a gaoler. And then, when she was almost in despair, Kate and Charles arrived and brought light and laughter into her life once more.

Kate had decided she wanted a little entertainment before motherhood made it impossible, and she and Charles were determined to enjoy themselves. They were so happy together that they had a kind of aura which spread to everyone about them. Not even

Roland was immune. He pulled himself out of his torpor and made a determined effort to be affable. The invitations which had stood unanswered on the mantelshelf were accepted and they began to go out and about.

Kate took Margaret out shopping for the clothes she had had no inclination to buy before; there had seemed no reason to deck herself in finery to sit at home alone, even though Roland had urged her to do so. Now she found herself buying gowns, petticoats, mantles, shawls, stockings, slippers, and even a new riding-habit with a military coat—all gold braid and frogging. Accompanied by Roland and Charles, the two young wives attended receptions, soirées and routs, and danced the night away at grand balls, and Margaret blessed her sister-in-law for making it possible.

'Roland never wanted to go out before you came,' she said one afternoon when Kate came to call on her after a shopping expedition which looked set to impoverish her husband if she repeated it many more times. Her town chariot was loaded with packages, many of them fripperies for her nursery, for the coming child meant everything to her. 'Do you suppose he was ashamed of me?'

'Heavens, why? You are beautiful, don't you know that? And you know how to go on. I am ready to wager you will be the belle of any ball you attend. He would not have married you if he did not think you could hold your own in Society.'

'But my background is not of the first order, is it?'

'Pooh to that. He may not like the Capitains, but there is no denying their name is as old and as respected in Society as the Pargeters'. And there is nothing wrong with the Donningtons, is there?'

'Not that I am aware of.'

'Perhaps Roly has other troubles weighing on his mind. Shall I ask him?'

'No, I could not bear him to think I was prying. Perhaps, one day he will tell me what is wrong.'

'It could be his wound troubling him,' Kate said thoughtfully. 'Charles told me it was very severe and he was laid abed for months with it. Do you think it could be that?'

'Oh, very likely.' Margaret seized this lifeline and resolved not to dwell on Roland's ill humours of the past while he was so obviously in excellent spirits now. 'He would never complain of it, would he?'

They were agreed on that, and Kate went on to talk of the rooms she was making ready at her Huntingdon home for her baby. There was about her a glow, something more than beauty, which shone from her eyes and embraced everyone. 'If it is a boy we shall name him George, after my father. I had thought of naming him for Roland, but I am sure you will want that for your son, and three Rolands in a family would be just too many.' She laughed and looked sideways at Margaret. 'You are not. . .'

Margaret smiled. 'Not yet.' She wanted Roland to be the first to know, and had as yet not found the right moment to impart the news that she was expecting a child. She was not sure how he would view it. He had never rescinded their bargain, never said, now you are my wife in truth, you do not have to go. The news might make him angry. He might even think she had somehow accomplished it on purpose to hold on to

him, though how she could have done it without the
hand of providence she did not know.

'There is time,' Kate said.

'Yes, all the time in the world,' Margaret agreed,
with a sinking heart. 'Are you out this evening?'

'We go to Ranelagh Gardens.' She seized Margaret's
hand enthusiastically. 'Say you'll come too.'

'I should like to, but I do not know if Roland——'

'Oh, of course he will. Really, Margaret, you must
not be afraid to stand up to him, bully him a little. He
will respect you for it.'

Margaret was not so sure, but in the event it was not
necessary; Roland agreed to meet Charles and Kate in
the pavillion at nine o'clock.

Margaret dressed carefully, wondering if tonight
would offer an opportunity to tell Roland her news.
Perhaps in the comforting darkness of the gardens they
might be alone together and she could whisper it. He
might even be pleased.

She wore a panniered gown of rose-coloured silk,
over a petticoat of silver net. Its stiffened bodice
emphasised a waist that had not yet begun to thicken,
and was embroidered with scrolls of leaves and flowers.
The low neckline was filled with lace for modesty's
sake. A froth of lace floated from the short sleeves.
Her hair was dressed high and wide with elaborate
curls down both sides and crowned with a head-dress
of feathers and trailing ribbons. A flimsy silver lace
shawl was draped over her shoulders to keep off the
chill of the evening air. On her feet were satin slippers
dyed to match her gown. Thus attired, she picked up
her reticule and chicken-skin fan and left her room to
await her husband in the drawing-room.

Roland, in his own room, submitted with scant patience to the attentions of his valet, who would not be hurried. His finger nails were burnished, his brows plucked a little, being too thick for Johnson's liking. He was powdered and painted, and a patch was set below his left eye to cover an old pin-prick of a wound which only the servant could see. Rings were put on his fingers, silk stockings on his muscular calves, pulled up and tucked under the ribbons that tied his white breeches below the knee. A cambric shirt was followed by a satin waistcoat and a cravat neatly tied about his throat. Then came the putting on of the burgundy velvet coat, so well fitting that this could not be accomplished by its wearer alone, and last of all, a wig was set upon his head and a buckle fastened above the ribbon which tied it back. He slipped his feet into his shoes and stood up, surveying himself in the mirror with a quirk of amusement. 'A veritable fop, Johnson. If the men of Winterford could see me now. . .'

'But you are not in Winterford, my lord, you are in town. Would you have me derided for a man who does not know how to dress his master?'

'No.' He smiled, and attached a quizzing-glass and a fob to one of his waistcoat buttons. 'Let us hope it pleases the ladies.' He meant one lady, as Johnson was well aware. He did not wait for a reply, but picked up his cane and hurried down the stairs to meet her.

'How charming you look,' he said, appraising her before taking her hand and bowing over it.

'And you, my lord, look very modish.'

He smiled, and offered her his arm to escort her to their town chariot which waited at the front door.

They were early and, as Charles and Kate had not

yet arrived, they spent the time wandering over the lawns, watching the fireworks, and the musicians preparing for the dancing which would take place in the pavilion when darkness sent everyone indoors. The gardens were crowded; couples walked arm in arm, nodding and swaying to acquaintances, or hurrying off down the many walkways to avoid being recognised; many a reputation had been lost in the gardens. Groups of people laughed and joked and flirted. There were fireworks and dancing bears and coloured lanterns in the trees, casting pale shadows which dipped and plunged as the wind stirred the branches. Margaret, her hand lightly on Roland's arm, strolled with him along the walkway towards the pavillion and their meeting with Kate and Charles, but she was in no hurry. Now perhaps was the time.

She went so far as to say, 'Roland, I——' but got no further. Kate and Charles were just ahead of them, talking to a middle-aged couple and a young lady dressed in the very latest fashion; her panniered dress was at least five feet wide, balanced by the height of her wig. The man laughed at something Charles had said, then turned and caught sight of Roland and Margaret. The laughter died on his face, though his mouth remained open a second or two longer before he snapped it shut. The others turned, and Margaret found herself subjected to the scrutiny of five pairs of eyes, three of which were decidedly unfriendly. Charles looked uncomfortable and Kate puzzled. The moment seemed to go on a long time before Roland turned on his heel and almost dragged Margaret away down an avenue of trees and out of their sight.

'What is wrong? Who were those people?'

'It matters not. Let us stroll a little longer; it is too warm to go indoors.'

'What will Charles and Kate think of our behaviour? We as good as cut them direct.'

'They will think I want to be with my wife; what else should they think?'

She wished it were the truth, but she knew it was not, though she dared not anger him by questioning him further. She could feel the tension in him as she took his arm to walk between clipped hedges and come out on to one of the lawns, where a troupe of acrobats was amusing the crowd.

'Shall we sit?' she asked, making for one of the seats which were spaced around the perimeter of the lawn. 'I am feeling a little faint.'

'Yes, of course.' He was at once solicitous. 'Would you like me to fetch you a cordial—ratafia, perhaps?'

'Please.'

While he was gone, she composed herself to tell him her news, mentally rehearsing how she would begin, imagining his reaction—several reactions, from pleasure to anger. She began to fidget, wanting to have done with it. It was too noisy to talk here; the crowd were laughing and applauding the performers. She rose and walked slowly in the direction Roland had gone, intending to meet him as he came back with her drink. The walkway was dark and there were couples sitting, even lying, in recesses in the hedges. She hurried on, eyes averted, towards some lights she could see a little way off. When she came near she realised that the lights were coloured lanterns swinging above a little pagoda. She had almost reached it when she heard voices and stopped. Not wanting to intrude, she turned to go, but then she recognised Roland's voice and was rooted to the spot.

'Now you know the truth, can you forgive me?'

'Now, as to that. . .' There was a tinkling laugh which could only have belonged to a woman being coquettish. 'Kiss me and I shall tell you whether I forgive you or not.'

'But I am married.'

'So when has that stopped a man kissing the woman he loves?'

'I ——' Roland became silent suddenly and Margaret was sure he was obeying the demand for a kiss.

'Now I may forgive you, if you tell me that you still love me.' Again the high-pitched laugh that assailed Margaret's ears like the wind in the reeds of the fen, foretelling a storm. 'Poor little mouse, she doesn't stand a chance, does she?'

'No, I am afraid not.'

Margaret, clothed in a misery which wrapped itself around her like a thick cloak, turned and hurried towards the pavilion, where there were other people, lights and music and gaiety. If she could only find Charles and Kate, they might be persuaded to take her home. She stopped suddenly. Mouse, was she? Didn't stand a chance—wasn't that what they had said? But she was Roland's wife and she carried his child; was she going to let them dismiss her so lightly? She turned and walked slowly back, meeting Roland and the girl as they came along the path together. It was the same fashionable young lady thay had seen earlier talking to Kate and Charles. She had her hand on his arm and was smiling. Roland looked grim.

'Why, my dear,' Margaret called, falsely bright, as

she hurried towards them. 'I had given you up for lost. Where is my cordial?'

'Oh, I am sorry. I'll fetch it now.'

'Do not trouble yourself, I am no longer thirsty.' She turned deliberately from Roland to survey the girl from top to toe. 'Are you not going to introduce your friend to me?'

He pulled himself together. 'Of course.' He turned to Susan, who had a triumphant gleam in her eye which made him angry; she had nothing to be triumphant about. 'My lady, may I present Mistress Susan Chalfont?'

Margaret gave no more than an inclination of her head, but Susan swept a low curtsy. 'I am pleased to meet you, my lady. Ro. . . His lordship has told me so much about you.'

'Indeed.' Margaret's voice was as cold as ice.

'Yes, it is so romantical. I wish you well.' Again that empty laugh. 'I am persuaded the Pargeters have the devil's luck when it comes to their women.'

Roland squirmed uncomfortably. When Susan had come upon him hurrying to fetch Margaret's cordial, he had seized the opportunity to speak to her alone and try to explain why he had married and why those early reasons were no longer true. And then Margaret herself had appeared and the whole thing had blown up in his face and he hated himself. He swept Susan an elaborate leg. 'Mistress Chalfont.' Then he turned to offer Margaret his arm. 'Come, my dear, we must find Charles and Kate.'

His manner angered Susan. She did not see why she should be dismissed in that fashion, even if he was married to the mouse. 'I shall come too,' she said, taking Roland's other arm. 'Mama and Papa will be looking for me.'

Thus all three made their way to the pavilion, but only Susan found anything to talk about.

'You must come to my ball,' she said. 'Both of you. I shall ask Papa to send you an invitation tomorrow. It is to be *masqué*. All the best people will be there. The house has been in a ferment for weeks. Our ballroom is not very large and the crush will be tremendous, but so much the better. Papa has engaged the very best orchestra and a new French chef. Of course, we had hoped to announce my betrothal, but that will have to wait.' She laughed suddenly and gripped Roland's arm tighter. 'But I do not mind; the best things are worth waiting for, and in the meantime I may flirt a little with whom I choose.'

'Indeed you may,' Roland said, because she had run out of breath and he felt that something was required of him.

'Oh, la, Roly.' She tapped his arm with her fan. 'Are you not even the tiniest bit jealous?' She leaned forward to speak to Margaret across his front. 'We are very old friends, Roly and I.'

'Indeed.'

'I spent some time at the Chalfonts' Derbyshire home, recovering from the wound I received at Culloden,' Roland explained to Margaret. 'It was due to the care I received there that I survived.'

Margaret forced herself to smile at the girl. 'Then I owe you a debt of gratitude.'

Susan seemed to find this statement amusing and could not answer for laughing. She was still giggling into her lace handkerchief when they came upon her parents, anxiously looking for her.

Sir Godfrey looked grim, but Susan ran to him and took his arm. 'Papa, all is well, truly it is. Roland has explained and it is oh, so thrilling. Do not be angry with him any more. Let me introduce you to Lady Pargeter.' To Margaret she said, 'My parents, Sir Godfrey and Lady Chalfont.'

Margaret curtsied but, before she could speak, Roland bowed stiffly. 'My respects, Lady Chalfont, Sir Godfrey. I must find my sister.'

'She has gone home,' her ladyship put in. 'She was feeling a little unwell—the heat, you know. Charles said you would understand.'

'Of course. Charles is right to be careful. I think we shall also return home.' He bowed again. 'Your servant, my lady.'

He took Margaret's arm and led her away. Behind them, they could hear Sir Godfrey remonstrating with his daughter and her spirited response.

'I believe Mistress Chalfont is a little spoilt,' Margaret said, testing the water. She wanted to find out more about the girl, but was reluctant to plunge straight in.

'A little, I think, but she is an only child and came to the Chalfonts late in life.'

'You did not tell me about them.'

'There was no reason to. Now, where is that good-for-nothing coachman? In the tavern, or I miss my guess.' They had come upon their coach, but of the driver there was no sign.

'You can hardly blame him if you decide to leave early,' she said mildly.

'No, of course not. Get in and I'll go and find him.' He opened the door and helped her up the step, then he was gone.

She settled herself against the velvet upholstery, but she could hardly sit still for the tumult in her breast. Susan Chalfont was more to Roland than a friend, that was obvious. Were they in love? Had they been lovers? She did not want to think of it, but she could not help imagining them in each other's arms, making love as she and Roland had made love. The thought of that sickened her. Had Roland quarrelled with the girl? Was that why he needed her forgiveness? Had he married Margaret simply out of pique? Married her for a year, married her intending the union should never be consummated? But it had been and she was with child and she did not know what to do. She fished in her reticule for her handkerchief just as he returned and seated himself beside her. Hastily she sniffed back her tears and waited while the driver climbed up and they moved off.

'Roland, why was Sir Godfrey Chalfont so angry with you?'

'Angry?'

'Yes. He could not bring himself to speak to you, and yet you say it was because of him you are alive today.'

'Perhaps I was not grateful enough.'

'That sounds unlikely. I am sure you always pay your debts.'

He laughed grimly. 'Oh, yes, my debts are always paid. I do wrong and I am punished.'

'What wrong have you done?'

'I have wronged you.'

Her heart began beating almost in her throat and her next words were breathless. 'Because you married me, knowing you loved Mistress Chalfont? And now you must bear the punishment?'

'Yes.' The answer was torn from him. 'I have wronged Mistress Chalfont too.'

She was determined to stay cool, not to let him know how hurt she was. 'Thank you for being honest with me,' she said quietly.

'You deserve no less.' His voice was cracked.

'And did I not deserve your honesty when you first met me?'

'For that I apologise.'

'Apologise! Is that all you have to say? You had a lovers' quarrel and you married me to spite her. Did you not think of my feelings at all?'

She thought it was as simple as that! Well, he would not disillusion her. 'You and I made a bargain,' he said. 'Feelings had no part in that, neither yours nor mine.' It was a foolish thing to say and he regretted his words immediately; they inflamed her even further.

'I tell you this,' she said as coolly as she could manage, though the effort was almost her undoing. 'I am glad we agreed this marriage of ours would last no more than a year. Glad, do you hear? Glad! Now, be so good as to stop the coach and get out. I cannot bear your company.'

He put his head out and called up to the driver to stop, then he opened the door and jumped lightly to the ground. 'Goodnight, my lady.' To the coachman he said, 'Take Lady Pargeter home. I will walk.'

The coach rolled away but he did not immediately follow it. Instead he went to White's, where he drank

a whole bottle of Rhenish which had little effect on
him. How could he have been so heartless, so uncaring,
so utterly mad? Yes, that was what it was—madness.
Two lovely women, and he deserved the wrath of both.
He should be put away in Bedlam, but instead he
joined a game of dice. He was too disturbed to
concentrate on cards, but dice required only luck and,
amazingly his luck was good. He won two thousand
pounds in the space of half an hour. It did nothing to
cheer him up.

'One would think you had lost a fortune, Pargeter,'
John Carstairs said, slapping him on the back. 'Why
the long face? You have a pile of guineas in front of
you which I'd give an arm for.'

'Take it,' Roland said. The young man lived beyond
his means and was always impecunious.

'What? Are you gone mad?'

'I believe I am.'

'Then it must be love.' He laughed. 'Don't tell me;
let me guess. You have found the perfect woman to be
your wife, but she will not have you?'

'I am but lately married.'

'Is that so? Then you have found a jewel of a mistress
and your wife does not understand about precious
gems, being new to the state of matrimony.'

Roland smiled, refusing to take the bait. 'Shall you
toss me for the pot?'

'No, thank you. I'll not stand against your luck
tonight.'

'Then I may as well go home to bed.'

Carstairs laughed. 'Whose bed? I know of a
lady——'

'No thanks, I am off ladies altogether. Give me the

company of men, preferably fellow officers. You know where you are with them.'

'Talking of the army,' Carstairs said suddenly, 'I heard that the Young Pretender's followers are rallying.'

Roland evinced a flicker of interest. 'They would never risk another invasion, not after Culloden. There can hardly be a man left to join them.'

'I'm told Cumberland thinks otherwise. I heard he was looking for you.'

'For me?' Roland queried. 'Why should he want me? My soldiering days are done. His Grace knows I left to take up my inheritance when my father died.'

He picked up the gold coins from the table, made a bow to the assembled company and left, with Carstairs's cheerful rejoinder ringing out behind him. 'Better a monarch that needs you than a wife who fetters you.'

He was fettered, but by his own hand, not his wife's, and he could see no solution. It was almost day again and nothing had been resolved and, added to that, his head was thumping. Culloden. That was where his troubles had started; why should he want to go through that again? It would be a good joke, if only it were not so serious.

Suddenly he was laughing, loudly and uproariously, so that windows were thrown up and night-capped heads came out to shout at him to be quiet, that there were some who had to rise for work in less than three hours, and if he wanted a pail of water thrown over his lovely suit, then he was going the right way about it. His laughter ceased as suddenly as it had begun and he went silently homeward.

What could he say to Margaret? Should he tell her the truth of why he had married her? But did he really know why himself? He only knew he loved her as he had never loved any woman, and that included Susan. Could he explain that what he had felt for Susan was gratitude, not love, and he had only recently recognised that? In Margaret's present mood, she would not believe it, nor understand. Only time might convince her. Time. But time was something they did not have. Half the year was gone. How, in the name of God, was he ever going to live without her?

CHAPTER SEVEN

MARGARET knew Roland would not follow the coach
home; she had driven him away with her shrewishness.
How could she have been so foolish? He had been
right to remind her of their bargain, because that was
all their marriage meant to him. He had never mentioned feelings, falling in love, or anything which could
bind him to her emotionally, and she had agreed to his
terms. He hadn't asked her to fall in love with him,
had not even expected it, and the fact that he had
shared her bed meant nothing; she was his wife and he
had a perfect right to do so. If only she had managed
to keep her jealousy to herself, they might have
remained on good terms. But was that enough?
Wouldn't she rather have nothing at all if she could not
have his love?

Penny helped her to prepare for bed but she knew
she would not sleep, and as soon as the maid left she
rose and went to sit at her bedchamber window, gazing
out across the moonlit scene, wishing she had never
gone to look for Roland in the gardens, never learned
about Susan Chalfont; and she wished fervently that
she had not taxed him with being in love with the girl.
But he had admitted it! Her anger, which had cooled
as she had sat looking out on the peaceful scene beyond
her window, rose to the surface again when she realised
how she had been used. To have married her simply
because he had quarrelled with Mistress Chalfont was

the outside of enough, especially as the quarrel, whatever it had been about, seemed to be over now.

The horizon was streaked with pink and the sky was changing from dark voilet to pale grey when she heard the night footman open the door to her husband. She heard him speak to the servant, then his steady tread on the stair and his footsteps in the corridor outside her room. It seemed as if he paused outside her door. She ran to it and flung it open, unsure of what she would say, but wanting reassurance, a return to amicable relations, if nothing else. He stopped and turned towards her.

She looked pale, with her hair tumbling about her shoulders and her eyes dark pools of seething emotion. And did she know that the diaphanous gown she wore was nearly transparent? God, what the sight of her did to him! He fought his own passion to drawl lazily, 'Still awake, madam? I had thought you would be asleep hours ago.'

'Sleep! How can you expect me to sleep after such an eventful evening?'

'Eventful, my dear? I thought it rather dull.'

She had intended to speak calmly, to be sweet and reasonable, but the way he stood there, surveying her with an attitude of indifference, if not actual boredom, inflamed her. Her good intentions vanished like a puff of smoke and she found her voice rising. 'You introduce your paramour to me and make me the laughing-stock of all London and you think that dull, do you?'

'Mistress Chalfont is not my paramour.' He seized her arm and propelled her back into her bedchamber. 'And if you insist on shrieking at me like a fishwife, then do it where we cannot be heard by the servants.'

'I am not shrieking.' She wrenched herself out of his grasp and stood facing him, her chest heaving. 'And you admitted you loved her.'

'So I did.' The effort to remain cool was proving almost too much for him, but he forced himself to speak calmly. 'That does not make her my mistress. She nursed me——'

'I know that. And nursing usually means beds and night apparel and——'

He threw back his head and laughed aloud. 'Margaret, I was too sick to know what was happening to me.'

'You laugh, sir. I am a joke, a wry jest, someone to amuse you when your love is not to hand. But now she is close by and you go to her and make a fool of me——'

'Go to her?'

'Yes, that is where you have been, is it not? Do not trouble to deny it, for I shall not believe you.'

His laughter died as suddenly as it had come. 'Very well I shall not deny it. And it is not I who make a fool of you, but yourself. You are behaving like a jealous harridan. It was not part of our contract.'

'Contract! We must not forget our contract, must we?' She spoke bitterly, suddenly weary of the fight. She lowered her voice. 'Why did you marry me, Roland? If Mistress Chalfont had quarrelled with you, could you not have taught her a lesson without going to such lengths?'

'We did not quarrel.'

'Then why did you not wed her? Why marry me? Explain that, if you will.'

'I cannot.' He took a step towards her, almost as if

he wanted to plead with her, but she could not trust herself to remain aloof if he came too close and she backed away against her dressing-table. 'Margaret, please listen. . .' He lifted a hand towards her, but she dashed it down, stinging her fingers on his signet-ring.

'It is a great pity you did not remember our contract when you took me to bed,' she went on, though she knew every word she uttered was making matters worse. 'There can be no annulment now.'

'I know,' he said quietly. 'I wronged you most grievously and I am sorry for it.'

'Sorry!' She stared at him with eyes dark-rimmed with fatigue.

'Yes, I wish I could make amends.' He stopped. How could he make amends? How could he undo the dreadful harm he had done to her?

'Nothing you say will make the least bit of difference,' she said, summoning the last vestige of her pride and tilting her chin upwards. 'We cannot cancel out what has been done and I must take my share of the blame for agreeing to marry you on those terms. I thought——'

'No!' It was almost a shout and for a moment disconcerted her.

'No?'

'You are not to blame.'

'Then may I remind you of the promise you made to me?' she went on, determined to finish what she had to say. 'You told me that in the eyes of the world you would be a loving husband until such time as our agreement came to an end. I believe it has some months yet to run.'

'I am not likely to forget it; it is engraved on my heart.'

'I wish you to keep your word.'

'Very well.' He smiled crookedly. 'While we remain in London, I will do my best to be a model husband. Who knows? I might even come to enjoy the role.' She knew he had been drinking, but not that he was so drunk he did not know what he was saying, and she was too hurt to detect the underlying bitterness in his words.

He went to the door, but stopped with his hand on the doorknob and turned back to her. 'But I give you fair warning—I do not submit easily to petticoat government, and you would do well not to provoke me as you have done this night.'

Without stopping to think, she picked up a scent bottle and threw it at him. It crashed against the wall and smashed, covering him in sweet-smelling lily of the valley. He strode across to her and took her shoulders in his hands, holding her at arm's length, his eyes glittering dangerously. He shook her once, throwing her head back, but then suddenly crushed her to him and brought his mouth down to hers in a kiss that began as a bruising punishment and ended in sweet passion. At first she held herself rigid, but she could not keep that up and found herself melting towards him, answering his passion with her own.

Suddenly, realising what was happening, he thrust her from him. 'I bid you goodnight, madam,' he said, ignoring the shards of glass and slipping out of the door before she could find something else to throw. He did not hear her sobs of frustrated anger and despair because she flung herself on her bed and stifled them in the pillow.

It had come, the dismissal she had been dreading, the reminder of their contract. How could she ever have been such a fool as to agree to it? She had sold her soul to the devil. She lifted her head and gave a cracked laugh; now she was becoming as superstitious as the people of the Fens. If only someone or something had given her a sign that she ought not to embark on a marriage which would bring her only grief, she might have been spared her present anguish. But omens had been singularly lacking when she needed them. Except the swans. According to Penny, they were a good sign. What was good about them, when they had lured her on to the ice? She was reminded of her great-uncle's words at the time. 'It is not I who wants her dead.' Had Roland wanted her death? No, that was ridiculous. No one could have done more to save her. And he had been extraordinarily concerned when she had cut her hand, and on many other occasions when she had had quite ordinary mishaps. It was the cut hand which had led to the marriage being consummated and the fleeting moments of happiness since then. Until now. Now he had shown his true colours and she was in torment.

She fell asleep at last and dreamed of falling through the ice, and woke up in a cold terror. Penny was standing over her with a cup of hot chocolate and the sun was shining through the window, picking out the clothes she had discarded the night before and making the shards of glass from the scent-bottle twinkle in a myriad colours. She sat up. 'What time is it?'

'All but twelve, my lady. Master Mellison is here

with Mistress Kate.' She had known Kate since baby-hood and could not cure herself of referring to her in the old way; 'Mistress Mellison' was foreign to her tongue.

'Tell them I'll be down directly. Is his lordship about?'

'No, my lady. He went out early. He said he would be back in good time to prepare for the ball and you were not to worry.'

'Ball?'

'Lady Chalfont's, my lady. Had you forgot?'

'No, of course not.' She could hardly believe that he still meant to attend it. 'Go and ask someone to take some refreshments to the parlour for Mistress Mellison and her husband. I will wash and dress myself. And then you had better clear up the glass. I am afraid I had an accident with it.'

Penny raised an eyebrow, but said nothing as she bobbed a curtsy and disappeared, leaving Margaret to complete her *toilette*. Whatever she did, she could not disguise the pallor of her cheeks nor the dark circles beneath her eyes, and make-up seemed to make her look worse. She gave up and washed it off, brushed her hair loosely about her shoulders and dressed herself in a chemise gown of blue muslin before going down-stairs to greet her visitors.

'Goodness, Margaret, you must have stayed at Ranelagh very late last night!' Kate exclaimed after Margaret had bidden them good-day and made sure they had wine and honey cakes. 'Have you been to bed at all?'

'We sat up and talked after we returned,' she said. 'I am afraid I slept late.'

'Is Roland still abed?' Charles asked. He was standing by the fireplace, resting his forearm on the marble shelf, within inches of the Chalfonts' gilded invitation card.

'No, he went out early. I am afraid I don't know where he has gone.'

She sounded so weary that Kate looked up in alarm. 'Margaret, what is wrong?'

'Nothing, nothing at all. I am simply tired.'

'Pardon me, but I do not believe you. Is Roland being unkind to you?'

'Not at all,' she said valiantly. 'What makes you say that?'

'When we first came to London you were worried about him. I remember you said he was reluctant to take you out and about, but I cannot see why you mentioned it. We have been everywhere in the last few weeks.'

'Yes. I was being foolish.'

'So what troubles you now? You can tell us.' She looked up at her husband. 'Can't she, Charles? Could it be that you are. . .?' Her eyes lit with happy mischief.

'It isn't that,' she said, then, unable to bottle it up any longer, burst out, 'Oh, it's Mistress Chalfont. She behaves so coquettishly with Roland and. . .'

'You disapprove. Quite right. I shall give him a wigging about it.'

'Oh, please don't. He is angry already. . .'

'Angry? Oh, surely it is no more than a harmless flirtation. He will leave it off as soon as he realises you are upset.'

Margaret looked up at Charles, who had ceased to lounge against the mantelshelf and now stood looking down at her thoughtfully. 'You know Mistress Chalfont, I believe?' she asked him.

Charles looked decidedly uncomfortable, which only confirmed Margaret's worst fears. 'She is a distant cousin of mine,' he said quietly. 'Roland met her when I took him to Chalfont Hall after he was wounded. We had carried him all the way from the Culloden battle-field, but he was in a bad way and I knew he could not survive many more days of being jolted about on a waggon. It was leave him behind or bury him before another day had passed, and it was then I remembered my mother's cousin. We took him there.'

'Mistress Chalfont nursed him. He told me that,' Margaret said. 'He also admitted that he loved her.' She paused to look up at him. 'Oh, you do not need to look so sheepish. I know it to be true.'

'But why did he marry you, if that was so?' Kate cried. 'It was monstrous of him.'

'I do not know.'

'He cannot still love her,' Kate went on. 'She is nothing compared to you. She is a spoilt child who does not like it because she cannot have her own way. Don't you agree, Charles?'

Her husband bowed but did not speak. He had suddenly realised that Margaret had fallen in love with her husband and that was something they had not foreseen. He felt desperately sorry. And guilty.

Kate laughed suddenly. 'But you have the last word, Margaret, dear; you are his wife. All you have to do is to remain calm, pretend you do not mind. It will all blow over and my foolish brother will come to realise what a treasure his wife is. Now, are you going to the ball tonight?'

'I do not want to.'

'But you must—there will be gossip if you don't. You will dress magnificently and hold up your head and defy the world.' She grasped both Margaret's hands in hers and laughed again. 'Roland loves you; I stake my oath on it. Now say you will come.'

A dozen times in the next few hours Margaret vacillated between wishing she had not agreed and determination not to be cowed. Her pride must sustain her. She went to bed in the afternoon in an effort to make up for lost sleep, knowing she had to look her best in the evening, but sleep eluded her until it was almost time to rise again, and then she dropped into a slumber so deep that Penny had to shake her into wakefulness.

She sat up and drank a dish of bohea tea, which revived her, and nibbled at a fruit-filled pastry, half of which she left, and then her lengthy *toilette* was begun.

She was bathed in rose-scented water, creams and lotions were applied to her body, her nails were polished, undergarments of finest lawn were slipped over her head, silk stockings were pulled on and fastened with ribbon garters. Next came a pale green satin petticoat, and then she was enveloped in a powder-cape and sat down before the mirror for Penny to dress her hair. It was brushed and taken high above her head over cushions to give it height and width, then twisted into curls about her ears; more curls were allowed to fall on to her shoulders. It took the best part of an hour before Penny was sufficiently satisfied to powder it. The air was thick with its dust, and maid and mistress soon found themselves coughing.

'Don't shake your head so!' Penny cried. 'You will have it down.'

'Then leave off throwing that powder about. Surely you have done enough?'

The fine particles settled at last and Penny set to with a paint-box; brows were drawn in, cheeks rouged, and a patch applied below Margaret's left eye, but Margaret would not allow her face to be painted white. 'No!' she said, with determination. 'Leave that for the dowagers. Besides, it looks dreadful when my face gets warm and it cracks.' She took off the powder-cape and turned towards the bed, where her gown lay lovingly spread out. Made of rose-pink brocade and heavy satin, its skirt was decorated with ruched silk, its low-necked bodice with fine tucks and silk bows. Matching bows finished the three-quarter sleeves. 'Is it time?'

'Yes, my lady. I heard his lordship go to his room over an hour since.'

The gown was slipped on, and the lace in the corsage and tumbling from the sleeves was frothed out. Her feet were encased in brocade slippers with jewelled heels, just as Roland entered the room, looking magnificent in a burgundy coat trimmed with silver braid, with pink satin breeches and a long, flower-embroidered waistcoat. The lace of his cravat was pristine and fastened with a diamond pin that glinted in the lamplight. There was another in the black bow at the back of his wig. He carried a small box in his hand.

He stood and looked at her for a moment, lost in admiration. She was beautiful, this little kitten of his, beautiful and poised, though her lustrous eyes betrayed her sadness. He smiled and moved towards her as Penny disappeared with the powder-cloak and the discarded day-clothes. 'My felicitations, my dear, you have excellent taste.'

It was not quite what she wanted to hear, but it was a compliment and she must be gracious. 'Thank you, my lord.'

'It came to me that you might not have much jewellery.' He thrust the box into her hand, almost tongue-tied. 'I hope you like it.'

She lifted the lid and gasped in delight. The box contained a necklace of rubies set in gold filigree. 'It is lovely!'

He lifted it out and went behind her to put it on for her. His hand brushed her neck and she almost cried out with the rush of desire that his touch generated. She wanted to twist herself round and fling herself into his arms, to beg to be kissed, to be taken in love as he had taken her in Winterford, but instead she stood very still, with a stiff little smile on her lips, while he fastened it. He bent to kiss her throat, almost negligently, before leading her to the mirror. 'See how it suits you.'

She could hardly stand for the tumult in her breast. But he was simply keeping his promise to behave like a loving husband, no more. And she must keep her side of their bargain. 'It is lovely, Roland, but so costly. . .'

'A mere trifle, my dear. Now, are you ready? There will be a fearful crush so I have bespoke a chair and will walk alongside; it will be easier than a coach.'

'Yes.' She allowed him to help her on with a lime-green domino and then picked up lace gloves, fan, reticule and velvet mask and put trembling fingers on his arm. 'On with the masquerade.'

It was a foolish thing to say and she felt him stiffen beside her, but his smile did not change; it was as if it had stuck that way, a little lop-sided quirk of a smile which could have indicated amusement but could just as easily have been a sign of displeasure. 'As you say,' he said, escorting her down to the hall where Johnson stood ready with his tricorne hat, gloves and cane. 'On with the masquerade.'

He was right about the crush. Long before they reached Mount street, they came upon such a tangle of coaches, carriages, horses and sedans that it was impossible to proceed. Grooms and footmen were shouting at each other, horses prancing and rearing; linkboys darted about, swinging their lanterns and threatening to set fire to many a priceless gown. Roland stayed close by Margaret's chair, fending off the crowds, some of whom were no more than sightseers come to catch a glimpse of finery they could never hope to wear. Gradually Roland cleared a path for Margaret's chair, and half an hour later they were admitted to the vestibule of Chalfont House, where Sir Godfrey and Lady Chalfont stood to welcome their guests.

Now that the moment had come to test her resolve, Margaret found herself shaking so much that she could hardly make the curtsy which was required of her. She was glad of her mask, which could at least hide her expression if not her identity, as she passed into the ballroom on Roland's arm and was greeted by Kate, who had arrived only minutes before and recognised the gown she had helped Margaret to choose.

'You look magnificent,' she whispered behind her fan. 'I said it would be worth it, didn't I? What did Roland say?'

Margaret glanced at her husband, who had moved a few paces away to speak to Charles. 'He was very complimentary.'

'There! I told you so!'

The ballroom was so crowded that there was hardly any room to make up the sets of all those who wanted to dance, and the noise of conversation and laughter was so loud that the orchestra could hardly be heard, but no one seemed to mind. Margaret found herself surrounded by young bloods eager to dance with her, and with a glance of enquiry at Roland, who nodded imperceptibly, she took to the floor. For the next hour or two she almost managed to forget her troubles and began to enjoy herself. Roland danced once with her, smiling for all the world as if he were enjoying it, but she could feel the tension in his body, as if he dared not allow himself to relax, even for a moment.

'You were right about the squeeze,' she said as they turned and met to perambulate, hand in hand, between the double row of dancers to the head of the set. 'I don't know how Sir Godfrey has squashed everyone in.'

He laughed. 'The bigger the crush, the greater the success of the occasion. You don't find it too much?'

'I think, after this dance, I shall go on the terrace.'

'Please take a shawl. I do not want you to catch a chill.'

She looked at him sharply because there seemed to be an unnatural emphasis to his words, but he was smiling and she decided she was being over-sensitive.

As soon as the dance had finished, she moved to the door, intending to find the room where the ladies' cloaks had been left. In the hall she was accosted by a young lady wearing a blue taffeta dress, heavily embroidered with silver thread and seed-pearls. She was holding a blue velvet mask before her face and Margaret did not, at first, realise it was Susan Chalfont.

'Lady Pargeter.'

'You recognise me?'

'Yes, you came in with Roly, and I'd know him anywhere. After all, I did nurse him.' She dropped her mask and laughed her tinkling, empty laugh. 'You are looking very flushed. Are you too hot?'

'Good evening, Mistress Chalfont.' Margaret inclined her head. 'I was going to find my shawl and take a stroll outside.'

'It will be in the ladies' retiring-room. Come, I'll show you.' She turned and led the way up the wide staircase with its carved mahogany balustrade. It had a small landing halfway up where the stairway divided into two and went up each side to a gallery which ran all round the hall. 'You must find London a very great change from the country.'

'Yes, indeed. But I lived in London before I married Roland.'

'Did you? And I thought he had met you near his home. You were in some difficulty. . .'

'Did he tell you that?'

'Why, yes. You were alone in the world and he felt sorry for you. And his grandmother urged him to marry you. You know why, of course?'

They had reached the gallery and were heading towards a door at the far end. 'I was unaware the Dowager Lady Pargeter had anything to do with it,' Margaret said, trying to keep her voice light.

'I assure you she did. She told Roland of the witch's curse, but I'll wager he said nothing of it to you.'

She could not help it; she stopped and clutched the banister. 'Witch's curse? What nonsense!'

'Oh, no, it is not nonsense. Generations ago a curse was put on all Pargeter heirs. Their first wives were condemned to die before they had been married a year, all of them without exception. Roland wanted to marry me, but he could not, or I would have been the one to die, so you see. . .'

'I do not believe it,' Margaret gasped. 'No one believes in witches nowadays.'

'Roland does. He is sure you will die before the year is out.' She stopped and turned towards Margaret, and there was a gleam of triumph in her eyes. 'In truth, he is counting on it.'

Margaret was bewildered. A grown man, and a soldier at that, someone who had faced cannon and sword, who maintained law and order over his domain and held the lives of hundreds under his rule—how could such a one be afraid of ill omens? But it explained so much that it had to be true. 'I've changed my mind,' she said, turning to go back downstairs. 'I do not need my shawl after all.'

Susan laughed, a high-pitched, unnatural sound, and grabbed Margaret's arm, pinching it painfully. 'You will die and Roland will get his wish and marry me. Nothing you do will save you.'

'I have heard enough! Let me go.' Margaret tried to wrench herself away and make for the stairs, but Susan reached out for her again, forcing her to turn and face her.

'Not so fast, my lady. Do you think I am going to

stand by and watch you with Roland, watch him smiling at you, even though he only does it for appearances sake? Do you think I can wait another six months to become his wife? I have always been impatient.' She took hold of Margaret's upper arms and began to shake her. 'I cannot wait that long.'

Margaret began to feel very frightened; the girl was crazed with jealousy. Her eyes glinted and she seemed to have the strength of ten as she pushed Margaret until she was leaning backwards over the banister. 'I mean to give fate a helping hand. After all, what is a month or two when you have all eternity?' And, before Margaret could do a thing to save herself, she was flung upwards and backwards over the banister and into the well of the stair.

Roland was talking earnestly to Charles in one of the card-rooms and did not immediately notice the commotion in the hall.

'I've got to break that curse,' he was saying. 'Even if Margaret refuses to speak to me again, I have to save her.'

'I'm sorry old fellow; if I had foreseen. . .'

'We none of us did and it was not your fault. I did not have to do as you suggested. Besides, it wasn't only you, it was Grandmama. She hated the Captains and saw the marriage as a way of being revenged on them.'

'Not you, though,' Charles said softly. 'Not this one.'

'No, not this one.'

'What can you do?'

'I went to the Bishop, thinking he might know how to get the curse lifted, but it is so old and not like a ghost which can be exorcised. There is no ghost, nor a haunted place either.'

'Is that what he said?'

'Yes. He also told me to give away all my worldly goods as penance; that if I owned nothing I would be absolved.' He gave a cracked laugh. 'He said he would be pleased to receive my wealth and possessions into the Church.'

'Into his coffers would be more accurate!'

'Perhaps, but do you think it would work?'

Charles shrugged. 'I do not know. What would you live on if you gave everything away?'

'Does that matter?'

'You have to provide for Margaret. Would he allow you to do that first?'

'He said it would defeat the object of laying the curse if I tried to cheat it like that. It was all or nothing.'

'You are surely not thinking of complying? My God, Roland, you would be a pauper.' He paused, looking thoughtful. 'I could perhaps. . .'

'No, my good fellow, I would not ask it of you. I wish there were some other way.'

'You may as well consult a wise woman. It would be more to the point.'

Roland smiled wryly. 'It might even come to that, because we cannot continue as we are.' The noise of shouting and racing footsteps at last impinged on their senses. 'What the devil is that?'

'Someone is calling your name,' Charles said, running and throwing open the door.

They came out into the rear of the hall and dashed towards the light, where a crowd thronged the stairs.

'Here he is,' shouted someone. 'Lord Pargeter, it is your wife. She has fallen. . .'

But Roland had already reached the bottom of the stairs and was pushing his way up to the half-landing. The crowd moved back a little so that he could see Margaret in a crumpled heap, and someone bending over her, endeavouring to bring her to her senses. He reached her in one bound. She was very pale and very still.

'What happened?' he demanded, kneeling and putting one arm under her shoulders to lift her head on to his thigh.

'She fell.' This was Susan, standing on the gallery above them. 'She caught her heel in her dress and toppled over.'

He glanced up at her briefly before turning his attention back to his wife. She was not dead, was she? He had not left it too late? He thought he saw her eyelids flutter and he breathed a huge sigh of relief. It was then he realised that her left arm was undoubtedly fractured; it was a strange shape and very swollen. He felt along all her limbs very gently but there did not seem to be any other broken bones. He put his other arm beneath her and picked her up.

'Bring her to my room,' Susan said.

He followed her with his burden, calling behind him, 'Someone send for a physician.'

Susan led the way into her own bedchamber, where Margaret was laid on the bed. She looked so deathly pale that his heart almost stopped. If only she would regain consciousness! If only she would open her eyes! 'Margaret.' His voice was a hoarse whisper. 'Margaret, look at me, please.'

'She's dead.' Susan's voice sounded unnaturally loud. He turned sharply to look at her. She was standing watching him with a gleam in her eyes which horrified him. 'She is, isn't she?'

'No, dear God, not that.'

'That's what you wanted, isn't it? The curse has come true. You are free.'

'No. Go away, please. Leave me alone with her.'

'I understand. You must act the grieving husband right to the end. But when you are ready I shall be waiting.'

He did not even hear her go, so engrossed was he with his wife. She must not die! She must live. He could not face life without her.

Margaret's eyes flickered open. 'Roland. . .' Her eyelids dropped again. She was alive! He turned as the door opened and a little man in a black coat and breeches, with a military pigtail wig, came into the room, carrying a bag which he put on the table and opened. 'She fell downstairs, I am told.'

'Yes. Her arm is broken, but she is so still, I believe there might be other injuries.'

'We shall see, we shall see.' The doctor pulled out a sharp little knife and a bleeding-cup.

'I do not want her bled.'

'Why not? It will clear any excess blood to the head.'

'Just examine her and bind up her arm.'

'Very well, but I will not answer for the consequences.'

He pushed Roland away and sat on the bed beside Margaret to run his hands over her limbs and around her head, then down her torso. 'She has a broken arm, as you said, and a bump on her head which is causing the insensibility.' He pulled open her gown and laid his head on her abdomen. 'Good. Good,' he said, then looked up. 'The child has a good strong heartbeat. I do not think we need to worry on that score. . .'

'Child?' Roland looked stupefied.

'Yes. There is no doubt she is with child. Did you not know?' He went to his bag and took out a splint and bandages and bound the broken arm.

'No.' Roland could hardly comprehend what the man was saying. 'How many months?'

'I cannot be sure until she has recovered sufficiently to answer questions, but I believe you can expect to be a father towards the end of the year.'

'My God!'

The doctor looked at him quizzically. 'You seem doubtful, my lord?'

'No, no,' Roland said, shaking his head from side to side. 'It is just that she did not tell me.'

'Oh, women do like their little secrets.' He held up the bleeding-cup. 'Are you sure? It will relieve the pressure on the brain.'

Roland was too bemused to maintain his objection and Margaret was duly bled, though she looked paler than ever when the doctor at last closed his bag and left, instructing Roland to make sure she was kept quiet and not excited in any way.

'When can I take her home?'

'Not until she has fully recovered her senses and that lump goes down.'

Margaret began to come round about half an hour later, though her head ached dreadfully and trying to move her arm was agonising. She was glad to swallow the dose of laudanum she was given and drift back into unconsciousness. From then on it was difficult to separate reality from nightmare. She felt herself being undressed by gentle hands, washed and made comfortable, but she had no idea of the passage of time, did not know whether it was night or day. She wanted to open her eyes, but her eyelids were so heavy that she could not force them upwards. She heard the murmur of voices, sometimes two or three, sometimes only Roland's, but she could not make out the words. And once she felt herself being lifted very gently and carried—she knew not where—but then decided she must have been mistaken because she was still in bed and she still could not see properly, and the gentle voice was still close by.

'Margaret, do you hear me? Live, my darling, live. . .'

It was Roland's voice and it was clearer now. But how could that be? He wanted her dead. He expected her to die. She had been pushed over the balustrade. Pushed. Had he known what Susan would do? Had he condoned it? She heard herself screaming, but she made no sound; the screams were in her head. She tried to struggle up, but could not lift her head. Better to die, better than lying here helpless. She sank back into oblivion.

The next time her eyelids flickered open, she was in her own bed in Pargeter House. She could see blue sky beyond the window, and her dressing-table with its little pots of make-up and her clothes-cupboard. She moved her head gingerly; the pain had gone. Someone was slouched in a chair beside her bed and it was a moment before she recognised her husband. He wore no coat or waistcoat and his cambric shirt was open at the neck and so creased that it looked as though he had slept in it. His chin was on his chest and, though his hair was held back by a ribbon, a dark lock of it fell across his forehead. He looked grey with fatigue and had several days' growth of beard.

'Roland?'

He started up guiltily, then, realising she had really spoken and it had not been a dream, leaned forward and took her hand. 'Margaret. Thank God, thank God.'

'How did I get here? I don't remember. . .'

'I carried you. I thought you would rather be in your own room.' He had not been at all satisfied with the treatment she had been getting from that fool of a doctor at Chalfont House, who seemed to rely too much on bleeding and tincture of opium. And Susan had been in and out on some pretext or other most of the day. Margaret had been in her room and Susan had been obliged to sleep in a guest room, so he could hardly exclude her. He had been very suspicious of her story that Margaret had caught her heel in her gown. He had undressed his wife himself and there had been no tear in the material of her skirt. He was thankful that she had tumbled no further than the half-landing. If she had gone over further along the gallery, nothing could have saved her from falling straight down on to the marble floor of the vestibule to her death.

'How long. . .?'

'Two weeks and three days.'

'Have you been there all the time?'

He smiled sheepishly. 'Most of it. Now you are going to get better.'

'Roland.' She paused. 'Before. . .before the accident happened, I had something to tell you about. . .'

'You are with child, I know. The doctor assures me the baby is unharmed.'

'Are you angry?'

'Angry?' He was puzzled. 'Why should I be angry?'

'It was not part of your plan that I should have a baby, was it? Now, if I die, you will lose your son too. . .'

'You are not going to die, do you hear?' His voice was a fierce whisper. 'You are going to live and so is our child.'

'Mistress Chalfont said. . . She told me. . .'

'Damn Mistress Chalfont!' he said with feeling, then more gently, 'Do not think of her; do not think of anything. Rest now.'

She smiled and drifted off to sleep again, but when she woke the next time Kate was sitting by her bed and there was no sign of Roland. She wondered if she had dreamed that earlier awakening as the true horror of her position came flooding back.

'Oh, I am so pleased to see you awake,' Kate said. 'You gave us such a fright.'

Margaret looked round the bright room. The window was open and she could hear bird-song. 'Roland was here. . .'

'Yes, we persuaded him that he really must rest.' She reached out and patted Margaret's good hand; the other was encased in splints and a tight bandage. 'He has been distraught with worry and has not left your side since it happened. We could get no sense out of him at all and he would not go to bed, but now you are mending and all will be well.' She paused. 'Do you remember what happened?'

'No.' She could not tell anyone what really occurred;

she could not say, Roland wants me dead and Susan pushed me over the balustrade. It was too outrageous an accusation for anyone to believe.

'Mistress Chalfont said you caught your heel in your gown and tripped. She tried to reach out to save you, but she was not quick enough. Roland carried you to her room, but as soon as you could be moved he arranged a litter to bring you home. Can you recall any of that?'

'Everything is a blur,' Margaret said, frowning a little. 'I seem to remember being carried and sometimes I heard voices, but nothing is very clear.'

'It doesn't matter now; you are going to get well.' She laughed suddenly. 'Why did you not tell me you are going to have a baby?'

'I wanted to tell Roland first, and somehow I couldn't find the right moment.'

'Foolish girl,' Kate said. 'When is it due?'

'In December.' Margaret smiled weakly. 'Somewhere near the anniversary of our wedding.' The date was significant, she realised. If there was any truth at all in the story Susan had told her about the curse, she was expected to die within a year of marriage. Her child might be born before that, but perhaps not. Perhaps she would die in childbirth. The drugs she had been given had dulled her senses so that she could view the prospect without emotion, almost as if it were happening to someone else. If Roland did not love her, she did not want to live.

She stopped her meandering thoughts abruptly. She did not believe in that nonsense, even if Roland did. She was young and strong and there was no reason why she should not have a healthy child and live to a ripe old age. But with Roland? If his plans were thwarted, would he cast her aside? Did she *want* to live with a man who wished her dead? If only. . . If only. . . She was so tired, so very tired. She drifted off to sleep again.

CHAPTER EIGHT

'IF ONLY I could see into the future.' Roland had washed and shaved and dressed properly for the first time in three weeks, although his naturally tanned face looked grey and his eyes were clouded with exhaustion. He was sitting in the breakfast-room with a pot of coffee in front of him from which he had just poured two cups. Kate had gone up to sit with Margaret, and Charles was sharing his breakfast. Not that he had eaten anything; these days he had no appetite.

'What would you have done?' Charles prompted him.

'I don't know. I would never have married her and condemned her. . .'

'Would you have married Susan?'

'No, I do not think so. Oh, not only because of that curse, but because I would have realised we just would not suit.'

'You have fallen in love with Margaret?'

'Yes, by God, and that can never alter.' He paused, thinking of Margaret as she had been at Winterford, lying in his arms after they had made love the first time, her body glowing and her lovely eyes dreamy with contentment. She was part of him, his other half, his *better* half, and without her he would wither and die. Perhaps it would be better if he did. 'Charles, I must have that curse lifted. I don't care how it is done, even if I die in the attempt.'

'Perhaps the worst will never happen; perhaps you are worrying for nothing. Curses can only harm you if you believe in them.'

'How can I not believe? It is not just me, is it? That curse is over a hundred years old and it has been true of every generation since it was made. Why should I be the exception?'

'I can only suggest you wait and see. After all, your wife has already survived near drowning and a fall that might have killed her. Perhaps that is a good omen.'

'Omens!' he exclaimed bitterly. 'Margaret does not believe in them.'

'There you are, then!'

'She didn't know about the curse, not until Susan told her everything and made it sound as if I wanted her dead. Curse or no, Margaret hates me for that, and who can blame her?'

'Can you be sure of that?'

'Wouldn't you, in her place? And if Susan pushed her. . .'

'I say, Roland, that's a bit brown, isn't it? You haven't been fair to Susan either, have you?'

'I am only too aware of it. But what would you have me do?'

'What you need is a rest. Why don't you try to get away for a while?'

'It is too soon for Margaret to be moved.'

'I meant without her. If you could part for a while, you might be able to get things straight in your head. . .'

'God, man, do you think I can walk away from her now? What do you take me for?'

'What good will your staying do? If you remember,

you had intended to leave her immediately after you married her. You said you could not face her, knowing what was to happen to her. . .'

'That was before. . .'

'Before you fell in love with her, I know, but that is all the greater reason for leaving her now. She has doctors and nurses in plenty, and if you are absent she may survive.' He paused to look into his friend's face. The anguish Roland was feeling was plainly evident; his face was ashen and drawn and there was a bleak look to his eyes. He was a man without hope. 'Which is more important, staying with her and trying to convince her you do not want her to die after all, or to go away from her and leave her free to live?'

'Do you think it will work?' A gleam of something akin to hope lit Roland's face briefly.

'What else is there?'

'Nothing.' A separation there would have to be, but, as Margaret had so rightly pointed out, an annulment was out of the question. He could simply set her up in a separate establishment and make generous financial provision for her and her child, as many a man had done before him when faced with the failure of his marriage, but usually the poor wife was ostracised and he did not want that for Margaret. Besides, she was carrying a Pargeter heir. She must go back to Winterford until her child was born. If he left her in sole possession of the Manor and stayed away from Winterford himself, then perhaps the evil lying so heavily on his soul would go away. She might survive, and their child too. But he needed a reason for leaving home which would satisfy Margaret, and any others with a penchant for gossip, and he thought he had it.

He stood up and left his friend without so much as a goodbye, and went bounding up the stairs to Margaret's room before his resolve could weaken.

She was sitting up in bed talking to Kate. For the first time since her accident she had a little colour in her cheeks and her lovely kitten eyes were showing signs of her former vitality. He forced himself to smile at her and strode towards the bed. Kate quietly withdrew, shutting the door softly behind her. He sat down on the edge of the bed and took his wife's hand. 'Now that's more the thing,' he said, raising the back of her fingers to his lips. 'How do you feel?'

'Better, thank you,' she said, wishing she could forget Susan's revelations and the clear knowledge that he did not love her after all, had never loved her.

'As soon as you are well enough to travel, I am taking you home to Winterford. You will do better there.' He did not seem to be the self-assured man she had married, nor was he the worn husband who had sat by her bed for three weeks looking dejected. There was a purpose about him, a new determination.

'I am well enough to go now.'

'Good.' He paused. 'I have to go out. We will talk about the arrangements when I return.'

'Very well.'

There seemed to be little else to say, and he dared not continue sitting on her bed holding her hand lest he weaken. He stood up, looking down at her a moment before murmuring, 'Forgive me,' and then left the room, calling to Johnson as he went. Half an hour later, dressed in a buff coat, buckskin breeches and top-boots, he left the house, riding his grey mare.

He rode to Horse Guards, where he knew he could find his former commander.

William Augustus, Duke of Cumberland, third son of George II, was still only twenty-six years old but he was a veteran soldier and had commanded the English troops at Culloden, when Charles Edward Stuart, pretender to the throne of England, had been so resoundingly beaten and where Roland himself had been wounded. He came forward with hand out-stretched as Roland handed over his hat, cane and gloves to a footman. 'Colonel Pargeter, how go you?'

'Well, Your Grace.' Roland bowed as he took the proffered hand.

'No ill effects from your wound?'

'None, Your Grace, but an itch. . .'

'Itch?'

'To exact revenge, Your Grace. I hear the Young Pretender does not know when he is beaten.'

'Ah, you have heard I have need of you.'

'Yes, Your Grace. I came to offer my services. Farming becomes wearisome.' It was far from the truth, but the truth was too complicated to explain. His Grace turned to a servant and ordered wine to be brought, then motioned Roland into the library. 'Sit down, Colonel.'

Roland obeyed and the Duke set about explaining what he required from the man who had served him well in more than one theatre of war.

'Not every dog of a rebel was killed at Culloden,' he said. 'Some escaped to continue their nefarious plotting. They gather in holes and corners, a few together, spreading their godless sedition, planning to overthrow their lawful king. They must be rounded up, destroyed.

His Majesty must be able to sleep easy in his bed an this country of ours is not to be bathed in blood.'

'Yes, Your Grace.' He paused to take a glass of wine from the tray the servant held out to him. 'Does anyone know where they are to be found?'

'Not precisely, but I have intelligence that they are making for the east coast, no doubt to take ship and join their infamous master in France. What do they call him, the "king over the water"? Zounds, that is one king who will never sit on an English throne. Find them and earn your sovereign's gratitude. Be one of them if it aids you.'

'A spy?' Roland queried, taken aback.

The Duke smiled, examining the liquid in his glass. 'If that is the only way.'

'But I am a soldier, Your Grace; I serve King George in uniform, with a sword in my hand and a pistol in my belt, face to face with the enemy. I know nothing of spying.'

'Nevertheless, I am persuaded you are the man we need. You know the region.'

'The east coast, you say?'

'Hull, King's Lynn, Lowestoft, Yarmouth—my informant could not be more specific.'

'They may not be intending to use a port at all, Your Grace. It is a smugglers' coast, full of little bays and inlets, and every man a sailor. Who is to tell who is loyal and who is not? It is a small step from smuggling casks to smuggling human cargo.'

'Exactly. That is why I need you. You know the people and their ways. It may be that there are only a handful of dissidents, no great threat, but on the other hand it might be a regular escape route, a network of

safe houses and a vessel that can come and go at will.'
He paused, watching Roland over the rim of his glass
with keen eyes. 'Will you do it?'

Roland bowed. 'I am at His Majesty's service.'

'Good.'

'I should like permission to escort my wife home to
Winterford, Your Grace. She had an accident. . .'

'Yes, I had heard of it. She is recovering?'

'Yes, Your Grace, but I am persuaded she will do
better at Winterford.'

'Then take her home. It will give you time to make
your peace with her. Methinks she will not be pleased
to part with you so soon after the nuptials.'

'She will understand.'

'Good. I will send word to tell you where and when
to go. Report back to me when the task is done.'

'Very well, Your Grace. I shall await your instructions with some impatience.' Roland put down his
glass, bowed low, picked up his hat and left. The die
had been cast; he could not in honour refuse to do as
he was asked, but it was very different from what he
had intended when he had offered his services. A spy!
A creature that neither side respected. A sewer-rat, a
worm, an animal of the night, living in holes and
corners, creeping up on the enemy from within instead
of facing him on a battlefield to fight and die with
honour. But perhaps that was all he deserved.

'Oh, Margaret,' he murmured as he rode back to
Pargeter House. 'You shall have your freedom, even if
it costs me mine.'

It was the beginning of August and a beautiful warm
sunny day when they returned to Winterford. The

roads were baked hard, jolting them from side to side as the wheels of their travelling-chaise lurched from one rut to the next. Margaret was glad when the last stage was reached and they were within sight of Winterford, not only because of the physical discomfort but because she and Roland had hardly had a word to say to each other the whole way. The closeness they had enjoyed for so brief a span before going to London had gone, and now there was nothing but a distant politeness. It was the same as it had been when he had first married her, before she had cut her hand, before they had made love for the first time. Two accidents with very different consequences. Not that she wanted him to make love to her now, she told herself, not after Susan Chalfont's revelations which he had not even troubled to deny. Could you hate a man and love him at the same time?

It was a very different Winterford from the one they had left. The trees were in full leaf, the pastures were lush, the grazing cattle sleek and well-fed, and the sheep in their summer coats nibbled at the myriad wild flowers, gold, blue, white, that decked the grass on which they fed. On the high ground, the barley she had watched being sown in the spring was being harvested. In each huge field, made up of many strips, bands of men worked their way along the rows with sweeping scythes, and behind them others gathered up the fallen cereal, tied it into bundles and built the stooks. Children ran behind, chasing the birds away and picking up scattered ears of corn and filling bags that hung round their necks. No school for them for several weeks. Already along the new dyke the reeds had begun to grow to protect the banks, softening its straight lines.

Yellow and blue irises grew in clumps near the water's edge. Ducks and geese swam and dived for food, just as if the drain had always been there. Above them, the great arch of the sky was a clear cobalt-blue with hardly a cloud to be seen. In such surroundings, how could she be anything but hopeful?

But hope was stillborn, she realised, when Roland told her after a silent dinner in which he had seemed to be weighed down by cares he could not share with her, that he intended leaving again.

She laid down her fork, her appetite gone, her heart beating so hard that she could hardly breathe; so he was going back to Susan, after all. She would not beg him to stay. 'When?' she asked, so quietly and calmly that he thought she would be glad to see him go.

'I don't know. There are arrangements to make. Perhaps not until after the harvest is finished.' His voice was flat; he could have been talking to his bailiff or one of his labourers.

Half of her wanted to cry out, to beg him not to go, to tell him she needed him by her side; the other half rejected him as a philanderer, a man who used her too badly to be forgiven for it, so that all she could manage was a stiff, 'How long will you be gone?'

'Some time. Five or six months. I will make arrangements for you to have sole rights to the income from the estate, to do as you please, just so long as you remain at Winterford.'

'Do as I please!' she exclaimed. 'You mean to leave me here alone?'

'You will not be alone. There are servants. . . .'

'It is not the servants I shall need when my time comes. Will you not be back before that?'

'No, it will be impossible.'

'Oh, I see. Like Mistress Chalfont, you are too impatient to wait——' It was out before she could stop it. She had told herself that she would never mention it, that she might have dreamed the story of the curse in her delirium, but she could not rid her mind of it. It was with her day and night; it coloured everything she said and did. She found herself watching him for signs which might confirm or deny its existence. His earlier silence had seemed grounds for believing it was on his mind too, and now he had announced he was leaving her, and that, as far as she was concerned, was proof enough.

'To wait for what?' he asked.

'To be free of me.' In spite of the tight rein she was holding on herself, her voice rose perilously close to hysteria. Her eyes were bright and there was a high spot of colour on each cheek. 'For me to die.'

So she believed it too, he decided. In spite of all her protestations that she had no faith in omens and curses, she was afraid. He wanted desperately to take her in his arms and comfort her, to tell her it was all a fabrication and he loved her, but in her present mood she would not believe him and it would make it doubly difficult to leave her. 'I pray fervently you will not,' he said.

'I do not believe you. Mistress Chalfont enjoyed telling me of that curse before she pushed me over the banister. You expected me to die, like your father's first wife and the first wives of generations of Pargeters before that. Did your grandmother fill your head with that superstitious nonsense? The old lady was mad— mad, and wicked too.'

She was determined to quarrel; so be it. If it made her feel better, then he would oblige her. 'I advise you to think carefully before you malign my grandmother or accuse Susan.'

'Think! I have had plenty of time to think while I have been ill,' she said. 'I have done nothing but think. I understand that bargain we made now. I was to be the sacrifice and if, by some chance, I survived, why, then I was to be paid off, the marriage annulled and no harm done. But the marriage has been consummated and annulment is out of the question now, and you couldn't wait, could you? Not when you realised I might be with child.'

'Margaret, you are overwrought.'

'The impeccable Mistress Chalfont had to give fate a helping hand,' she rushed on, like a runaway horse with the bit between its teeth. 'Only I didn't die, I survived. She must have been very disappointed.'

'You imagined it. Susan would not——' He stopped, unable to go on because she had only voiced his own suspicions. He wished heartily that he had not told Susan about the curse, but he had hoped to make her understand, not only why he had married Margaret in the first place, but why he had since come to love her. Susan, who had always been used to having her own way, had not believed his change of heart. That night in the gardens, she had said she would fight for him. And she must have spun a plausible story to her parents in order to persuade them to invite him and Margaret to the ball. If only they had not gone!

Margaret laughed harshly. 'You mean I imagined she was disappointed, or imagined she pushed me? You know, at first I thought I *had* dreamed it, especially when my head ached so dreadfully that I could not even think clearly. What did you use to keep me under? Laudanum, was it? Poppy-seed tea? What I cannot understand is why you did not have the courage to go through with it; why, after all that, you took me home and nursed me back to health.'

'Because I love you, woman!' he shouted.

They sat at opposite ends of the dining-table and stared at each other in silence with his words hanging between them like tangible things, to be picked up and thrown back, except that she had lost her way between her loving and her hating and could find nothing to say.

'Margaret,' he said at last, getting up and moving round the table to sit beside her. 'I beg you to understand. I had heard about a curse when I was growing up. To me it was just a family story told over the fire in the winter. I did not know the details, and it was only when I told my grandmother I wanted to marry that she reminded me of it. I was persuaded that I ought to marry a stranger as a sort of safeguard.'

'But why me? What had I ever done to you?'

'Nothing, nothing at all. You were a Capitain.'

'And that was enough?'

'It was because of a Capitain that the curse was uttered in the first place.'

She was calmer now. 'Hadn't you better tell me the whole?'

'I told you the Pargeters and the Capitains were on different sides in the Civil War——'

'So were many neighbours and friends, but they didn't go round putting curses on each other——'

'There was more to it than that. Please don't interrupt. It is hard enough as it is.'

She fell silent and he went on. 'My ancestor, John Pargeter, was betrothed to Anne Capitain. The marriage had been negotiated between the two families and had everyone's approval, but when the fighting started John Pargeter raised a troop of villagers to support Parliament and set off to march to Peterborough with them. He was denounced by one of the Capitains, who had given their allegiance to the King. The little troop was ambushed and only John himself survived, and that only because the attackers knew he was to marry their kinswoman and she had pleaded for him to be spared. It is hardly surprising that John broke off the betrothal. Anne still loved him and when he subsequently married a local farmer's daughter, called Rosalind, she could not accept it and went a little mad. On John's wedding-day, in the church, she swore in front of half the village that within a year of the marriage John's wife would die.'

So attuned was Margaret to the story, so sympathetic to those unhappy people who had lived a hundred years before, that she could almost hear the demented woman shrieking. Poor Anne! But to swear a curse, a dreadful omen, and in church too, was asking for the wrath of God. 'And it came about, just as she said?'

'Yes.'

'It could have been coincidence, nothing evil at all.'

'But it didn't stop there. It happened at a time when Matthew Hopkins, the witch-hunter, was at his most powerful, and he heard this story and had Anne arrested. There were plenty of people to give evidence against her—after all, her family had been responsible for the massacre of many of their menfolk. She was sentenced to hang. It was on the gallows that she refused absolution and predicted that the same fate would befall all those who dared to marry Pargeters.'

'Poor woman!' Margaret said. 'Vilified because of a love which took no account of war and allegiance to King or country. Is it any wonder she was deranged?'

'No,' he said slowly, realising that he was almost crazed himself. 'But what she predicted came to pass.'

'A fairy-story,' Margaret said, though her heart was beating uncomfortably fast. 'Do you sit there, a grown man, an educated man and a soldier, and tell me you believe it?'

'It has been true ever since 1646 when it was made, so my grandmother told me, and I have no reason to doubt her word.'

'Then you *do* expect me to die before the end of the year?'

'No!' He was almost shouting, but pulled himself together and went on in an almost normal voice, 'I am persuaded that if we separate, if I go away, the curse will be broken.'

'Why should that be?'

He gave a twisted smile. 'Because a Captain will once again be in possession of the Manor. I, a Pargeter, am capitulating; the Capitains have won.'

'And you are simply going to walk out and leave me?' Her voice was flat, registering no emotion. She was too numb to feel anything. 'I don't call that love; I call it cowardice.'

He stood up so suddenly that his chair fell back with a clatter. She saw his clenched fist rise and then drop to his side. 'I think we have said all there is to say, my lady,' he said, in a voice so cold, so devoid of any kind of hope, she found herself shivering. 'Now please excuse me; I have a great deal to do.'

Then he was gone and she remained in her seat, staring at the overturned chair. He had sentenced her to death, a sentence which he seemed incapable of revoking. Or perhaps he didn't want to. He had not expected Susan Chalfont to tell her about that curse, but when she had he must have realised he could not stay and watch her die. But how was she to die? Illness, accident, childbirth, murder? No one had explained that. And why, in the name of God, had he made her his wife in truth as well as name? He had said he loved her. No, he had shouted it angrily, in a fit of temper, not gently and lovingly, as a man ought. But he could be gentle and loving; he had it in him to be everything she desired. He had pulled her from the ice when he could have left her to drown, had carried her tenderly home and put her to bed. And he had taken her from Chalfont House, where she would undoubtedly have died from an overdose of laudanum, if not her injuries, and had sat by her bed and begged her to live. That must have been guilt; it could not have been anything else.

Was she even going to survive the next three months? Should she stay in her room, never going out, waiting, watching for the blow to fall? She began to laugh crazily, filling the room with the crazed sound, unable to stop herself. He had almost succeeded in making her believe she was doomed. She was not going to die, she was going to live. She was going to live in order to confound him. He would stay away until their first anniversary and then he would come home to find her alive and well and the mother of his child. And then what? Reconciliation? No, that was impossible. Divorce? That was unthinkable. Her laughter suddenly turned to tears as she contemplated a future without him. She wept with her head buried in her arms on the table, wept and wept until she had no more tears to shed.

She lifted her head at last. Everything was as it had been before—the dinner-table with its plates and dishes; the overturned chair; the closed door through which he had disappeared and on the other side of which servants waited for her summons; the curtains at the window, beyond which her blurred vision could see sky and lawns and ducks waddling. The summer day had not ceased to be a summer day; there was no great tumult in the sky, no thunderclap. Everything was normal. She got up slowly and went to her room, where she washed and changed into a cool silk gown, put a light shawl about her shoulders and went out. She would not cower at home; she would go out and meet her fate with her head up.

Penny followed her at a discreet distance because she knew she would be in trouble from his lordship if she did not. Margaret realised she was there, but pretended she did not. She wanted to walk alone, to breathe deeply, to stand and watch the great bowl of fenland sky, with its light clouds chasing each other on a zephyr wind, to look into the water and see her own reflection alongside the images of the drooping willows, to try to understand the reason behind it all, to calm herself. She was only a tiny particle of God's creation and it was He who dictated who should live and who should die, not some half-demented woman. She turned for home.

Roland watched her from the window of his bed-chamber and his heart ached for her. He wanted to rush down and say he had changed his mind, that he would stay with her and they would fight the demon together. But it was no longer a simple matter of whether or not he believed in the curse; it was all about trust and faith and love, and she could have none of those for him. She knew Susan had tried to kill her and she believed he had condoned it. Perhaps he had; perhaps by taking Margaret to Mount Street and allowing Susan to take her upstairs he had given Susan *carte blanche*. He felt as guilty as if he had done the deed himself. No woman with any spirit would forgive that, and Margaret had more than her share of spirit. She was walking along the road from the village now with her head held high and a smile on her lips for everyone she met. How could she smile? Did she know something he did not? Where did she find her strength? He was glad of it; she would need it in the weeks and months to come.

In the early autumn days that followed, Roland was more taciturn than ever. His behaviour veered from an over-solicitous concern for her well-being to a crabbiness which he did not seem to be able to control. His remedy for that seemed to be to disappear for hours on the fen. If he found her company so distaste-ful, she wondered, why did he delay leaving? Why not go at once? Could it be that he was waiting for a summons from Susan Chalfont?

She tried not to think about that, and directed her restless energy into preparations for re-opening the school as soon as the children could be spared from the harvest fields, and to looking after the welfare of the villagers, doing her best always to appear cheerful and at ease, though the effort often exhausted her. Wherever there was hardship, she was there with a basket of provisions and clothes; wherever there was sickness, she was there with medicines and a cool hand; wherever there was a dissent among the women, she was there to see justice done.

'The villagers have taken you to their hearts,' Roland said one day when, for a change, he had come home for dinner. 'I do believe there isn't one who would not die for you.'

'They respect and admire you, my lord, and as I am your wife——' She stopped, wondering if she had said the wrong thing. Would it remind him that he wished it were otherwise? 'Besides, I like to do what I can for them.'

'But you must not tire yourself. Remember, you have been very ill, and the child. . .'

'I am perfectly well,' she said, putting her hands over the bump in her abdomen and feeling the baby kicking. 'You do not have to coddle me, you know. Everything is perfectly normal.'

Now she really had said the wrong thing. His face clouded and he hurried from the table, saying he had forgotten that he had promised Barnard that he would look in on one of the horses which was foaling.

It was like living on a knife-edge, she decided. And 'normal' was the very last word to describe their marriage. She sighed and went to the kitchen where Cook, with help from the village women, was preparing a feast of beef and mutton, fowl and fish, fresh-baked bread and home-made ale for the harvest horkey which

was to be held in the big barn behind the Manor as
soon as the harvest was finished. There was no shortage
of things to do, but nothing seemed to take her mind
off her troubles.

She was standing beside Mistress Coulter when the
last sheaf of corn was taken from the harvest field,
decked with flowers and ceremoniously brought to the
barn and nailed over the door, where it would stay
until the following harvest. 'It guarantees a good year,'
Mistress Coulter told her.

'More omens?' Margaret queried, unable to stop
thinking of that fearful curse.

'A good one, though.'

'What do you do if you want to break a spell?'

'Why, you consult the wise woman, my lady.'

Margaret had heard of her before. She lived in a
cottage on the edge of the fen and dispensed nostrums
and spells to everyone who cared to consult her. A
hundred years before, she would have been condemned
as a witch, just as Anne Capitain had been, but now
she was simply tolerated.

'Do you want to consult her, my lady?' the woman
went on, looking at Margaret knowingly. 'Do you want
to know if your baby will be a son or a daughter? She
can tell you, you know.'

'No, I do not mind which it is. I shall be happy with
whatever God sends me.'

'Amen to that. It don't do to meddle, does it?'

'No, it certainly does not,' Margaret said fervently as
all the villagers, dressed in their Sunday best, crowded
behind the cart carrying the decorated sheaf and
poured into the barn.

Roland, for once, was in a genial mood, joking with

the men and paying compliments to the women. He made a speech, praising the workers and telling everyone the harvest had been a good one, and, with the new dyke, they need not fear the fields being flooded in the coming winter. He was cheered to the rafters and then held his hand up for silence again. 'I have to go away on the King's business, but I leave my affairs in capable hands.' He turned to smile at Margaret, then faced them again. 'I charge her to look to you and I charge you to help her all you can. Believe me, I would not go at such a time if it were not imperative. God bless you all.'

There was silence and they looked at each other, wondering what to make of this announcement, then one of them called out, 'Aye, my lord, you may depend upon us.'

After that there was a general scramble for the food, and when they had eaten their fill the tables were pushed to one side and a fiddler began to play for country dancing. Margaret felt too heavy and cumbersome to dance, but she watched for a while, sitting with the older women, tapping her feet to the rhythm until Roland, noticing she was tired, came to take her home.

It was late afternoon on the following day, when she was out walking with Penny, that she remembered her conversation with Mistress Coulter and decided to go and see the wise woman. It was not that she wished to consult her about her own particular demon, but it would be interesting to find out why the fen people set such store by her. Roland was busy elsewhere—she suspected he was deliberately keeping out of her way—and she had nothing to occupy her before supper, so she set off along the drove which led to Sedge House, with the protesting Penny several paces behind and getting further behind with every yard they went.

Halfway along the lane, she turned off on to a narrow path which lay higher than the summer field—ground which was dry in summer and submerged in winter—to a little creek on the edge of the permanent fen. The cottage stood by itself, surrounded by an osier-bed. It was in good repair, bright curtains hung at the windows and the door stood open. A cat, sunning itself on a bench beneath the eaves, stretched and yawned as she approached, and jumped down to rub itself against her legs. She bent to stroke it.

'She likes you,' said a cheerful voice. 'That's a good sign.' Margaret looked up to meet the blue-eyed gaze of the woman who had come to the door. If she had expected to see a bent old crone in voluminous black clothes, she was doomed to disappointment. The woman was plump and middle-aged, wearing a brown linen skirt and a flowered cotton blouse. On her greying hair she wore a crisp white cap.

'I am Lady Pargeter,' Margaret said, looking round for Penny, but the girl had stopped at the corner and would come no further. 'I heard you lived here alone and I thought——' She stopped suddenly.

'And I am Janet Henser. I have been expecting you.'

'Expecting me?' Margaret queried. 'How can you have been been? I decided to come only a few minutes ago.'

'Everyone visits me sooner or later. Come in, my lady; sit and rest a while.'

After a moment's hesitation, Margaret ducked her head to go through the low doorway of the cottage and found herself in a bright room furnished with a table, a chair, a bench, and a bedstead. There was a rug on the dirt floor and a kettle boiling on the fire. A shelf under the window held a collection of bottles, odd-shaped lumps of wood, small pieces of bone, a bowl containing pins, and an array of herbs. Everwhere was spick and span. The cat had wandered inside and was now curled up on the bed, washing itself.

'Sit, please,' Mistress Henser said, busying herself with the kettle and a teapot. 'I will make you some herbal tea. Now do you wish to consult me or have you come simply from curiosity?'

'No, no,' Margaret said quickly, seating herself on the chair. 'I am merely making a social call.'

'As you wish.' She poured tea into two cups and handed one to Margaret. 'Drink it; it will soothe you while we talk.' She sat on the bench opposite Margaret and looked at her closely. 'You are disturbed.'

'Not at all. Why should I be?'

'My lady, you should never lie to a wise woman.' She smiled. 'Your husband has already been to see me.'

'Roland came here?' Margaret could not keep the surprise from her voice.

'Why not? He was greatly troubled and needed help.'

Margaret could hardly believe that Roland, who was Lord of the Manor and a Justice of the Peace, should stoop to consulting such a one. But he had behaved so oddly lately that she knew it to be true. 'He told you about the curse?'

'It was already known to me, my lady.'

'What did you tell him?'

'I offered him a solution, but as he had no faith in it

there was little point in proceeding. And besides, the ingredients were impossible to find.'

'What ingredients?'

Janet chuckled. 'We needed a lock of hair, or nail parings, from the person who made the spell, but as she died over a hundred years ago and has no marked grave we would have had to substitute something else— perhaps something of you, my lady, as she was your ancestor. This would have to be sealed in a small glass bottle together with some apple-pips and pins, and placed in the back of the fire.'

'It would explode.'

'Yes, it would, and when it did that it would blow all the evil away.' She shrugged. 'If his lordship had had sufficient faith it might have worked.'

'I believe he was right to be sceptical.' She paused, wondering what else Roland had had to say. 'Did you advise him to leave me?'

'He had already hit upon the idea, but I agreed it had some merit.' She leaned over and stroked her cat, which began to purr loudly, reminding Margaret that witches often had cats as familiars—demon helpers. She stopped her foolish thoughts when Janet spoke again. 'He must go. It is necessary to appease the evil influences which were at work when the curse was made.'

'When does he go?'

'Very soon now, my lady.'

'He has told you this?'

'No, but I know it.' She watched as Margaret's good sense fought with her doubts, and added, 'You have the power to bring him back when the time comes.'

'How can I?'

'By willing it.'

Margaret forced herself to smile. 'I fear he goes to pleasanter company than mine and, if he does not want to return, there is nothing I can do about it.' She gave a cracked laugh. 'Nor anything you can do either.'

'No, my lady, not if you do not wish it. You have to have faith.'

'In your spells?'

'No, in yourself.'

Margaret was puzzled. She had expected a different sort of person, someone who looked the part, and she had expected incantations and potions and dire warnings, none of which had been offered. 'Tell me, how did you come to be a wise woman?' she asked.

'I inherited the power from my mother, who taught me how to use it.' She smiled. 'Have no fear, my lady, the force is not used for evil. I try to do good. If the people come to me for their remedies and I am able to help, that is all I ask.'

'With witchcraft.'

Janet Henser smiled. 'No, simple faith, my lady.'

'If that is all, why do you need all these things?' She indicated the objects on the shelf. 'Why exploding bottles?'

'Faith needs something tangible, something the suppliant can do or hold, or have me do, to reinforce it.'

'Then it is not faith.'

'Indeed it is, my lady, just as the parson's collar, the candles on the altar and the taking of bread and wine in communion strengthen the conviction of those who believe in God.'

'You set yourself up in competition with God,' Margaret cried angrily, jumping to her feet. 'That is the worst kind of blasphemy. You will burn in hell for it.'

The woman seemed unperturbed. 'Each to his own, my lady. I am a believer, just as you are. There are many paths to God; we each have to find our own.' She paused and looked up at her visitor. 'Do you have faith, my lady?'

'Of course I do.'

'Then trust in it, my lady. Believe that all will be well, and it will be.'

'Is it as easy as that?'

'No, it is not easy. Your will has to be even stronger than the beliefs of those who think otherwise. Even though he does not wish it, your husband is convinced you will die. He cannot help it. You must overcome his conviction with a stronger one. Now, please sit down again and drink your tea.'

Margaret did not know why she obeyed; there was no hint of compulsion, no threat, no piercing eye, no coercion at all, and yet she sat down again and drank her tea and, after a little while, she felt calmer.

It was strange that Mistress Henser and the Reverend Mr Archibald should both give her the same advice, both tell her that she should have faith. But faith in what? God? Yes, she had that. Faith in the omens? Perhaps, but also faith in herself, in her own strength to overcome evil.

She was not going to give in; she was going to fight. She would go on living, not just for the next few months but for years and years, and she would have a healthy child, one who would never know about a curse put on the family by a vindictive woman all those years ago.

CHAPTER NINE

It was late when Margaret left the cottage, and growing dusk, but she told herself she was not afraid and the darkness held no terrors. Penny, who had had neither the pluck to follow her mistress into the cottage nor the courage to leave her and go home alone, was waiting at the end of the track, tense and fearful. Margaret smiled at her and took her hand. 'Come, Penny, home for supper. I am famished.'

Moonlight lit their way. It threw shadows across the path, shadows of the windmill with sails slowly turning, so that there was continuous movement around them, first light, then deep shadow, then light again, and the very earth seemed to be alive. The creaking of the buckets and splash of water as it was tipped into the drain sounded loud in their ears. A frog croaked near at hand and an owl hooted somewhere towards the village.

'Oh, my lady, we shouldn't have come,' Penny sobbed. 'If we was to meet that hateful black thing. . .'

'What hateful black thing?'

She looked round fearfully and dropped her voice to a whisper. 'Black Shuck, my lady.'

'Nonsense! There is no such thing.' Margaret spoke sharply, but she could not deny that she was nervous and would have felt more so if she had not had Penny for company. Talking to keep up the girl's spirits also bolstered her own. She was glad when they at last turned in at the gate and made their way towards the lights of the Manor. Almost at once the great doors were thrown open and Roland hurried across the courtyard to meet them. Behind him stood several menservants.

'Where have you been?' His face was white and drawn and his eyes seemed almost feverishly bright.

'There is no cause for alarm,' Margaret said, calm now that she was within the circle of light coming from the big house. 'We went visiting and stayed too long.' She gave a cracked little laugh. 'Surely you were not concerned about me?'

'You know very well that I was,' he said in a fierce whisper, not wishing to quarrel in front of the servants. 'I was about to send the men out looking for you.'

'Well, I am home now, so you may dismiss them.' She turned to her maid, who stood shaking behind her. 'Come, Penny, I must change for supper.' And with that she walked past her husband into the house with her head in the air, apparently cool and in control of herself.

Once in her room, she sank on her bed and sat staring into space. How much did Janet Henser really know? She had said that Roland still meant to leave, had said it was necessary. What had she meant by that? She smiled slowly as Penny busied herself fetching water, soap and towels for her to wash; she was being almost as foolish as her maid, believing in ghostly dogs and will-o'-the-wisps. By the time she was ready to go to supper in a simple gown of yellow silk, she had convinced herself that Mistress Henser was no more than a rather eccentric woman, with no powers above those of any other mortal.

Roland was waiting for her in the drawing-room. He was reading a letter but folded it away when she appeared and put it into the depths of his coat pocket. Her new-found confidence plummeted when she realised he was dressed for travelling in a dark green coat, frogged and braided, over a long green double-breasted waistcoat. His knee-breeches were buff and he wore riding-boots. He looked strained, as if he had not slept properly for some time.

'Is there anything amiss?' she asked, trying to keep the tremor from her voice.

He had spent the last three weeks in a state of ferment, waiting for the summons from London, wanting it and yet dreading it. There had been days, bright, sunny days, when everything had seemed so right that he had begun to think the omens were favourable and he could safely stay with Margaret.

He had begun to wish he not been so foolish as to volunteer his services to his old commander. On other days, the heaviness on his spirit could not be lifted and he could not wait to get away, to find some relief in action. Now it had come, the letter telling him to make haste to Scotland. Scotland! It might just as well have been the other end of the earth. And he had to break the news to Margaret and risk another confrontation like the one they had had when he had first broached the subject of leaving. He hardly knew how to begin. He took a deep breath. 'The time has come to leave.'

'Now?' She was surprised how calm she sounded. 'You will surely not get far tonight?'

'Far enough,' he said. There seemed no point in

delaying; it would not mend anything. Everything had been done that could be done, orders issued about the running of the estate, instructions given for Margaret's comfort, and everyone from the bailiff to the pot-boy had been charged, on pain of dismissal and worse, to guard her ladyship with their lives. Johnson had finished the packing and had been sent to the stables to have horses saddled, one for him to ride, one to be led carrying his pack, and another for Johnson himself, who had announced his intention of accompanying his master whether his lordship willed it or no. 'I would have gone earlier if you had not been missing.'

She gave a crooked smile. 'I suppose it is no use my asking where you are going?'

'I am afraid I cannot tell you.'

'Cannot or will not?'

'I can't, Margaret, I do not know.'

'Are you not even going to leave a direction where you might be reached?'

'No, I do not know where I shall be. I have left instructions for the management of the estate and the outdoor servants with the bailiff. He is trustworthy and you need not worry about anything. And, naturally, in the house, your word is law.' He took his tricorne hat from Johnson, who had come to the door to tell him the horses were at the front door, but he did not immediately put it on. Instead he stood looking at her, unable to drag himself away. He took a step towards her and reached for her hand; in spite of the warmth of the day, it was cold. 'Margaret, I know I do not, can never, deserve your love, but I pray that one day you will find it in your heart to forgive me.' He bent his head to kiss her, but she turned her face away, knowing that if she allowed that small gesture her self-control would snap and she would dissolve in a flood of tears. She had to harden her heart if she was to survive.

'Please do not let me delay you, my lord,' she said stiffly.

He swept her a bow, clapped his hat on his head and strode out to his waiting horse. He did not look back. He dared not.

The weeks passed slowly and the days grew shorter and cooler. The leaves on the chestnut-trees by the village green turned to yellow and then deep ruby-red. The alder beds changed from emerald to bright gold and the reeds began to die back, but the autumn sunsets were glorious, streaking the huge skies with fire. Margaret, now in her sixth month of pregnancy, never tired of watching them.

The stubble fields, picked clean by the gleaners, had been ploughed and the wheat-seed sown, and now that the threshing was done and the grain taken to the miller, there was little to be done on the land. The villagers returned to their life on the fens.

Margaret kept herself busy with the school and charitable work and long walks over field and fen, ignoring Penny's lamentations that she should rest more and think of her child. She *was* thinking of it; convinced that she carried a boy, she was determined that he would grow up strong and fearless. Winterford was her home and it was her son's heritage; nothing could take that from him. He would learn to love the Fens as she had come to love them, to look after his people and earn their respect. He would not be weighed down by dread of curses as his father was.

She had heard nothing from Roland at all and did not know for certain where he was, but she was convinced he had gone to Susan. After all, that was why he had married her in the first place, to leave him free to marry the woman he really loved. She smiled grimly whenever she thought of them together; he would have a long wait for his freedom because she did not intend to die. She had never felt better. Plenty of fresh air and a walk every day kept her body healthy, and keeping ahead of her pupils exercised her mind. Sometimes she wondered what her husband would do when he came back and realised she had not been beaten by that old superstition. *If* he came back; he might decide to stay away. She would not let herself dwell on it and instead concentrated all her energies on giving her child the best start in life that she could. Whenever the thought came to her that the year was not yet over and she still had some way to go before she could truly say she was safe, she remembered her talk with Mistress Henser and told herself, 'I will have faith.'

There was no shortage of people to talk to; servants obeyed her every whim and the village children, now they had become used to her, chattered away like the magpies which flocked on the fields. Their parents, although more reticent, would always spare time for a chat, but, for all that, she was achingly lonely. Occasionally she went into Ely or Cambridge, where she browsed round the bookshops, and once she went to Huntingdon to visit Kate, but Kate was not well, being close to her time, and she did not have the energy to entertain. Though she made Margaret welcome, it soon became plain that she wanted to be alone with her husband, who cosseted her dreadfully, and Margaret returned to Winterford feeling depressed and more isolated than ever.

She was feeling particularly despondent on the afternoon she met Nellie in the village. It was a raw day in November with a heavy mist creeping up over the low-lying land and obscuring everything further away than fifty yards. Nellie, bewigged and painted, had brought a pony to be shod and was standing in the warmth of the blacksmith's shop, when Margaret passed on her way from visiting Mistress Reeve, an old woman who was suffering horribly from the ague.

'My lady.' There was a certain insolence in the greeting and the way Nellie bowed her head, making the rakish feather on her riding-hat brush her cheek.

'Good morning, Mistress Capitain.' She had no idea if that was how Nellie liked to be addressed, but as she did not know her surname, she could not call her by it. 'How go you?'

'Well enough.' She moved aside so that Margaret might feel some of the warmth from the furnace. 'You are well, I see.' Was it simply a friendly enquiry or was there more to it than that, an element of doubt or surprise?

'Why, yes, I have never felt better.'

'Not long to wait now?'

'Six weeks.'

The blacksmith called over his shoulder to his son. 'Kit, fetch a stool for her ladyship. Where's your manners?'

A stool was fetched and Margaret sat down, holding her cold hands towards the fire. Nellie stood and watched, a smile playing about her lips.

'And his lordship, he is well?' she asked.

'I believe so.'

'Where is he now?'

Margaret looked up at her sharply, but could define nothing from Nellie's expression, perhaps because her face was so heavily painted. She hesitated before saying, 'In London, on business. Why do you ask?'

'No reason. You must be lonely without him.'

'A little, but I keep myself busy.' She paused and smiled; there was no reason at all why they should not be friends. After all, if she was going to put an end to the hatred and anger, where better to begin? 'Would you like to visit me at the Manor one afternoon? Or perhaps I could come and see you. My uncle would not object, would he?'

'You ran away once—why come back?'

'I did not like my uncle's guests.'

'No more don't I. They leave and others come, but they don't get any better. You would not like them, my lady.'

'Why do you stay with him, Nellie?'

The girl shrugged. 'Where else would I go? I can't go back where I came from, can I?'

The question found an echo in Margaret's own mind. Going back was never an option. 'Could you not find work, some way of earning a living. . .?'

The girl laughed. 'Whoring. No, thank you, my lady.'

Margaret looked at her, standing just inside the door, pretending not to care, and felt a great deal of sympathy. 'Is that how you met my uncle?'

'No. Not exactly, though who's to say it wouldn't have come to that? I worked in a tavern where he came to drink and gamble. He said I took his fancy. He was good to me, bought me presents, took me out. Then, when he said would I like to come home with him to the country, I couldn't wait.' She laughed harshly. 'I didn't know it would be like this. Mistress Clark left weeks ago, and I am an unpaid housekeeper, no more. Not that I'm much good at that. My mother was a whore and I never learned. . .'

'I am sure you do your best. Did my uncle never mention marriage?'

'Oh, he did at the beginning but that was only to get me down here. He wanted a hostess who wouldn't ask too many questions.'

'About his guests?'

'That and. . . No, I ain't saying nothing.'

'Are you afraid?'

'You would be, if you could see them. Huddled together over the card-table, whispering. And they've got knives and pistols.'

'What are they whispering about?'

'How should I know? They shut up when I go near. But I reckon they're up to no good.'

'Why does my uncle have them there? Entertaining them must cost a deal of money.'

'They don't stay long when they come, and they pay him well.'

'Why do we never see them in the village?'

'Because they arrive by boat and leave by a different boat. Henry will do anything for money, but he'll pay with his life one of these days. This last lot are worse than all the others. Filthy and dressed in rags when they arrived, and they must be given hot water and

clothes and fed and anything else that takes their
fancy. . .'

'Then you must stay with me and not go back. I'll
deal with my uncle.'

'No.' Nellie stood up to go. 'I wish I hadn't told you.
Henry ain't all that bad; it's just that he's hard up. If
you go interfering, he'll get into trouble and I'll be
blamed. I thank you for your interest, my lady, but
there ain't nothing you can do.'

'Have you no family you could go to?'

'No, nor money either. Besides, Henry would kill
me.'

They were alike in that, Margaret thought—no home
and no money and dependent on men who did not care
what became of them. But Roland would never offer
her violence; in that he and Henry were different.
'Surely not?'

Nellie laughed but there was no humour in the
sound. 'No, I jest. But best leave well alone, my lady.'

Margaret was puzzled, but before she could ask any
more questions Nellie turned and took the reins of the
newly shod pony before dipping Margaret a slight
curtsy. 'Henry was up later than usual last night and
snoring his head off when I left,' she said. 'I must get
back before he wakes up and misses me.' And with
that she led the pony to the wooden block outside the
door, mounted and disappeared into the fog.

'I hope she does not miss her way,' Margaret
murmured.

The blacksmith laughed. 'She may miss her way but
that animal won't. Have no fear for her, my lady.'

'Does Master Capitain never come into the village?'

'Rarely, my lady, unless it be his cellar runs dry,

then he might visit the Crown. That woman——' he
jerked his thumb in the direction Nellie had taken
'— buys his provisions for him and his guests, though
why anyone should want to visit such an out-of-the-
way place God only knows. Beg pardon, my lady,' he
added, suddenly remembering that he was speaking of
her kinsman.

She smiled, bade him good-day and set off home,
musing about her uncle and his succession of visitors.
She did not think Nellie had been joking, whatever she
said. The girl was afraid of Henry Capitain. But why?
She decided she ought to find out, but when she arrived
home she found that Kate had arrived in her absence
and Nellie and Henry Capitain were pushed to the
back of her mind.

Her sister-in-law had come with a carriage-load of
baggage, a wet-nurse, a nursery-maid, a coachman and
a footman, besides her personal maid, and all had to
be accommodated and looked after, but Margaret was
overjoyed to see her.

'Kate, how well you look!' She moved to embrace
her and then held her at arm's length to look her up
and down. 'Your figure has quite returned.' She turned
to take the four-week-old baby George from his nurse
to cuddle him. 'He is beautiful, just beautiful. How
long can you stay?'

'Two or three days. Charles has business in
Newmarket, something to do with bloodstock sales.
He has taken the coach and will call for me on the way
back.'

'Oh, how marvellous! We can talk and talk to our
hearts' content and no men to interrupt or become

bored.' She summoned servants to make rooms ready and light fires, and handed the baby back to his nurse.

'Is Roly not home yet?' Kate asked, following Margaret up the wide, carpeted stairs.

'No,' Margaret said, then added quickly, 'Shall we eat in the dining-room or my sitting-room?'

'Oh, in your sitting-room. It is cosy in there and we can draw the curtains and shut out the fog. Do you know, we could hardly see our way and I was afraid we would end up in the river? As it was we nearly ran into a chaise coming in the opposite direction; we both had lanterns but neither could see the other. I didn't want Charles to go on tonight, but he insisted on going as far as Ely. I think he was going to meet someone at the Lamb.'

'I am sure he knows what he is about,' Margaret said as Kate drew breath. 'I'll leave you to change your dress and see George and his nurse settled. Come to my room when you are ready and we can have a good gossip.'

She knew that a gossip would entail explaining why Roland had not yet returned home and admitting she did not know where he was; she did not see how she could evade it. On the other hand, it was possible that Kate knew more than she did. She might know where Roland was and what he was doing.

They dined at a small table drawn up near the fire, and Kate spent the first half-hour regaling Margaret with tales of baby George and his dazzling progress, but the time eventually came when she had almost exhausted the topic, or it might have been that she became aware that she had not once asked Margaret how she was. She stopped suddenly. 'Oh, forgive me,

Margaret, I have been prattling on and you haven't said a word. Tell me, how are you?'

'Very well. Why should I not be?' Margaret's answer sounded sharper than she intended it to be and she laughed. 'How could I not be with everyone looking after me so well?'

'Have you felt the baby kicking?'

Margaret smiled. 'Oh, yes, he kicks quite a lot.'

'He? You know it is a male child? Did you ask Mistress Henser?'

'No, I just think it is a boy.'

'What a pity Roly is not here to share your joy. Charles used to love putting his hand on my stomach and feeling George kicking.' She paused. 'Roland will be home soon, won't he? I cannot think what is so important that it keeps him away at a time like this.'

'I expect he is busy.'

'But where is he?'

'You do not know?' Margaret looked up at her sister-in-law, wondering whether she dared confide in her.

'No, or I would not have asked.'

'I believe he is with Mistress Chalfont.'

Kate dropped her fork on to her plate with a clatter and stared at Margaret with her mouth open. 'Susan Chalfont!' she said at last. 'I don't believe it. Why would he go to her? She is nothing but an empty-headed, spoilt child.'

'She nursed him when he was all but dying.'

'Nursed him!' Kate scoffed. 'The servants nursed him. She simply sighed over him when he began to get better. He cannot have been taken in by that.'

'She obviously has qualities we can neither of us see,'

Margaret said. 'He once admitted to me that he loved her.'

'Oh, that must have been ages ago, before he met you. It is all over and done with.'

'I wish that were true.'

'I shall ask Charles when he comes back. He will know.'

'Please don't.' She paused, then took a breath and went on quickly, 'Oh, Kate, it is so complicated and so silly.'

'You quarrelled. It must have been serious to send him away like that, especially after your accident. I could have sworn then that nothing could have dragged him from your side.'

'It wasn't exactly a quarrel. It was about. . . Oh, please don't laugh. It was about a witch's curse made a hundred years ago.'

'I am not going to laugh,' Kate said. 'Who was cursed and why?'

'Roland, or more specifically Pargeter heirs and Pargeter wives. Surely you have heard the tale?'

'Oh, there was a story I heard when I was little, but I never really took any note of it. Fen people are always putting spells on each other. It is part of their folklore.'

'So I have since discovered. But I also realise that many people take such things very seriously.'

'Roland? Surely not.'

'I am afraid so.'

'Then you had better tell me all about it.'

So Margaret did, haltingly at first, and then more freely, pouring out her misery, forgetting all about the roast duck growing cold on her plate. 'You see,' she said at the end of the recital, 'what I never considered was that I should fall in love with Roland.'

Kate had listened without interrupting but now she exploded into wrath. 'Roland should be horse-whipped. That a brother of mine, whom I loved and looked up to, could dream up such a devilish plot is past comprehension,' she said. 'And why, in heaven's name, did you agree to marry him?'

'I have asked myself that time and time again,' Margaret said, pushing her plate with its congealing food away. 'At first I told myself it was because I was penniless and had nowhere to go after I ran away from my uncle, but I knew that wasn't true even before the wedding; I had worked for a living before, I could have done it again. The truth was I fell in love with Roland almost from the first and I hoped that in time he would come to love me and confide in me.'

'He must have been mad,' Kate said. 'That wound he suffered addled his brains.'

Margaret smiled wanly. 'It was a chest injury, close to the heart, not a head wound.'

'Heart! He has no heart. How could he? How could he do it to you?'

'I believe old Lady Pargeter put the idea into his head when he told her he was thinking of marrying Mistress Chalfont. She was the one who explained the details of the curse.'

'Grandmama.' Kate smiled. 'She was always fore-casting doom; I truly think she enjoyed frightening people.'

'But she was your grandfather's second wife, wasn't she?'

'And what is so unusual about that?'

'And your father married twice too, didn't he?'

'Papa's first wife died in a fall from a horse. According to stories I have heard, she was a little mad and rode astride all over the country on a huge black stallion which was too strong for her. She put him to a hedge one day and he simply refused to jump. There were no children, so Papa had to marry again to produce an heir.'

'Roland?'

'Yes, followed by me. Mama was never well after I was born and died when I was about eight. Papa did not marry a third time. He used to laugh and say twice was enough for any man, and what did he want another woman in the house for when he had me?'

'You make everything sound so normal.'

'But it is normal, Margaret. Men often marry twice; it is the way of the world. And how can you be sure the myth did not grow up as a result of these second marriages, not the other way about?'

'I never thought of that.'

'You know, Margaret,' Kate said thoughtfully, 'I think you have come to believe a little in this evil prediction.'

'I don't want to.'

'Then fight it.'

'That is what I am trying to do. Mistress Henser says all I need is faith.'

Kate laughed. 'So you did go to see her!'

'Only out of curiosity, to see what she was like. I wanted to find out why people believe in spells and superstitions.'

'And was your curiosity satisfied?'

'In a way. At least, I felt calmer when I left.' She

paused. 'Kate, I am determined to live and prove the curse is wrong for my son's sake.'

Kate lifted one finely drawn brow. 'Not for your own?'

'I care little for myself if Roland does not love me. And since he left I have become convinced we have no future together. He said as much to me on that last day.'

'I cannot fathom him,' Kate said. 'He never used to be so unfeeling. When we were children he was so good to me. He understood how unhappy I was when Mama died, and tried to make up to me for her loss. He took me out on the fens and taught me how to pole a boat and we went "babbing" for eels with worms tied to lengths of worsted. The eels catch their teeth in the wool, you know, and it makes them easy to pull out. We went riding together in the summer when he came home from school; he is a superb horseman. He is a good shot too, and his fencing master said he was one of the best swordsmen he had ever taught. But he could be gentle too. I remember once he became quite distraught when Wheeler, the gardener, had to drown some unwanted kittens. Roland fought him for them. Papa was angry and said he should not interfere with the work of the servants and if every kitten was allowed to live we should become overrun with them. Roland would never hurt another living thing—so why did he marry you if he truly believed in that curse?'

'Love makes us do strange things sometimes,' Margaret said, remembering, with a pang, that Roland had once referred to her as a kitten. 'He wanted to marry Susan Chalfont and he did not want her to die; that was his only consideration. And my mother was a

Capitain; that seemed to have some bearing on it too.'
She gave a cracked laugh. 'I was as expendable as one
of those new-born kittens.'

'No, you are not.' Kate reached out and took
Margaret's hand. 'You are my friend and I love you
and I will fight for you, if no one else does. My foolish
brother may do as he pleases. Tomorrow we will begin
delving.'

'Delving?'

'Yes. First we will go to the church and examine the
registers and make certain of our facts; we do not know
that Papa's first wife died within the year, nor
Grandpapa's either, and if they didn't, then the story
of the curse is flawed from the start. Then we will
search the house. There must be letters and papers
about the place. If such a curse exists we must find out
the exact words; we may even discover an antidote.'
She stopped to face Margaret. 'Now, is that not better
than relying entirely on faith?'

Margaret laughed shakily because it was so comforting to have someone to talk to about it, someone as
level-headed as Kate. Even if they found nothing, it
would occupy her mind and make her believe she was
doing something constructive.

Next morning she was not so sure. When they took
a walk to the church and began their search of the
parish registers, they very soon confirmed that not only
had Kate's father and grandfather married twice within
the year, but so had two generations before that. David
Pargeter, who had been born to Rosalind in 1646, a
few months after Anne Capitain had been hanged as a
witch, married in August 1670. His wife had died giving
birth to a son, Miles, in June 1671. They could find no

record of David's having married again. Miles himself was married in 1692 and his wife, Caroline, had died of a fever only three weeks after the wedding.

'Look at this,' Kate said, pointing down the funeral records. 'Dozens of people died in the village in 1692; there must have been an epidemic. Caroline was one of many.'

'But it happened within the year, just as predicted,' Margaret put in, turning pages. 'Was Miles your grandfather?'

'Yes.'

'His first wife died within a month of the wedding.'

Miles had subsequently married Matilda—the Lady Pargeter Margaret had known—who had borne him two children—a daughter, who had died in childhood, and a son, George, who was Roland and Kate's father. George's marriage to Janet in 1716 had lasted a day short of the year and he had married again in 1719. Roland was born in 1720 and Kate eight years later. Matilda, of course, had outlived all her relatives except Roland and Kate. The stone over her tomb still looked very new.

'And Papa's lasted a year all but a day; that proves nothing. Every single one is easily explained.'

'Do you think all those wives knew about and believed in the curse?'

Kate shrugged. 'Who knows? Perhaps we will find out when we search the house.'

As soon as they returned home, Kate flung off her bonnet and cloak and ran up to the nursery to see George. He had a very reliable nurse and all the other servants were more than anxious to spoil him, but his mother could hardly bear to be parted from him. Her first action whenever she had been away, even if it had only been for an hour or two, was to reasssure herself that he was well and happy. That done, she returned downstairs to join Margaret for dinner.

'Nurse took him out in the garden,' she said, helping herself from a dish of partridges. 'She said he loved all the ducks waddling on the lawn and laughed when they squabbled over the crumbs from the kitchen table.'

'Kate, he is barely four weeks old. You can hardly expect him to be amused by ducks.'

'But he is very knowing,' Kate protested. 'I can see a change in him every day. Oh, he is going to be clever, I know it, and I shall be so proud of him.' She stopped suddenly, thinking of her sister-in-law's coming child. 'Oh, Margaret, you must conquer that terrible curse.'

'So you believe in it too.'

'No, no.' Kate's protests did little to comfort Margaret. 'But we love you and need you. Your baby will need you. . .'

'And I shall need you when my turn comes.' Margaret smiled, though it was not altogether convincing. When anyone spoke of the future, it made her wonder how much of that she would have. Would she see her child change from day to day, grow up into manhood? And what about his father? Would he ever come home?

Roland brought the black stallion to a halt at the end of the gallop, where a belt of trees stood between the town and the open heath. 'Good fellow,' he said, patting the horse's neck. 'We will do well together.' He turned to walk the animal back to where the horse-dealer and the faithful Johnson stood waiting for his verdict. The horse had taken his fancy as soon as he'd seen it. Of mixed Barb and English stock, its long muscles, deep chest and firm hocks told him it was a stayer and the proud neck, flaring nostrils and lovely expressive eyes were evidence of a turn of speed he might have need of if his enemies recognised him or tumbled to his intentions.

It had taken weeks to track them down and he had only been able to do that by pretending to be a loyal follower of Bonnie Prince Charlie, a name the traitorous Scots had given their master. Flora Macdonald had helped the prince to escape to France and been arrested for it, but Roland knew there were others helping survivors of Culloden to leave the country, where they would be free to plot another return of the 'king over the water'. Following a trail which had often grown cold, he had come down from Scotland to East Anglia, taking each day as it came, working his way into the confidence of the remnants of the Jacobite following, being passed from one safe house to another, until he had arrived at a small village on the cliffs north of Lowestoft. But he had been too late. The four men he had been following had scrambled into a rowing-boat and pulled out to where a Dutch sloop waited to take them on board. Cursing the ill luck which had delayed him on the road, he had returned to the house where he lodged.

'I missed them,' he had told his host, a fat brewer, who had been the one to arrange for the men to be taken on board the sloop by his brother, who owned the rowing-boat.

'I did tell ye they wouldn't wait. Will ye stay to see if

any more arrive? I'll not risk life and limb arranging an escape for one man.'

'No, I understand,' Roland had said. He had no intention of going to France or anywhere else; his instructions were to prevent anyone else from doing so. 'I must find other means of leaving.'

'Course, if you are anxious to be gone, there are other routes.'

'Then you'd best be telling me about them. I have urgent dispatches.'

The brewer had been reluctant to speak because the different routes were kept secret and he only knew about them from snatches of conversation he had overheard, but in the end Roland, with a huge bribe, had elicited all he knew. He had turned back inland, but the horse which had bravely carried him hundreds of miles was done for and he needed another, and so he had stopped at Newmarket to buy one. Now he trotted back to meet the dealer, satisfied that the stallion was just what he was looking for.

Half an hour later, with Johnson on a bay a few paces behind him, he was riding along a rough track, which went by the name of a road, towards King's Lynn, knowing he would pass very close to Winterford on the way. Dared he stop? Dared he go home? He longed to see Margaret, to satisfy himself that she was well, to be there when their child was born, but if leaving her had lifted the curse, then going back would bring it down upon her again. Besides, he had a very good idea that a message had been sent ahead of him to the next safe house to warn his new hosts of his coming, and, if he did not arrive at the expected time they would become suspicious and go out looking for him. It was too dangerous to deviate from his given route. But if only he could send Margaret a message he would feel easier.

He was so immersed in his thoughts that he did not hear the coach and was not aware of it coming round the bend until it was almost too late. In a flurry of neighing horses and locked wheels, the carriage came to a halt only feet from him, and it was due to Roland's competent horsemanship that he was not unseated.

'You crazy fool!' Charles opened the door and put his head out. 'D'you expect the whole road to yourself?' He stopped suddenly. 'My God, Roland! What are you doing here?' He looked at Roland's rough coat and battered tall hat, his patched breeches and scuffed boots, his matted beard and filthy cravat. His appearance was in sharp contrast to the magnificent animal he rode. 'What happened to you, man?'

Roland grinned. 'You see before you Captain Robert MacDougal.'

'Who is he?'

'Me, you dunderhead.' He dismounted and walked leisurely over to the carriage. 'You very nearly killed me.'

'You should watch where you're going. Why are you wearing those rags? Surely you can afford to dress like a gentleman?'

'Oh, that would never do. I have been on the run since Culloden, putting up wherever I could find a friend and, when I could not, sleeping by the wayside. It is small wonder I look like a wayfarer.'

'I do believe you are gone mad. Come, tie the horse on behind and get in the chaise. I'm on my way to Winterford to fetch Kate. I'll take you home.'

'No. I am expected elsewhere and I cannot be seen with you.'

'No one can see us—the road is deserted.' He jumped down and took Roland's arm. 'If you won't get in the coach, let's walk a little, because I do not intend to leave here until I hear what you have been doing since you left home. You do remember leaving home?'

'To fight at Culloden, yes. You were with me.'

'No, after Culloden.' Charles heaved a sigh. 'I suppose you can recall what happened after the battle—your wound, Chalfont Hall, coming home, getting married, all that?' He turned to face his friend, wondering how he was going to tell him, if he had really lost all recollection. He did not relish the task at all. He looked up into Roland's face and suddenly became aware of the light in the other man's eye. He burst into laughter. 'Oh, you devil. You really had me thinking you had lost all memory. . .'

'Would that I had, or, better still, would that it were a nightmare and I about to wake up.' Roland sounded morose. 'But tell me, how is Margaret?'

'Come home and see for yourself.'

'No, I cannot. The year is not yet up and I have not completed my mission.'

'Mission? I had thought you were back in uniform.'

'Does it look like it?'

'No, a more bedraggled-looking sight never met my eyes. What happened to you?'

'I shall tell you, my friend, but only if you swear not to breath a word to a living soul. . .'

'But Margaret and Kate——'

'No!' It was almost a shout. 'I am not proud of what I am doing. When it is finished. . .'

'You will come home?'

'How can I? Margaret must hate me for what I did to her, and even if the year passes and she survives——'

'Of course she will survive!'

'—she will not take me back,' he went on, ignoring Charles's remark. 'I do not blame her. I am the lowest of the low. I cannot even ride into battle with my head up, but must slink about like a rat in a midden-heap. I sacrificed her for a whim. And I hurt Susan.'

'Do not worry about Susan; she soon found consolation. I heard only this week that she is to marry Sir Bartholomew Fletcher.'

'He is an old man.'

Charles laughed. 'But rich. You may safely forget her. But Margaret. . . Margaret is another matter. She does not hate you, she loves you.'

'I wish I could believe it.'

'Oh, you may believe it. When you left, she almost pined away, but she is a courageous woman and rallied miraculously. She will break that curse, Roland. I'll lay odds.'

'When the year is at an end, an it please God to spare us both, I will come home if she sends for me, not otherwise. I leave the Manor and all its contents to her.'

'And your child?'

'And to our child.'

'Am I to tell her that?'

'She knows it already. Now I must be off.' He turned to go back to where Johnson stood holding his horse.

'But you have not told me where I can contact you.'

'I will send you word,' Roland said over his shoulder as he mounted. 'Goodbye, my friend.'

'God fare thee well,' Charles said, but Roland did not hear him; he had already gone, cantering along the road and turning off down a rough bridleway which led over the heath.

CHAPTER TEN

THE next day the weather was so bad, with rain and gales blowing round the chimney-pots, that there was no going out even if they had wanted to, and Margaret could not dissuade Kate from taking the opportunity to search the house for evidence of the curse. As soon as breakfast was over, she pushed her chair away and stood up. 'Come, I think I know where to begin our hunt.'

She would not be denied, and Margaret reluctantly followed as she led the way from the dining-room, across the hall to the door which opened on to the east wing. The only room in use on that side of the house was the schoolroom, and though Margaret had looked round the others she had not explored them thoroughly.

'This used to be separate living quarters for the Dowager,' Kate said. 'But when my mother died and Grandmama resumed control of the household she moved back into the west wing and this part of the house was shut up. It was always dreadfully expensive to heat.'

'But there is very little furniture. Where would papers be kept?'

'We'll start in the attic,' Kate went on. 'I seem to remember some chests and trunks being taken up there years and years ago, when my grandmother moved. She would never allow anything to be thrown away.'

Margaret followed her up some stairs, along a landing and up another flight to a series of little rooms high up under the roof, where it was possible to stand upright only in the centre. Here they found discarded chairs and stools, faded curtains and old pictures stacked against the walls. Margaret moved one or two to face the dormer window so that she could see them better. 'These are filthy,' she said. 'It is almost impossible to make out the figures.'

'The best ones are hanging in the hall downstairs,' Kate said. 'These must be of poorer workmanship.'

Margaret picked up a piece of cloth and gently rubbed it over one of the portraits. 'But this is far from inferior; it is very well-drawn. The sitter is very thin of face and her eyes are sad. Her hair is scraped back into a coif and she is wearing such plain clothes that it makes her look gaunt. I suppose it could be one of the wives who died. Their successors would hardly want them hanging where they could see them every day and be reminded they were not their husbands' first choice.'

Kate seemed hardly to be listening. 'That's true. Look, there are documents in this chest.' She delved into it and pulled out a sheaf of papers, holding them to the candlelight. 'Goodness, this is signed by Oliver Cromwell. It says

> To John Pargeter, Baron, by reason of his faithful service to the cause of Parliament, to be held in perpetuity for him and his heirs, those lands north of the parish boundary of Winterford and lying south of Sedge Fen, from the dwelling known as Sedge House, and between the Bedford River to the west and the drain known as the Winterford Cut to the

east, lately in the possession of James Capitain and sequestered by Parliament for non-payment of taxes. The said James Capitain is required to vacate and surrender such lands one month from today. Signed Oliver Cromwell, on this seventh day of August, 1646.'

She turned to Margaret. 'Supposing the Capitains had been looking to the marriage of their daughter, Anne, to John Pargeter, to restore the land to the family, then it would have been a bitter pill to swallow when it did not take place.'

She began rifling through the chest again. 'There are records here of acquisitions and sales of other strips of land, dotted all over the fields. It looks as though my Pargeter forebears were trying to consolidate their land and enclose their boundaries. There are copies of wills here and bills for cattle and horses and a travelling-chaise. Oh, and here is the receipt for a portrait of Rosalind, Lady Pargeter. Which one was she?'

'According to Roland, that was the first one, the one Anne Capitain cursed.'

'I do not remember seeing a record of her death in the church. Surely, if the curse story was true, then she would certainly have had to die within a year of her marriage?'

'Yes.' Margaret sat heavily on a nearby stool; she was little more than a month to her lying-in and today she was more than usually tired. 'Perhaps she moved away from the village.'

'Why should she do that? It was her home. We must delve a little deeper.' Kate bent to the chest and produced a small leather-bound book. 'A journal, or I miss my guess,' she said, opening it. 'Look at this entry.

The curse lies heavy upon me and I pray daily that it will be lifted from me. An if that cannot be, then let me alone bear the burthen of this terrible evil and let it not pass to my child. If it please God to grant me a healthy son, I shall die in peace.'

'Oh, Kate, the poor woman,' Margaret said. 'I feel dreadful prying into her private thoughts.'

'Yes, but she has been dead these many years. What I should like to know is when and how she died.'

Margaret did not answer because her attention had been caught by a letter. The careful script was her mother's and she picked it up with shaking hands. Dated 1715, it was addressed to George Pargeter. She read:

This was your mother's doing. I do not know what makes her hate me so. I am not nor ever have been a Catholic, but if I were I would not have kept it from you, whom I love. But you believed the lie and that is more than I can bear. I am going away. Perhaps one day, when you and I are forgotten, things will change and love will replace hate. . .

The rest of the letter had been scratched out and over it in another hand had been written, 'We cannot change our destinies.'

Margaret could no longer see the words for the tears which gathered in her eyes. 'Poor Mama,' she whispered. 'Nothing has changed.'

'I'm sorry, what did you say?' Kate asked, but Margaret was in another time, another place. She was at her mother's bedside, helplessly watching her die. Had Mama ever been truly happy after leaving her home? Was that why she had suggested that Margaret should go to her uncle? She could not have known that history would repeat itself. Sitting in that dusty attic, Margaret lived again her journey to Ely, her flight from her uncle's house, her arrival at the Manor and Roland's strange proposal. She went over their conversation again and again, word for word, and wondered if it had all been ordained. Then who had ordained it? A loving God or an evil witch?

'Margaret, what is it?' Kate's voice penetrated her thoughts at last. 'Are you ill?'

'No, but I am a little tired.'

Kate was immediately penitent. 'Oh, my dear, how remiss of me. I was carried away by all this.' She paused. 'Shall we ask to have the chest brought down to your room? Then we can look through it at our leisure and you won't have to climb these stairs again.'

'If you wish.'

Margaret was not at all sure she wanted to know any more. Everything they had uncovered so far had only served to verify the story of the curse. She told herself it made no difference to her own conviction, but she could not stop herself thinking about all the people who had been involved—Anne Capitain, bitter and disappointed, Rosalind, who had so obviously believed she was about to die, and John Pargeter, with all his newly acquired land. Could he have found any pleasure in it? Handling Rosalind's journal and reading the faded words she had written a hundred years before, and that poignant letter from her mother to the man she loved, had brought the evil into the present, made it more real. For the first time since she had spoken to the parson about it, she felt its force. She knew what Rosalind had meant when she had written of the curse lying heavily upon her. Margaret felt weighed down by it.

As soon as they returned downstairs, she asked to be excused and went to lie down. She really was tired, in body and in spirit, but she could not rest. She imagined Rosalind, big with child, just as she was, going about her daily life around the Manor, visiting the village, preparing for the coming of the infant and wondering if it would ever be born and, if it was, whether she would live long enough to hold it in her arms. Where had John Pargeter been when all this was happening? Had he been by her side, supporting her, or had he turned his back on her? That picture she had seen—was that of Rosalind? What had happened to her? Margaret was torn between her need for reassurance and her fear of uncovering something she would rather not know. Could anything at all be gained by continuing the search? She was sure it would make no difference to the final outcome.

She said as much to Kate when she joined her for dinner, but Kate simply smiled and said, 'You can't mean that, Margaret. Surely knowing the truth must help? The boxes have been brought down to the library and the weather is no better. It will occupy the rest of the afternoon.'

In the warmth and light of the occupied part of the house, and with the matter-of-fact Kate for company, there seemed little to be afraid of, and Margaret gave in and followed her sister-in-law to the library as soon as the meal was over and George, who had been brought down to see his indulgent mama, had been returned to the nursery.

It was in the library that Charles found them, surrounded by dusty papers and documents, books and pictures, which smelled mouldy. Both women had smudges of dirt on their faces. He stood a moment in the doorway looking at them, before Kate saw him and ran to throw herself into his arms to be kissed. 'Charles! I did not expect you so soon.'

'Evidently not,' he said laconically. 'Shall I go away again?'

She laughed and dragged him forward. 'No, I missed you. You'll never guess what we have been doing.'

'Making yourselves very dirty,' he said, smiling and bowing over Margaret's hand. 'How are you, Margaret?'

'Well, as you can see.' She spread her hands to encompass herself and the cluttered room.

He wished Roland could see his wife now. Pregnancy had made her more beautiful and she had a glow about her; she did not look like someone about to die. And yet there was a sad depth to her eyes, which he guessed was caused not so much by fear of the curse as by the prolonged absence of her husband. He wanted to reassure her, but did not know how to explain that he had seen Roland not twenty miles away when he was thought to be with his regiment. From the little Roland had told him, such knowledge might be dangerous.

Margaret sent a servant to tell the cook there would be three for supper. 'Sit down,' she said to Charles, indicating a chair. 'We will put these away and talk to you instead. Did you have a successful trip?'

'Yes, I bought a beautiful matched pair of bays for

the carriage, and a brood mare.' He paused and looked round the room. Every available space was littered with papers. 'What are all these?'

'Margaret is going to write a family history,' Kate told him, her enthusiasm shining in her eyes. 'We found all these things in Grandmama's chest but they are all in a muddle, so we were putting them into date order.'

'And have you found anything of interest?' He picked up a piece of paper. 'This has become so damp it is hardly legible,' he said. 'Something I can't decipher, then "dying by her own hand. . ." More smudges. "Must be buried outside the confines of the churchyard. . ." Is it all like this?'

'Some of it is,' Kate said. 'Some we cannot read at all and some of it is in Latin. It will take years to sort it all out.'

He looked up at Margaret, thinking of the curse; five more weeks and it would have run its course, for good or ill. She caught his eye and smiled as if she had read his thoughts. 'Yes, Charles, years.' She took the paper from him, but there was no date, nor indication of the writer, though she guessed it might be the parson of the time. But who was he writing about? Who had died by her own hand? Could it be the unhappy Rosalind?

'Margaret told me the most extraordinary story,' Kate told her husband. 'That's why we went in search of the chest, to prove it.'

'And did you?'

'You haven't asked what the story was.'

'If you are referring to the curse of the Pargeters and Roland's fear of it, I know it.'

Kate looked at him in surprise. 'You do? Why didn't you tell me?'

'I was sworn to secrecy. And it was for Margaret or Roland to tell you, if they wanted you to know it.'

'Margaret has told me now and I am thoroughly ashamed of my brother. If I knew where he was, I would go to him and tell him so.'

'I doubt it would help. You could not make him feel any worse than he does already. He loves Margaret.'

'And I suppose it is a measure of his love that he leaves her just when she needs him most?'

'Yes, exactly.' He turned to Margaret. 'I don't know when he realised he loved you but, having married you, he didn't know what to do. It was like being caught in one of those eel-traps you see on the fen. You go in forwards and the way becomes narrower and narrower, but there is no backing out.'

'I am the one that's been caught,' she said tartly. 'I was lured into a trap just as the wild ducks are lured by decoys.'

'Please don't judge him too harshly; he was badly advised,' he said.

'By his grandmother, I know.'

'And also by me. I was the one who suggested he should marry a stranger until the curse had run its course. What I did not bargain for was that Roland would fall in love with you and you with him. The idea was that you should separate immediately after the wedding and not meet again until ——'

'Until Margaret had died,' Kate put in. 'Oh, Charles, not you too? Oh, I think I begin to hate you. . .'

'No, Kate, please,' he begged. 'I am penitent. I would do anything. . .'

'Can you lift this dreadful evil?' she demanded, eyes glinting angrily.

'No, or I would.' He turned to Margaret. 'Can you forgive me?'

He looked so thoroughly miserable, Margaret took pity on him. 'Nothing is going to happen,' she said, packing the papers back in the chest which stood open in the middle of the room. 'I am perfectly healthy and so is my child. There is nothing to forgive.'

He breathed a sigh of relief. 'It is more important that you absolve Roland because he will not return until you do.'

'And I will not make myself the laughing-stock of Society by going on my knees to him. I have my pride.'

'What has Society to do with it?' he asked, genuinely puzzled.

'He is with Mistress Chalfont, is he not?'

'Whatever gave you that idea? He has returned to the service of his country. He wants you to live, Margaret, and he believes the only way is to leave you in possession of the domain of Winterford, as a kind of restitution. There is no one else; I'll take an oath on it.'

Margaret was so taken by surprise that she could only stare at him. She had been so sure that Roland was with Susan, and she had used that conviction to harden her heart against him, but if he was somewhere else entirely, if he really did love her. . . Oh, what a dreadful mess it all was! 'Then where is he?'

'He rejoined his regiment and was sent on special duties,' he went on, collecting up more papers to put in the chest. 'I do not know if he *can* come home.'

She dropped the bundle of documents she had been

gathering up into the chest. 'Have you seen him? Since he left here, I mean.'

'Yes, very briefly, but he could tell me nothing.' He could not tell her that he thought Roland was behaving recklessly, that he was trying to punish himself for what he had done to her. He might even be trying to get himself killed in order that she might live. Why else would he be riding about the countryside pretending to be a fugitive? 'I asked him to come home, but he said he must carry out his orders.'

'If he wants to be reconciled, then he has only to come home and say so,' she said. 'But it must be before the year is out. I want some evidence of his faith in himself and in me. Now I suggest we go in to supper.'

They abandoned the chest and the musty papers and went through to the dining-room to eat, and after that they played cards and Charles gave them a tune on the flageolet, and the research was forgotten. Margaret did not return to it until two days later, after Kate and Charles had left, and then only because the chest stood in the middle of her boudoir floor and she had to walk round it every time she crossed the room. Its unfinished business seemed to accuse her. She put an apron over her grey wool round gown and opened the lid.

Here was a family's history, encapsulated in faded letters tied with ribbon, official-looking documents, sealed with wax, private journals, never meant to be seen by strangers, hidden pictures, maps and plans. What could she learn from them, except the anguish of a family under threat? Did she want to pry into that? She picked up Rosalind's journal and turned the pages, but she did not read it; she had seen enough. The present was more important than the past. Life was for

living now and that was what she must do. She put the
journal back and shut the lid; let the memories lie. She
stood up, took off the apron and went to find a couple
of footmen to take the chest back to the attic. Then
she put on a warm cloak, tucked her hands in a fur
muff and went out for a walk.

An east wind blew across the fens from the North
Sea and stung her face; it whipped at her skirts and
froze her toes. Even the ducks seemed to be huddled
together under the lea of the boat house. The sky,
though as immense as ever, was low with heavy clouds,
which chased each other across the heavens like giant
grey horses, manes and tails flying. Winter was at hand
and the seasons would soon have come full circle since
that fateful day when she had stepped down from the
stage at Ely. She had been penniless and homeless
then; was it any different now? She could spend
Roland's money, he begrudged her nothing, and she
had a roof to shelter her, but was it home?

It was her child's home, she told herself, putting a
hand over the bump in her abdomen which could no
longer be hidden, even by voluminous clothes. Whatever happened to her, it was his heritage. She stopped
to rest, leaning against the wall which surrounded the
grounds of the Manor, and felt the baby kick inside
her. 'Kick, my son,' she murmured. 'Kick for all you
are worth, for you will need to be strong to live here.'

It was too cold to stand still. She moved on, walking
across the sloping lawn to a part of the garden which
had been allowed to grow wild. In the spring she would
tidy it up, cut the grass, plant some flowers—roses
perhaps—and herbs for the kitchen. In the spring. . .
Would she see the spring? She pushed the melancholy

thought from her and walked on, picking her way carefully over uneven ground. She looked up to see a heron swoop and almost tripped over a stone slab. At first she thought it was part of an old pathway, but then she noticed that it had been engraved. She stooped and brushed aside the accumulation of lichen and moss to read the words.

Here lyeth Rosalind, Lady Pargeter, departed this life on the seventh day of December 1646. May God have mercy on her soul.

She had stumbled on Rosalind's grave! It was Rosalind who had killed herself and then been denied a last resting-place in the churchyard. But she was not at rest; Margaret felt her presence very strongly. There was no escaping it, no relief from the evil of that curse; it was everywhere. She scrambled to her feet and ran into the house, as if the unhappy woman's spirit pursued her. It seemed to be saying, It could happen to you. You will be next, and then your son's wife and his son's wife, if he should be fortunate enough to have one. There is no breaking that awful prediction. Why don't you do as I did? Why prolong the anguish?

Stumbling up to her room with her hands over her ears to shut out the voice, Margaret knew that she was near to breaking-point. The legacy of that curse had finally conquered her will-power; she could no longer fight it. Faith had deserted her. Tomorrow, she would leave. But where could she go? How would she live? Where would her child be born? Her son. Roland's. She hated him. She loved him. She wanted to die. She wanted to live. She did not know what she wanted. She flung herself on her bed and buried her face in the pillow.

She stayed in her room for more than two weeks, never going out and eating hardly anything. Penny could do nothing with her. Sometimes she cried, sometimes she raged in anger; at other times she talked aloud as if an unseen ghost were arguing with her, and now and again she fell to her knees and prayed for deliverance. She slept during the day and was wakeful at night, sitting shivering at her window in her nightgown and cap, staring out across field and fen with unseeing eyes, watching for another dawn, wondering if today would be the day. If Penny had known where to find him, she would have sent for his lordship, for it was apparent that her ladyship was losing her mind.

And then her release came in the shape of a fat little man in black breeches and a long black coat. He arrived in the village in a hired chaise and booked into the Crown before asking the whereabouts of the Capitain residence. Directed to Sedge House, he set off along the drove, but returned almost immediately and knocked on the door of the Manor.

A footman sent Penny to find her mistress before he would allow the man to step over the threshold. Penny returned from her errand to say that her ladyship was not receiving visitors and she was to take a message.

'Please tell her ladyship my mission is of the utmost importance,' he said pompously. 'Messages simply will not serve. And I am not accustomed to being kept waiting on doorsteps.'

The footman relented and allowed him into the vestibule, where he paced up and down while he waited for Penny to return a second time.

'Her ladyship will be down directly,' she told him breathlessly. 'Please wait in the parlour.'

Margaret appeared half an hour later. Dressed in a grey gown which flowed freely from a high yoke and with a simple coif over tresses which had been brushed but not powdered, she seemed to glide down the stairs and along the hall, a ghost of her former self. It was apparent to the little man, who watched from the open door of the parlour, that she was ill. She was deathly pale.

He bowed over her hand. 'My lady.'

'Do you come from my husband?' she demanded, because that was the only reason she had agreed to see him.

He looked startled. 'No, my lady. I do not know his lordship. My name is Jacob Lovett. I am a lawyer.'

'If this is legal business, should you not be speaking to my husband?'

'No. It is you I have come to see.'

'Then state your business. I am afraid I am not in the best of health and can spare you only a few minutes.' She sat down heavily on a settle and motioned him to a chair.

'Time,' he said with a sigh. 'Everyone is concerned with time these days, rushing about like a heap of ants. No one stands still. It has taken me months to find you.'

'Why were you looking for me?'

'Before I answer that question, I have one or two of my own. A formality, you understand. I need to know your mother's name.'

'My mother? She died almost exactly a year ago. Her name was Felicity Donnington.'

'And your father? What do you know of him?'

'Very little. He was, I believe, a merchant. His name was Richard and he died in India—Calcutta, I think it was—soon after I was born. My mother brought me back to England. I do not remember India, nor my father. Why are you asking about him?'

'Because, my lady, he did not die when you were a child. I surmise your mother told you that to cover the fact that she had left him.' He paused, watching her carefully. 'You did not find life easy, you and your mother?'

Margaret could hardly take in what he was saying; it was so different from what she had always believed. 'No, but we managed.'

He smiled slowly. 'The irony of that is that your father became a very rich man.'

'Where is he now?'

'He died in August '46.'

'But that was only fifteen months ago!'

'Yes, and in England. He came back, knowing his end was near and wanting to find you. He passed on before that could be accomplished. In his will, he charged me to find you and apprise you of your inheritance.' He stopped speaking when it looked as though Margaret would faint. 'Shall I call your maid?'

Margaret pulled herself together with an effort. 'No, please go on. How did you find me?'

He smiled. 'By dint of much searching and questioning. I managed to trace where Mistress Donnington went when she first returned to England, and from then it was a long quest, going from address to address, workplace to workplace, until I found the lodgings where she died. But no one knew what had happened to you. I was told the place of your last employment, but you had left there and it seemed I was doomed to failure. Then I made the acquaintance of a Mistress Tolliday, a friend of your mother's.'

'Yes, they worked together before Mama became too ill to work.'

'She told me she thought your mother had an uncle, though she did not know his name or where he lived. It was a slim hope but I pursued it. Your mother's name had been Capitain. I worked it out from there. I have just come from Henry Capitain's house.'

'This is unbelievable.'

'I have credentials, my lady.' He bent to pick up his bag. 'All you need. And a copy of the will. You are a very rich woman.' He pulled out a sheaf of papers and handed them to her, but she was too dazed to read them. 'The money is yours, my lady, to do with as you please. Unless you wish it, your husband cannot touch it.' He looked round the luxurious room and smiled. 'Though it appears he is not in want. . .'

'No.' She was in a dream; none of it was real. She had had too many sleepless nights and eaten too little and now she was having fantasies. But if it was true? If it was true, she had been a rich woman even before her mother died. If she had known, she could have bought her medicines, found somewhere more comfortable for her to live out her last days. There would have been no need to come to Winterford, no need to enter into that terrible marriage contract with Roland. And now there was no need for her to stay. Suddenly she began to laugh, a cracked, high-pitched sound which brought Penny to her side at once.

'You have upset my lady,' she told the little man in

a fierce whisper. 'I must take her to her bed.' She helped Margaret to her feet and put her arm round her to guide her across the room.

Margaret turned to her visitor, who had gathered up his papers and come to his feet. 'Master Lovett, I beg you to avail yourself of our hospitality. I will order dinner for you and we will talk again after I have rested.'

She pushed Penny away and walked unaided to the stairs, with her head high. She was an independent woman, a proud woman, and it was about time she took control of her own life. There would be formalities, of course, but as soon as she could, she would leave Winterford, go somewhere quiet to have her child, and after that she would make a life for herself somewhere where superstition was not rife, where the fate of Rosalind Pargeter could not haunt her. Away from Winterford she would begin to feel better.

But it was not as easy as that. She had commitments to the villagers and to the school; in Roland's absence they looked to her for help and guidance. And without someone to oversee them, what would happen to the servants, and Penny in particular? Penny had a family in the village; she would not want to leave them. And Nellie bothered her; she must do something for her. Take her away from her uncle's influence. According to Master Lovett her uncle had several visitors. 'Very unsavoury characters they are, if you pardon my boldness, my lady,' he said the following day, when they were sitting together going over her plans, plans he did not altogether agree with. She was throwing money away as if she did not expect to live to enjoy it. 'I am indeed glad you are not domiciled with him, for he would have had his hands on your fortune in the blinking of an eye.'

'The Capitains suffered great losses for their beliefs,' she said mildly. 'They were once as rich and powerful as the Pargeters, but they lost everything when they sided with the King in the civil strife.'

'Did they not get it back with the Restoration?'

'No. The Pargeters were well-received at court; they were allowed to keep their gains. The Capitains were granted a small annuity by Charles II in recognition of their services. It hardly seems fair.'

'It was a hundred years ago.'

She smiled wryly. 'Fen people have long memories, Master Lovett. I want to help my uncle.'

'How, my lady? You have a fortune, but it is not limitless and he would only drink and gamble away anything you gave him.'

'He is not as black as he is painted, I am sure of it.'

He sighed heavily. 'Very well, my lady, though it is enough to make your father turn in his grave.'

She chuckled suddenly. 'He will not be the only one turning in his grave, if I have my way.'

He looked puzzled. 'I beg your pardon?'

'It does not matter.'

She signed the papers he had brought with him and he took his leave to return to London, promising to be back within a week with all the formalities completed. 'But I urge you to think carefully before you give any to your reprobate uncle,' he said. 'I do not care for his manner at all.'

Left to herself, Margaret mused on the problem of her uncle and Nellie. It was a way of keeping her from brooding over her own troubles. They had not gone away, simply changed their character. Money was no longer the reason why she was forced to remain in Winterford; she had the resources to go wherever fancy dictated. Roland's undertaking to look after her, so long as she remained at the Manor to have her son, no longer mattered. Roland. He was never far from her thoughts. If he had been here, she could have discussed her new-found independence with him, asked him what he thought of her plans to benefit the village and build a proper school, enlisted his help over Henry and Nellie. She smiled wryly. If he had been at home, she would perhaps not be making plans to leave.

She could not send for Henry because he would not obey. There was nothing for it but to go to him. Penny would make a fuss, but Penny would have to do as she was told.

In the event, Penny's mother became ill and Margaret sent her home. 'I can manage without you for a day or two,' she said. 'Mothers are very precious people. Go and stay with her until she is better.'

As soon as the girl had gone, Margaret ordered horses to be harnessed to the curricle and went to her room to put on her warmest gown, fur-lined boots and a long cloak with a hood, for it would be cold driving along the drove beside the cut. By the time she returned downstairs the groom had brought the vehicle to the door.

'I will drive myself,' she said, stepping into the vehicle and picking up the reins.

'But, my lady, his lordship——'

'His lordship is not here, Barnard, but I am, and you will obey my orders. Tell Cook I expect to be back for dinner.'

She flicked the reins and, before the startled man could do anything, she was bowling out of the gates and on to the road into the village. At the crossroads she turned along the drove beside the cut, making for Sedge House, smiling to herself. She was independent now, she could do as she pleased, and if it pleased her to visit her uncle, then she would. Roland had left her to manage on her own; he could hardly complain if she did. She had hardly covered half the distance before her bravado began to fade; her uncle might be less than civil to her. He might not even let her in the house. She remembered her talk with Nellie in the blacksmith's shop and almost turned back. But the road was too narrow to turn in and she had to go on.

'Where is your courage?' she asked herself. 'Words can't hurt you. And he can't be bad through and through. He sent you that wedding-gown, didn't he? And he came to help when you fell through the ice. Roland could not have managed on his own.'

She passed Mistress Henser walking towards the village from her cottage. She stopped and looked up at the carriage as it passed, but Margaret was too concerned with keeping the curricle on the narrow road to do more than bid her good-day. The horses had not been out for a day or two and they wanted to exercise their legs; it was all Margaret could do to control them. She brought them to a shuddering stop outside Sedge House and had to sit a moment before she could stop shaking enough to get down.

'You are a fool, woman!'

Margaret looked up from tying the reins to a post, to see her uncle framed in the doorway, wearing a long

brown coat and thick breeches and hose. She answered
his scowl with a smile.

'I came to see you, Uncle.'

'Can't think what for.'

She finished securing the horses and went over to
him. 'I never thanked you for sending me the gown,
nor for helping Rolànd pull me from the dyke.'

'It's a little late for that, don't you think?'

'Better late than never,' she said. 'Aren't you going
to invite me in?'

'Better not. Better go back the way you came.'

'That is hardly civil of you. I want to talk to you.'

'What about?'

'About you and Nellie. . .'

'What has she been saying about me?' His bright
little eyes peered at her suspiciously. 'Little slattern!
It's a lie, whatever it is.'

'She has said nothing. I want to help you both.'

'Help us!' His many chins wobbled as he threw up
his head and laughed. 'What can you do? You cannot
even help yourself.'

'Yes, I can. I have come into money——'

'Money, eh? Then I suggest you use it to shake the
dirt of Winterford from your feet. You haven't got
much time left to do something to save yourself, have
you?'

'It is cold on the doorstep,' she said, ignoring his
reference to the curse and trying to peer past him into
the house. She thought she could see figures in the
background.

'She's not going away, man,' someone said behind
him. 'Better let her in.'

Henry stood to one side and Margaret stepped into

the hall, and immediately wished she had not. There were six men there. They were as unlike the guests she had met on her previous visit as any men could be. The ones she had seen had been fops, dressed in silks and satins and only interested in pleasure; these were roughly dressed, unshaven and altogether more menacing. No wonder Nellie had been afraid.

'Take her horses round the back and put them out of sight.' The man who spoke was a little less scruffy in appearance than the others and obviously used to command. His order had been addressed to a boy, who scuttled away to obey.

'There is no need for that,' Margaret said. 'I am not staying long.'

'We say how long you stay, my lady.' The man grinned suddenly. 'Now you are here, you can be useful to us.'

'Leave her alone,' Henry said. 'She is no good to us. Look at her—she's practically dropping her brat.'

'You think we should let her go?'

'Why not? She will not harm you.'

'Oh, I think she will. I think she will go straight to the militia.'

'What are you talking about?' Margaret asked.

'Nothing,' her uncle said quickly. 'James will have his little joke.'

'This is no jest,' the man said, while the others looked on, saying nothing, doing nothing, but Margaret noticed their hands straying to the pistols they kept in their belts. She began to be very afraid and backed away towards the door.

'Oh, no, you don't, me beauty!' The man her uncle

had called James sprang forward and seized her arm.
'You stay here.'

'Let me go! You have no right——'

'I have whatever right I choose to take,' he said, and
pushed her roughly towards the other men. 'Tie her
up.'

Margaret struggled ineffectually as two of them tied
her hands behind her and dragged her off to the back
parlour, where they pushed her into a chair and stuffed
a piece of cloth torn from the tablecloth into her
mouth. Then they left her and locked the door.

She got up and went to the window, but it looked
out on to the fen and the only signs of life were a few
wild ducks and a heron or two. She could not expect
help from that direction. She went to the door and
listened. There was no sound. If only she could untie
her hands, she might be able to make her escape. She
looked round the room. It was furnished with a table
and half a dozen chairs, a settle and a cupboard. There
was a meagre fire, beside which lay a poker. Could she
pick it up and, what was more to the point, could she
wield it? She had to free her hands before she could do
anything. Where was Nellie? They could escape
together if the girl could pluck up the courage to help
her. She began kicking at the door. No one came to
her and she gave up, exhausted, and sank on to the
settle.

How long would it be before she was missed? If
Penny had been at the Manor, it might not have been
long, but her maid was with her mother. The groom
might think to tell someone when the curricle did not
return, but it would be hours before they thought of
coming to Sedge House to look for her. Oh, why had

she insisted on coming alone? Why had she come at
all? Her uncle did not care what happened to her; he
had made only a feeble attempt to stop the men tying
her up. He was as afraid of them as Nellie was. Who
were they? She did not think they were welcome
visitors. Nellie had been right; there was something
going on and she was in mortal danger.

Was that curse at work? Was this to be her end? It
was strange how her frame of mind had changed in a
few short weeks from disbelief to belief, from confidence to fear. She supposed that living at the Manor,
in an ancient house, surrounded by things from the
past, it was hardly surprising that she had become as
superstitious as the fen people. And so much had
happened to her—falling through the ice, the accident
with the knife which could have been a great deal more
serious, being toppled over the banisters, and now this.
She had fought against it, right until the time of finding
Rosalind Pargeter's gravestone. She was too weary to
go on fighting. Was it time to give up, to let the curse
take over? But how could she do that, when there was
a new living being growing inside her, a child she must
protect at all costs?

CHAPTER ELEVEN

MARGARET heard the door being unlocked, and the leader of the men came in and stood looking down at her, a crooked smile on his face. 'Quiet now, my lady?' he queried.

She nodded.

He bent and ripped the gag from her mouth, knocking her head back and making her feel ill. 'You keep quiet and I'll leave it off.'

'I'll be silent.' She looked up at him, but his expression did not soften. 'What do you want from me?'

'Now who's to say you won't prove useful?'

'Money? I'll give you money if you let me go and allow Nellie to come with me.'

'Do you take us for fools? No, my lady, we have other uses for you.' He grinned suddenly. 'I had not thought of taking a hostage until you arrived so opportunely. . .'

'A hostage? Why do you need a hostage?'

'Safe passage,' he said. 'We are going to take you with us on a little voyage.'

She bit her lip to stop herself crying out. A voyage meant the sea and a foreign country, France perhaps. They were obviously fugitives, but from what? She must remain calm. She took a deep breath. 'Who do you suppose will pay a ransom for me?'

'Your husband, my lady.'

She began to laugh hysterically, rocking herself back and forth while the tears streamed down her cheeks.

'Pray share the jest,' he said.

'My husband,' she said between her sobs. 'My husband will not pay. He wants me dead.'

'It's true,' Henry said, coming into the room behind her. 'You will be doing him a favour if you kill her.'

The man spun round. 'Do you think I was born in your stinking fens? Do you think I am as stupid as you are?' He raised his hand and dealt Henry a violent blow to the side of his head which put him on his knees. 'Be damned to that for a tale. I begin to believe you are not to be trusted.'

'I have been a loyal servant of the Young Pretender and risked my life for his cause; what more do you want? Let the woman be—she is great with child. For the child's sake——'

'What care I for English brats?' He kicked Henry as he struggled to his feet, spread-eagling him on the floor. 'Now, get up and fetch the girl. We want something to eat before that lighter gets here, and provisions packed for the journey.'

Henry scrambled up and hurried from the room, muttering to himself about ingratitude, and whose house was it anyway, but the other man ignored him.

'You do not need me,' Margaret said, trying to speak calmly, though her heart was beating so loudly that she thought they must hear it. 'No one bothers about my uncle's guests—they come and go as they please—but if you take me, then the servants at the Manor will come looking for me.'

'I care nothing for your servants, my lady; my concern——' He stopped and turned as one of the other men came into the room. 'The boat's been sighted, sir. It's making its way up the cut.'

'Then get everything on board.' He hurried from the room issuing orders, and Margaret heard the men scurrying about to obey. She crept from the room and along the hall to the door.

'Oh, no, you don't!' One of the men came after her and grabbed her arm.

She struggled in his grasp, shouting at the top of her lungs, hoping someone might hear her. He slapped her face hard and then his hand was pulled away by Nellie, pouncing on him from behind. He yelled and turned to hit her. Henry came waddling along the hall to her aid, jumping on the man, and then everything was pandemonium as other men came in and began laying into Henry and Nellie, battering them about the head and body with the butts of their pistols and kicking them where they lay. Margaret, horrified, tried to go to their aid, but her hands were still tied. She kicked the man who held her and then tried to bite his hand. He yelled and hit out at her. She was saved by James. 'Stop that! Bring her to the boat.'

'What about him?' The man indicated the unconscious Henry with the toe of his boot. 'And the girl.'

'They're dead. Leave them. Come on; we've no time to lose if we're to catch the tide at the sluice.'

Margaret was gagged again and half dragged, half carried out of the house, across the garden and down to a large flat-bottomed boat which was tied up at the landing-stage. She made a last despairing attempt to stop them taking her on board, but they were prepared to manhandle her if she did not go willingly and, remembering her child, she shrugged them off and walked on board, her head high, but her spirits as low as it was possible for them to be.

Roland reined in at the Winterford crossroads and looked about him. There were few people to be seen at that time of day, most being about their business, but he knew he had only to go to the smithy or the basket-maker's, or one of the cottages, to find someone to talk to him. Any one of them would be able to tell him if his wife was alive and well. She might even have had their child a week or two early. She might even have died! It was something he would not allow himself to dwell on; he had left home in order to save her and he had to believe that that was possible or he could not live with himself. But anyone he spoke to would wonder why he did not go home and see for himself how she was; indeed, they would be shocked that he had even stopped to ask. Why should he not go home? Just for an hour or two, not to stay. He had hoped that absence might ease the pain but it had only made it worse. He wanted to be with Margaret more than he had wanted anything in his whole life, except that she should have that curse lifted from her and live to grow old. Could he ride up to the Manor, just to catch a glimpse of her?

His quarry had gone to ground somewhere in the area but he had no idea exactly where. There were so many lonely habitations, so many isolated little islands in the fens, that they could be anywhere. They could have reached the coast and been taken aboard a ship. Was he on a wild-goose chase? Would he not do better to go back to his royal commander and admit failure?

He patted his horse's neck. 'Which way, Satan?' he murmured. 'Home, back to London, or on to Lynn?'

'My lord?'

He turned to see who had spoken and found himself looking down at the upturned face of Janet Henser. 'Good-day to you, Mistress Henser.'

The woman smiled. 'So, you are come home?'

'Is there any reason I should not?'

She shrugged. 'It is for you to decide whether it is wise to do so, my lord, not me.'

'I do not intend to stay. I came only to reassure myself that Lady Pargeter is well.'

'And risking all.'

'I begin to think I was wrong to leave. . .'

'It was decreed from the first, my lord. Everything is ordained from our first breath to our last.'

'How can you say that? You are the one with incantations and cures, potions and remedies. You counselled me to go away. You convinced me. . .'

'That too was ordained. If you had not gone away, you could not come back. And that is important.'

'You talk in riddles. I will go home.' He turned his horse to leave her.

'Your wife is not there,' she called after him.

The horse pranced as he tugged on the rein to turn him back. 'Not there? Then where is she?'

'I saw her driving your curricle down the drove towards Sedge House.'

'Sedge House!'

It came to him like a revelation; Henry Capitain's strange visitors, who arrived and departed and whom no one ever saw, were fugitives! It was clear as day now; Capitain was a Jacobite sympathiser and helping to ship the remnants of Charles Stuart's rebel army out to join him. Sedge House was a place of safety for them while they waited for a ship. That was where his quarry had gone to ground. And Margaret had gone there! Was she one of them or simply an innocent bystander? 'Why was she going there?' he demanded.

'I am not your wife's keeper, my lord. She goes where she pleases. I simply passed her on the way.'

'Did you see anyone else, apart from her maid and the groom?'

'I saw neither maid nor groom, nor anyone else. She was alone.'

'Go to the Manor, alert the grooms, fetch my lady's maid and wait for me there.' He rapped out his orders to Johnson but he did not wait to see if they were obeyed; the words were hardly out of his mouth before he spurred his horse to a gallop. Margaret would not help that rascally uncle of hers, would she? And even if she did, would she know what she was getting into? He smelled danger; it filled his nostrils and made his heart beat so that he found it difficult to breathe. Margaret. Margaret. He pictured her with Henry Capitain and that band of ruthless insurgents he had been following for weeks, and felt sick with apprehension. What would they do to her?

The horse thundered along the drove alongside the dyke, covering the uneven ground as sure-footedly as a mountain goat, with Roland bent low over his neck, urging him to greater effort. He had to reach her and reach her fast. 'God, let me be in time,' he muttered. 'Don't let this be the end.'

But he was first and foremost a soldier and he was not so distracted as to throw all caution away. There was little cover, but he had been a fenman all his life; he knew how to move invisibly among the greys and browns of the reeds that grew along the water's edge. He stopped short of his goal, tied his horse to a willow and crept forward on foot. There was a lighterhouse tied up at the landing-stage, normally used as the lead vessel of a gang of fen lighters, taking a cargo from Cambridge to Lynn, calling at every little waterside village and town *en route*. It was usually pulled by a strong horse, ridden by a boy, but it also had a mast and a small sail for those occasions when the wind was in the right direction, and a little superstructure in the middle which served as a house for the crew of two or three. Today the lighterhouse was without its usual string of vessels. Roland could see no one on board and he dared not run across the open ground to reach it. He darted for the corner of the house, intending to use it as cover. It was then that he saw the door was open and there were two bodies lying in the hall, one of which was female, judging by the heap of pink silk and the slipper-clad feet.

'Margaret!' He turned away from the lighter and ran into the house, his heart in his mouth, and bent over the motionless forms. One was Henry. Roland realised he had been battered to death at the same time as he pulled him off the woman. It was not Margaret, but Nellie. He was so relieved that he found himself crying. And then she moaned. There was so much blood about, it was difficult to tell which of the two it had come from. He lifted her head on to his knee, and his riding-breeches were immediately stained with gore which oozed from a wound to the back of her skull.

Her face, beneath its paint, was badly bruised and her breathing laboured.

'I'll get help,' he said, looking round him, expecting to be surrounded by a dozen ruffians at any moment. Where were they? Why had they done this?

'Tried to stop them,' she muttered through swollen lips. 'Tried to stop them. . . Henry. . .'

'Where is Margaret? Where is my wife?'

'Getting away. . . Go after them. . .'

He did not need to know who 'them' were. 'Where is Margaret?' he repeated, more concerned with his wife's whereabouts than where the men had gone.

'Took her. Go after them. They mean to. . .'

He hesitated only a moment before pulling a cushion from a chair and laying it under her head. 'I'll be back.'

He dashed out of the house, uncaring whether he was seen or not, and ran towards the landing-stage. But the lighter had gone. He saw its red sail over the top of a bed of osiers as the wind took it out of the cut and into the river. He ran down to the boat-house in the forlorn hope that there might be a rowing-boat there, or that Margaret might have been left. He was disappointed on both counts and stood uncertainly at the water's edge for a moment before turning back to the house.

Nellie had not moved and her eyes were shut. He went to her and squatted at her side to take her hand. 'Mistress Capitain, can you hear me?'

'Yes.' Her voice was becoming weaker.

'Where were they taking her?'

'To the coast. Boarding a ship. . .'

'I have to go after them. You understand? I have

asked my man to fetch help. Someone will come. Can you wait?'

Nellie managed a crooked grin which was grotesque in that poor damaged face. 'I ain't going nowhere.'

He ran upstairs and into the first bedroom he came across, pulled the blankets from the bed and took them down to cover her. 'I'm going back to the village to get help. . .'

'No time. They'll go. . .through the sluice. . .'

He knew the significance of that. To get to the coast the lighter would have to 'shoot the eye' of Highmere Sluice, which was about fifteen miles downstream where a tributary joined the Great Ouse. In times of heavy rain or when the snow melted, the gates were shut to hold the flood-water on the higher reaches of the river and protect the downriver fields from inundation, but when the tide turned the gates were opened to allow river traffic through to the coast. The fugitives would have to approach at exactly the moment the tide turned so that the lighter could be carried through the open gates on the ebb. If they arrived too soon or too late, they would have to wait at the inn on the towpath until the tide turned again. The lighter was already well on its way with a favourable wind. The men would have unhitched the towing-horse and taken it on board until the cut turned and they could no longer make use of the sail, when they would take up the tow again. He had to reach the sluice-gates before they did, but he did not like leaving the injured girl.

'Are there any servants to help you?'

'No. . . Mistress Clark left. . . Could not stand Henry. . . He's dead, ain't he?'

'Yes.'

'Thought so.' She sighed and shut her eyes. 'What are you waiting for? Go, can't you?'

'Yes.' He patted her hand and dashed from the house towards the willow where he had left his mount.

He was barely in the saddle when he saw Janet Henser coming back along the drove, her basket on her arm. She was about to turn on to the track which led to her cottage when he hailed her. 'Mistress Capitain has been hurt,' he called. 'Do what you can for her. I am going to Highmere Sluice. Tell the men.' And with that he was gone, almost galloping along the drove away from the river and taking an old path across the fields.

'Go, Satan, go!' he said, digging his spurs into the animal's flanks. 'If you ever wanted to fly, now's the time to do it.'

While he was on the bridle-paths between the open fields, the going was good, but before long he had to strike out across marshy terrain. There were places where the silt of ages had accumulated to make paths a few inches above the level of the fen, but in winter these were not well-defined, especially if there had been heavy rain. He had to rely on instinct, watching the reed-beds and the willows, making note of where the osiers had been harvested, for that was usually a sign of civilisation. He walked the horse, looking for the hoof-marks of cattle, which could usually be trusted to find a firm way. He rode carefully, curbing his impatience and the temptation to make the horse go faster, for one false footfall would send him and his horse into the mere.

He found his way on to higher ground at last, and stopped a moment to look across at the river, curving away in the distance, but there was no sign of the red sail. Was he ahead of the barge or behind it? Would the sluice-gates be open or shut? If they were open, the barge would simply glide straight through into tidal water. Once that happened he would not be able to keep it in sight, nor catch it up until it reached the coast. He had a vision of the fugitives sailing the barge right out to sea and taking Margaret on board ship with them. She was heavy with child. If anything happened to her. . . He gritted his teeth and spurred his horse.

He dashed through villages, past cottages and farms, over fields, jumping hedges and ditches, hardly noticing them. The stallion carried him on and on, mile after mile, until its sleek black coat was a white froth of sweat and its great strength was almost spent. It had been a good buy, that horse, he thought as he lay over its neck; it was a pity to ruin it, but that could not be helped. Margaret was all he could think of. Margaret and that damned curse. This was it. This was how the fifth Lady Pargeter was doomed; you could not go against fate. But even while his mind was busy with pessimistic thoughts, he was urging the exhausted horse to greater effort. He would not give in. He would fight it to the end.

His mount was slowing and he knew it would do no good to use his spurs; the poor beast had given his all and no man could ask more than that. How much further? There was the river in sight again, winding its way through a small hamlet. Could it be Highmere? He turned towards it and there was the sluice. The gates were open but there was no sign of the barge. He dismounted and ran to a small clunch cottage by the water's edge, banging on the door with his crop.

'Has there been a lighterhouse through here?' he demanded of the bent old man who opened the door.

The old fellow took his clay pipe from his toothless mouth and grinned. 'Hundreds,' he said. 'Which other way would they go?'

'I mean today. In the last hour or two. You're the tollman, aren't you?'

'Yes, and I ain't taken any tolls since noon.'

Could they have reached here that quickly? he asked himself. Or had the old man mistaken the time? 'What manner of men were on board? Did they have a lady with them?'

'A lady? No, unless they hid her in the sacks. Six lighters in the gang, there were, carrying grain.'

He breathed a sigh of relief. 'The one I want to stop is a lighterhouse on its own. It has a red sail.'

'And why do you want to stop it? Where's your authority?'

'I have the authority of the King.' He produced a piece of paper from his pocket and waved it under the man's nose, guessing he could not read. 'I want the gates shut.'

'Very well, but if you have a riot on your hands from upstream, on your own head be it.'

Between them they cranked the gates shut, after which Roland gave the man a guinea to rub Satan down and feed and water him.

'Reckon you've rid that animal to death,' the old fellow said, pocketing the coin. 'But if you're willing to pay to have horse-meat rubbed down, then who am I to quarrel with that?'

'Go and do it,' Roland commanded. 'And then disappear. Go spend your guinea in the tavern.'

The tollman led Satan away and Roland settled down behind the bank to watch and wait.

The lighter had made good time at first, but the wind had died and they had reverted to being towed. While the haling-way was clear they made steady progress, but landowners had frequently built fences right down to the water's edge and that meant the horse had to jump the obstruction—and, once they joined the river, the towpath frequently changed banks and the horse had to be swum across to pick up the tow on the other side. Margaret, tied to a post in the cabin, wished there were more obstacles to slow them down, though she had little hope of rescue. No one knew where she was and it could be days before the bodies of Henry and Nellie were discovered and, even then, no one would connect that incident with her. That she was in mortal danger had been brought home to her when she had seen how savagely the men had attacked her uncle and poor Nellie, who had only been trying to defend her. These men would not hesitate to kill her too.

There were six of them. Two, the man called James and another whose name was Iain, seemed educated, but the other four were no more than ruffians and they spoke with an accent which she found difficult to understand and they frequently lapsed into a foreign language which she guessed was Gaelic. One of them was no more than a boy, with a mop of curly hair and frightened eyes, whom the men called Robbie. They were all dressed in rough tweed and wore no cravats or wigs. They had taken turns to ride the horse and open lock-gates, but there had always been at least two of them in the little superstructure, watching her.

'You will not be harmed so long as you behave yourself, my lady,' James had said.

She forced herself to sound calm, to hide the terror which had turned her legs to jelly and her insides to water. 'What are you going to do with me?'

'You will be taken aboard a fishing-smack when we reach the coast.'

'Why? I am no use to you, you must see that.'

'You are our safe passage. Your fine husband will offer us no violence while you are on board.'

'How can he know where I am? He has been away for weeks; what makes you think he is anywhere near?'

'We do not, but it is better to be safe than sorry.'

'Oh.' She would not admit, even to herself, that she had been hoping they knew something she did not about her husband's whereabouts, but the disappointment was hard to bear.

'He has been a thorn in our flesh for too long,' he added with a grim laugh. 'Now we have turned the tables, and until we are safe away we shall continue to hold you. If you behave yourself, I will have you rowed ashore in some lonely spot on the Norfolk coast. Sooner or later someone will come along and pick you up.'

'I do not think I can wait that long,' she said, pushing her hands into her abdomen. 'My child will pick his own time to come and I think it might be very soon.'

He looked her up and down as if assessing whether she told the truth, but decided it would be more convenient to disbelieve her, at least until there was more positive evidence. 'Then you had better pray he is in no hurry, my lady.'

One of the other men put his head in the door.

'Sluice coming up, sir. The gates are shut and the water is rising.'

'Shut?' He got to his feet. 'Damnation. Pull in and send Charlie to find the tollman.' He turned to Margaret. 'Keep out of sight, do you hear? One false move and I'll have your feet tied too.'

Charlie came back with the news that the tollman was nowhere to be found.

'Then take one of the others and open the gates yourselves. And make haste or the tide will turn before we're through.'

Two men disappeared behind the sluice while the barge rocked on its mooring-rope by the bank. For several minutes, while the others watched, nothing happened. James shouted impatiently, but there was no answer. He turned to the others. 'Iain, go and see what has happened to that weak-kneed couple of no-good sheep-herders. If the water keeps rising we'll be floated on to the fields.'

The man obeyed, leaving only the rebel leader and two others on board. Margaret could just see the back of James's head as he peered towards the sluice-gates, but she could not see where the other two were. For the first time she was alone in the little cabin. If any more left the lighter, could she escape? She looked round for some way of loosening her bonds, but before she could do anything there was a shot and she saw all three men dive for cover behind the bulwarks.

Someone was trying to stop the men escaping. Margaret strained at her bonds to get closer to the little window, but all she could see was a few feet of the barge's side.

'Iain, what goes on there?' James shouted, but there

was no answer from his henchman, nor any more shooting.

Margaret heard him swear, and then the door of the cabin was opened and he strode over to untie her from the post. 'Come.' He grabbed her arm and propelled her out to the bows. 'Open the gates, whoever you are!' he shouted, pulling Margaret forward. 'The lady will die an you do not.'

Nothing happened; no sound came from the other side of the gates, which remained firmly shut, nor was there any sign of the three men who had been sent to open the sluice. The river-level was rising behind it and threatened to overflow the banks. Margaret shivered with apprehension. 'Tell whoever it is to open the gate,' James ordered her, lifting his pistol to her head.

She tried to speak, but fear had closed her throat and she could do no more than croak.

'Shall I go and see?' queried one of the men who remained on board.

'No, we've already lost three.'

'They may be trying to open the gates. Mayhap they've stuck.'

'Then they would have answered my call.' He took Margaret's shoulder and forced her in front of him, pulling her up on the step so that she was in full view of anyone in the vicinity of the sluice. 'I mean it!' he shouted, raising his pistol to her temple. 'One more killing makes no odds.' He gave a cracked laugh. 'Two killings in one. I care no more for unborn Englishmen than I do for full-grown ones.'

Slowly the gates began to open and, when they were wide enough to allow the barge to pass through, a figure that could only have been one of the rebels who had left the boat appeared on the bank and waved them on. 'That's better,' James grunted, relaxing his hold on Margaret. 'Why the devil did he take so long?' He turned to take her back to the cabin. 'Get back inside.' He pushed her in without coming in himself to tie her to the post. He shut the door but she noticed he did not lock it.

She heard him shout to the man on the bank, 'What's happened to the others?'

The answer was indistinct, and then James said, 'Get back on board; we've lost too much time already.'

Margaret went to the window. They were gliding through the sluice and would soon be in wider water and riding on the ebbing tide. She could feel their speed increasing. The man on the bank leapt on board and Margaret caught sight of him as he landed. It was Roland! She gasped and hurried to open the door, but checked herself in time. If she went out now and distracted him, she could put them both in danger. On the other hand he had three men to overcome, and if she went to his aid she might shorten the odds. She stood indecisively with her hand on the door-latch, straining her ears for sounds of a struggle which would tell her Roland had been recognised.

At first there was nothing, and then running feet and shots, two in quick succession. She could stand idle no longer; she wrenched open the door but went no further. Roland was struggling with James, rolling over and over on the empty deck. She could do nothing but watch with her hand to her mouth. One of the other men lay dead, his pistol a few inches from his out-stretched fingers. She crept towards it, inch by inch. She had to reach it, though she did not know how to fire it if she did, but simply having it might help. She picked it up just as Roland sat astride James and, picking up his head, crashed it to the ground, rendering him unconscious. He scrambled to his feet in time to see Margaret stoop and grab the weapon. He walked over to her, breathing hard.

'I think I can make better use of that, my lady,' he said, smiling and taking it from her shaking fingers. 'Are you hurt?'

'N-no.'

A shadow momentarily blocked out the sun and Margaret looked up to see one of the men who had left the barge earlier climbing over the side behind her husband. 'Roland, look out!' she shouted. 'Behind you!'

Before the words were out of her mouth, he had whipped round and fired. The man dropped back into the water with a splash. 'I evidently did not hit him hard enough,' Roland said laconically, then touched the motionless form of James with the toe of his boot. 'Are there any more?'

'There were six altogether, but three went to open the gates. . .' she began.

'Dead now,' he said.

'This one who was their leader and that one you. . .' She pointed to the man whose gun she had taken. 'There is one more.'

He turned to scan the craft. Young Robbie was cowering in the furthest corner of the stern.

'He's only a boy,' Margaret said. 'And frightened to death.'

She looked on as Roland went to take the lad by the shoulder and pull him to his feet, glad that he was not rough with him. 'Go!' he said, reaching into his coat pocket for his purse. 'Here, take this and get as far away as you can while you have a whole skin.'

The boy grabbed the guinea and dived over the side. Margaret smiled as he scrambled up the bank and ran off through the village. 'He'll catch his death of cold in wet clothes,' she said.

'Better than dying on the end of a rope.'

Now it was all over she was shaking like an aspen and her legs would not support her. She felt her knees buckle. 'Roland. . .' The whole boat seemed to tip up as blackness enveloped her and she slid towards the deck.

Roland caught her and picked her up, taking her into the rough cabin and laying her on one of the bunks. 'Oh, my poor, poor darling,' he said, rubbing her hands and gently slapping her cheeks to bring her round.

She opened her eyes at last to see her husband's face bending over her. His eyes were soft and misted and a muscle twitched in his jaw as if he was trying to control some overpowering emotion. He had his arms around her shoulders and her head was nestling against his coat. 'Roland.'

'I'm here, my love.' He bent to kiss her gently. 'Thank God they did not harm you. . .' His voice was husky.

She was dreaming, she told herself; she had died and gone to heaven; he didn't sound like Roland at all, certainly not the Roland she knew. That one had been self-possessed, sure of himself and what he believed in; this one sounded less sure, but oh, so much more endearing.

'Roland, how came you here?'

'I rode.'

'But how did you know where I was? Those men. . .
Uncle Henry and Nellie. . .'

'I found them. I'm sorry, my darling, but Henry
Capitain is dead.'

'I thought he must be. They were so brutal. He came
to my rescue.' She was perfectly capable of sitting up,
and walking too, but it was too comfortable lying in his
arms. 'Nellie?'

'She was alive when I left her, though badly injured.
Janet Henser will look after her.'

She had forgotten seeing Mistress Henser on the way
to Sedge House, but the meeting had been providential. 'She told you where I was?'

'Yes.'

'You went to see her, didn't you? You went to ask
her about that. . .that dreadful prediction. She told
you to leave home, didn't she?'

He smiled ruefully and kissed her again, making her
wriggle happily in his arms. 'I hoped that if I made
restitution to all those Capitains who had been denied
their birthright over the years you might be reprieved.'

'But there was only Uncle Henry left. And he's dead
now, isn't he?'

'Yes, I am afraid so. But there is still you. Margaret,
I could not let you die. . .'

'I am not going to die. Not for a very long time. Did
Mistress Henser not tell you to have faith?'

'Yes.' He was shamefaced. 'I must have been mad.'

She smiled and lifted a finger to trace the outline of
his chin. 'So strong, so manly and so gullible.'

'You don't understand. If you had lived in Winterford all your life. . .'

'Oh, I do understand, Roland. I very nearly succumbed myself, nearly gave up. I was going to leave. . .'

'When? How?' He looked round the lighterhouse. Through the open door the sun still shone, but it shone on the lifeless bodies of the Jacobites. 'Not with these delinquents? Oh, Margaret, were you so desperate to escape from me?'

She laughed suddenly, a happy sound that made his spirits soar with new hope. 'No, not with these men and not from you. From Rosalind. I found her journal, you know, and her grave in the garden. She seemed to haunt me more than anyone. My faith faltered and I was afraid. . .' She sat up and turned towards him. 'I wanted desperately to get away and then I learned my father had died quite recently and left me a great deal of money, enough to keep me and my child comfortably for life. I was able to go wherever I liked, but I couldn't—not while there was a chance you would come back to me. I found any number of excuses to postpone the decision. I kept hoping you would return, that everything would be all right. I wished I had never heard of that awful curse. . .'

'You do not wish it any more heartily than I do. I told Susan about it because I hoped she would understand, not just why I married you, but why I had come to love you. . .'

'Do you?' she murmured, lifting her hand to trace the outline of his jaw with her finger.

'Yes. More than life itself.' He caught her hand and

put it to his lips, kissing each finger one by one and making her tingle with desire.

'Is that why you were doing your best to throw it away, chasing all over the country after Jacobites and taking them on at odds of six to one?'

'How do you know all that?'

'Charles told me you were on a special mission, and when those men spoke of my husband being a thorn in their flesh I knew it.' She paused. 'There aren't any more, are there?'

'If there are, I am not pursuing them. I am coming home with you. I intend to be there when our child is born.' He laid a hand on her abdomen. 'You are quite sure he is all right?'

'Absolutely. But what about. . .' She stopped, not wanting to put a name to it. 'You know what.'

'To hell with it. We will fight it together, you and I.'

She smiled. The threat seemed insubstantial now that they were facing it together. He had said he loved her and that was enough to give her hope. If she had to die, then she would rather it was in his arms. 'Mistress Henser said it was simply a matter of faith,' she said. 'And she is the wise woman, after all.'

'Faith,' he repeated softly. 'I have been a fool, haven't I?'

'We both have.'

'Let's go home.'

Ten minutes later, they found Satan in the stable at the back of the tavern. He was contentedly munching hay, none the worse for his gruelling race. Reluctant to make him carry them both, Roland went to the tavern to try and hire a cart so that Margaret might ride in comfort. It was then that he looked up and saw a crowd coming down the rutted road towards him. He recognised several of his own servants, riding mounts from the Manor stables, and there were Winterford villagers too, Silas Gotobed and Marcus Clark among them. Johnson had obviously disobeyed his instructions to go home and wait for him there. He had retrieved the curricle from behind Sedge House and was some way behind the others. Roland smiled and waited for them to come up to him.

'Better late than never,' he said, grinning. 'There's a lighter on the tideway needs turning round and taking back to Ely.'

'You caught them, my lord?' This was Johnson, pulling the curricle to a stop outside the tavern.

'Yes. Five of them. Dead as mutton, I'm afraid. Two lying down by the sluice-gates, the others on board.' He turned to Silas. 'Take Johnson and Marcus with you and take them to the Bishop's gaol. See if they can be identified. Then back to Winterford Manor. I'll take my lady in the curricle.'

Thus Margaret and Roland returned to Winterford, leading a cavalcade of villagers, all in high spirits and pleased to have their lord back among them, pleased too to see her ladyship looking so happy. She sat beside her husband, her hand tucked into his arm and her head on his shoulder, content to let the future take care of itself. Faith, Mistress Henser had said. Was hers strong enough? She would soon know.

Margaret's son was born on Christmas Day, just as the sky across the fen was streaked with the grey light of a new dawn. He weighed seven and a half pounds and was perfect in every detail. Roland, who had been pacing up and down the corridor outside Margaret's bedchamber most of the night, was allowed in at last, and dashed to kneel at his wife's side and take her hand in his. 'My dearest. . .' He could hardly speak for the emotions which assailed him. 'Are you. . .?'

'Perfectly well,' she said, lifting his hand to put it to her cheek. 'Nothing can touch us now.'

'No, of course not.'

She smiled, detecting the slight note of doubt in his voice. 'This is Christmas Day, Roland, the birthday of Our Lord; how can anyone born on such a day be anything but blessed? Little Roland will grow into a fine man, just like his father. Can you doubt that?'

'And you?'

'I too am blessed.' She stopped and laughed softly. 'Roland, do you know what else has come to pass?'

He looked mystified, then broke into a grin, then threw back his head and laughed. 'We have been married over a year—four days over the year.' He bent his head and kissed her longingly. 'We have nothing to be afraid of.'

'Perhaps we never did have,' she said. 'Love cast its spell on the day we met and that is stronger than any witch's curse.'

'I wish I had understood that,' he said, bending over and kissing her tenderly. 'Can you forgive me?'

'Oh, Roland, do not blame yourself. It is history. Let's not delve into it.'

'Mistress Henser said I had to go away in order to come back; I see what she meant now.'

He was still sitting by her bed, with his hand in hers, when Charles and Kate arrived in a flurry of excitement, bringing baby George and a retinue of servants, to spend Christmas and the New Year at Winterford. It was going to be a joyful time.

Years later, when Margaret's growing family meant it was necessary to open up the east wing and make it habitable again, the old chest containing the family archives was re-discovered, but this time there was no threat attached to it and Margaret spent several days happily sorting the contents, knowing they could no longer trouble her. One sheet of paper attracted her attention. It was right at the bottom of the chest and yellowing with age, but parts of it were still readable.

. . . she will not have him long. Before the year is out, she will be dead. Mark my words well. The Pargeters will not be allowed to forget this betrayal. I, Anne Capitain, will not rest in this life, or after it. My spirit will not sleep until the Capitains once again rule Winterford Manor. . .

This was what everyone had been so afraid of. This was Anne Capitain's curse in her own words. It was the last sentence which had worried old Lady Pargeter most; she could not bear to think of the Pargeters losing their home and their land to the Capitains. Margaret smiled slowly as she replaced the paper in the bottom of the chest. How easy it was to misinterpret predictions! When the Pargeters and the Capitains became united, a Capitain would rule Winterford. Her son. Roland's heir. There never had been anything to fear. 'Rest in peace, Anne,' she whispered. 'All is well.'

LEGACY *of* LOVE

Coming next month

THE DEVIL'S MARK
Joanna Makepeace
Winchester 1238

Her father would not arrange a marriage for her, and Janeta Cobham refused to become a nun…she had no alternative but to run from the convent that had been her home for so long. It was her good fortune that she was aided by Bertrand D'Aubigny, landless knight, who proved to be her entrée to the court at Winchester. How could Janeta know, caught up in the intrigues of Court, that more would be revealed than her growing love for Bertrand? Secrets that would put her in mortal danger…

THE ABSENTEE EARL
Clarice Peters
Regency 1817

Viola Challerton, Lady Avery, had survived the scandal which had followed in the wake of her wedding to the Earl of Avery, one year ago.

Less than two hours after their vows had been exchanged, Richard, Lord Avery, had absconded, and was not expected ever to return.

When he unexpectedly *did* return, Viola quickly learned that little had changed—except for herself…

LEGACY *of* LOVE

Coming next month

THE FLAMING
Pat Tracy
England 1865

Rancher Morgan Grayson stood to inherit a fortune—*if* he married his uncle's spinster sister-in-law. And spirited Anya Delangue was hardly the frumpy Englishwoman Morgan had expected. In fact, he was willing to bet that this businesslike alliance would heat up in no time…

Anya was appalled by her brother-in-law's plan—and intrigued! Though Morgan was a bullying ruffian from a savage place called Texas, his wooing was a heady experience. But could she chance that the untamed American's desire would deepen into the lasting love she had always longed for?

BODIE BRIDE
Isabel Whitfield
California 1879

Margaret Warren had hoped to spend her life 'guiding' her unruly family. But when her saloon-keeper father tired of her teetotalling bossy ways, well-meaning Margaret found herself bartered into wedlock with irrepressible miner John Banning. She gritted her teeth and promised to honour and obey—but love was another matter entirely!

John knew his prickly wife would have to be won over, and he relished kindling the banked fires beneath Margaret's cool exterior. Yet when their explosive attraction sparked genuine panic in her, John feared that one wrong move could send his new bride running scared…

MILLS & BOON

Always & Forever

This summer Mills & Boon presents the wedding
book of the year—three new full-length wedding
romances in one heartwarming volume.

Featuring top selling authors:

Debbie Macomber ♥ Jasmine Cresswell
Bethany Campbell

The perfect summer read!

Available: June 1995   Price: £4.99

GET 4 BOOKS
AND A MYSTERY GIFT

Return the coupon below and we'll send you 4 Legacy of Love novels and a mystery gift absolutely FREE! We'll even pay the postage and packing for you.

We're making you this offer to introduce you to the benefits of Reader Service: FREE home delivery of brand-new Legacy of Love novels, at least a month before they are available in the shops, FREE gifts and a monthly Newsletter packed with information.

Accepting these FREE books and gift places you under no obligation to buy, you may cancel at any time, even after receiving just your free shipment. Simply complete the coupon below and send it to:

HARLEQUIN MILLS & BOON, FREEPOST, PO BOX 70, CROYDON, CR9 9EL.

No stamp needed

Yes, please send me 4 free Legacy of Love novels and a mystery gift. I understand that unless you hear from me, I will receive 4 superb new titles every month for just £2.50* each postage and packing free. I am under no obligation to purchase any books and I may cancel or suspend my subscription at any time, but the free books and gifts will be mine to keep in any case. (I am over 18 years of age)

1EP5M

Ms/Mrs/Miss/Mr _____

Address _____

_____

_____ Postcode _____